Shadows & Wings

[A Fugue]

By Niki Tulk

Small House Press

Printed in the United States of America
First published 2013

ISBN-10: 0985842806
ISBN-13: 978-0-9858428-0-2

Digital edition published in 2013
eISBN-10: 0985842814
eISBN-13: 978-0-9858428-1-9

Small House Press
www.smallhousepress.com
www.nikitulk.com

Cover Design: by Mark Tulk, 2013
"Death of a Bird." by A.D. Hope

For
L. G. Mengersen

&

for the travelers, the immigrants, and the exiles:
we are strong.

The Death of the Bird

For every bird there is this last migration:
Once more the cooling year kindles her heart;
With a warm passage to the summer station
Love pricks the course in lights across the chart.

Year after year a speck on the map, divided
By a whole hemisphere, summons her to come;
Season after season, sure and safely guided,
Going away she is also coming home.

And being home, memory becomes a passion
With which she feeds her brood and straws her nest,
Aware of ghosts that haunt the heart's possession
And exiled love mourning within the breast.

The sands are green with a mirage of valleys;
The palm-tree casts a shadow not its own;
Down the long architrave of temple or palace
Blows a cool air from moorland scarps of stone.

And day by day the whisper of love grows stronger;
That delicate voice, more urgent with despair,
Custom and fear containing her no longer,
Drives her at last on the waste leagues of air.

A vanishing speck in those inane dominions,
Single and frail, uncertain of her place,
Alone in the bright host of her companions,
Lost in the blue unfriendliness of space,

She feels it close now, the appointed season:
The invisible thread is broken as she flies;
Suddenly, without warning, without reason,
The guiding spark of instinct winks and dies.

Try as she will, the trackless world delivers
No way, the wilderness of light no sign,
The immense and complex map of hills and rivers
Mocks her small wisdom with its vast design.

And the darkness rises from the eastern valleys,
And the winds buffet her with their hungry breath,
And the great earth, with neither grief nor malice,
Receives the tiny burden of her death.

—*A. D. Hope*

Fugue:

(n): A complex form of composition, associated most strongly with the Baroque period, and particularly with J.S. Bach, where a melody is played in a number of voices. At the beginning of the piece, each voice is introduced in turn by playing the melody, after which it consists of a mix of counter-melodies, accompaniment passages, periods of rest, and returns to the main melody (often transformed in some way).

(n): A dissociative disorder in which a person forgets who they are, and may leave home to create a new life; during the fugue there is no memory of the former life; after recovering there is no memory for events during the dissociative state. A dissociative fugue usually involves unplanned travel or wandering, and is sometimes accompanied by the establishment of a new identity.

Prelude

(n):An introductory piece of music, preceding, most commonly, a Fugue.

*O*n the edge of a lonely, sleeping city, a stoic breakwater crouched against the beating tide. Seabirds and refuse haunted its cold harbor, which at this hour held only a few deserted fishing boats and a rusting barge. A man stood on the rocks, hushed as a cormorant transfixed by fish beneath the water, his eyes to the North Sea. The hem of his coat trembled, and he wore a felt cap pulled close over his ears. From a distance he could have been mistaken for a pylon, he stood so still—more a thought, than a man.

After a long time, he pulled a brown paper parcel out from under his coat. His hands fumbled at the wrapping in the early morning chill that permeated the crevices in his clothing. On coming closer, much closer, one might have seen that the man's fingers were chafed and hardened. As he worked, languid gray water slapped the stone below him, the wind blew sharp with the stench of rotting fish.

The man paused, and sniffed from the cold. He glanced up for a moment, and then quite suddenly knelt on the unforgiving stone. He spread out his collection of objects, then gathered each one, gently, as if folding a love letter. He straightened each item as he pressed one down upon the other.

Then he began once more to wrap his bundle.

Low clouds spat on the man's wad of brown paper, staining it and interfering with his hands. The dawn had whitened; he could hear rough voices and the sound of metal on wood.

The man pulled a length of string from the pocket of his coat and clasped it in his teeth, as he began to fold the now damp paper. He completed the wrapping and—as best he could in the spruce wind—tied his string neatly around it in an even, careful cross. He tied a knot, then a bow.

It looked like a gift.

He got to his feet and blew on his hands to warm them, listening as he did so to the rising swell, and the stuttering motor of a fishing boat.

Should he kick what he had wrapped, or hurl it into the tide? He turned again to the waves, and realized that if he loosed it here, the parcel would merely spiral in the current and catch on the rocks. What he needed, he knew now, was the deepest water he could find.

A seagull skimmed above him, its high, harsh cry sliding over the water. He watched the bird land soundlessly on a gray wooden pylon. The man shifted his eyes back to the parcel in front of him; then, with the sudden agility of the cormorant, he grasped and thrust it under his coat.

He would have to take a boat.

Part One: Allemande

(n): A German dance in 4/4 time, often the first dance in a Baroque dance suite and generally moderate in speed. The Baroque Allemande, although a dance, often favored an imitative, ornamented texture rather than strong dance rhythms.

1.

Australia

Summer, 1979

Lara was seven, the age when children look more like insects than humans, with their thin torsos and too-long arms and legs. Her dusky, tangled hair fought with ties that bundled it into loose braids, and the strap of her overalls kept slipping off one narrow shoulder. She had steady, gray eyes that often made adults feel uncomfortable. She didn't mean to, of course, but she could never help herself from studying people's faces and trying to imagine what they were really thinking. But a slight sprinkling of freckles and a smile that would suddenly dart out and warm her face offset the seriousness that sat so oddly on her young visage. Well-meaning adults termed her precocious. Other adults, not quite so kind, called her proud. Other children, more often than not, just left her alone. Most of the time.

Lara was relieved she was home-schooled now, where it no longer mattered so much what others thought of her, or did to her. She sometimes allowed herself to remember life in the first grade: the bruises and tears, the spiraling dance of jeering girls. Recess had been Lara's time to play hunted rodent to the marauding felines with their painted claws, hissing at her funny clothes and big words. With her father's research taking him for months at a time overseas, and her mother's decision to live with Lara's grandparents when he was away, it had made sense to take Lara out of school. She was so grateful, she almost didn't care that her last day had meant another ruined lunch and her ears clogged with snarled recitations of her physical faults. Her Oma and Opa never called her buck-toothed, or ugly—or any of the other 21 names on the secret list Lara carried inside her.

But now it was summer, and armed with rucksacks and gingerbread men, Lara and her younger sister Jen stepped cautiously along the track to the gully. The long, dry grass raked at the girls' bare legs. Lara stopped to look up and squint under the shade of her hand. Jen, too busy watching for snakes as she walked, bumped straight into her.

"Watcha looking at?" Jen muttered accusingly, rubbing an imagined bruise.

"The sky."

There was a pause while Jen considered the significance of this.

"What's up there?" she asked, curious now. The bruise vanished.

"Shhh … I'm imagining something," hissed Lara.

Jen squatted patiently on her haunches, tucking a sun-bleached strand of hair behind her ear. She didn't take offence at Lara's tone—she knew that often her older sister was involved in serious matters that demanded her full attention and Jen's patient understanding. She waited.

Lara pointed upwards. "There! There it is!" She sucked in her breath with excitement.

Jen looked up but couldn't see anything. In frustration, she dug around in her backpack with chubby five-year-old fingers, and began to eat one of her gingerbread men.

The hawk leaned into the wind and circled above their heads. Its feathers were the color of dust and stone. Lara breathed in the smooth, almost liquid movement of its body through the sky. Her heart beat faster. The hawk tilted its soft, brown head toward them. Lara raised her head further and held out her arm—could it land there? The dreaming lifted her, she no longer touched earth. The hawk soared beyond her fingers.

"*Auf Wiedersehen!*" she called to the faraway bird, as it dipped away to the south.

"What does *Auf Wiedersehen* mean?"

Lara, always ready to play the teacher with her younger sibling, picked up a stick and wrote the words in the dirt. "See how you spell it? It means 'See you again.' Opa and Oma say it."

Jen knew best how to end these sorts of lessons quickly. Hankering to go to school was one thing; bearing with the intellectual discipline of an older sister was quite another. Jen nodded sagely, appeared to think deeply for a moment, and then asked, "When did Mum say we were to be back?"

Ignoring the question, Lara threw the stick away. They proceeded to scramble their way down a steep slope, scratching themselves on the sharp points of Iron Grass. Around them the gully walls rose higher as they descended ever closer to the creek. Caves like eye sockets, hollow and sepulchral, dotted the cliffs. Opa said there were Aboriginal paintings there. He also said the caves were dangerously high, and that not until she was older would Lara be allowed to explore them.

Lara and Jen gazed up silently at the indentations in the cliff face, and shivered involuntarily. The ancient hand-prints were a reminder that the gully hadn't always been theirs. And it needed to be their place. Nobody else's presence seemed right, even if others had been there hundreds, even thousands, of years before.

The earth flattened into uneven, tussocky mounds, then the creek abruptly presented itself. The excitement of the water, with its husky, determined gaiety, meant the caves were forgotten.

"Quick," instructed Lara, "the jars!"

Jen pulled off her rucksack, dipped her arm inside, and pulled out one glass jar at a time. Today they were going to hunt frogs.

Lara's hands trembled with excitement as she opened the screw-top lid and placed it within easy reach in her pocket. The first step was to bend close to the water without falling in and collect some water in the jars. Then it was time for action.

Intensely focused, they moved stealthily across the rocks and stepping stones. Every so often they heard a subdued croak. The children would stop, then bend slowly and carefully toward the target—until they could see the tiny, plastic form clinging to a shelf under the water. Then they struck, child-hawks, fingers like talons.

The girls didn't always manage to hold up their jars in triumph, but they had enough success to scramble along the river's edge with an elated spring in their steps. They felt powerful and alive as they collected creatures in glass; yet with this pursuit came an unexpected tenderness. At the end of the day, the children loosened the screw-top lids and gently poured the contents back into the creek. They watched the shiny creatures plop like wet pebbles, and cause a quickly dispersed ripple. Finally, empty jars in hand and a reassuring sense of their own magnanimity in their hearts, they ate the remaining gingerbread.

As they wiped the sweet crumbs from their mouths and headed back up the hill, Lara stretched out a hand to brush the tops of the grasses and remind herself how prickly they were, trying to turn her thoughts to something other than her aching leg muscles. The shadows of the trees gave way to warm evening sun, draping like soft cloth across her shoulders.

In front of her, Jen's small legs plowed upwards. Lara could hear her own ragged breathing. She played the what-if game. What if they just kept walking on up the street and hitched a ride to some other city? What if they turned around and camped the night in the gully, catching fish from the creek, and eating the blackberries that occasionally trespassed onto the park? What if they ran away and caught a plane to somewhere else? Germany? Lara's imaginings got her up the hill and left her with an odd, curling sensation in her stomach, as if she were about to step onstage.

The road rose to meet them, flat and comforting, so they swung in beside each other. The two girls ambled toward home, chatting in the contented languor of the summer afternoon, before finally turning into the side driveway of their grandparents' place.

Once on the grass that stretched in a tousled carpet toward the back veranda, the girls took off their shoes. Lara, wobbling on one leg and shaking road gravel from her sandal, could see the front of the house, where a heavy wooden door opened onto a slick lawn. That was the formal entrance, the trim grass spread as smoothly as their grandmother's Hungarian tablecloth, with a water fountain as its centerpiece and red geraniums embroidered around its neatly hemmed edges.

Laughter wafted across to them from an open kitchen window, and they heard the tinkling and hissing of their mother and Oma bottling hot apricots into glass jars. Occasionally a checkered tea towel waved like a flag, and the rich accent of their grandmother, and the higher melodic voice of their mother dipped and rose again like birdsong.

Lara loved this house, the old family home in which her mother had grown up. The house was the color of honey, built of golden rocks hewn from the nearby gully, and shaped lovingly into a home where their grandparents had built a life amid the dry wildness of the Australian bush. Chapped mortar gripped the stones, one upon the other, so that the windows seemed in danger of being forced outward by the walls' tight embrace. The very top windows let in the glimmering of the faraway sea, beyond a ridge of hills that kept the gully nestled within their reddened cliffs, and the city at a safe distance beyond.

Opa appeared along a narrow stone path that wound its way through a terraced garden toward the orchard. He carried a shovel, and his hands were filthy. Between his dirt-caked fingers swung a plastic bag, frothy tops of silverbeet[1] peering over its sagging edge. Lara grimaced. She hated silverbeet—especially the way Oma boiled it. Hopefully it was her mother's turn to cook tonight.

---

1   Chard

Opa smiled at them from under his felt Akubra hat.

"Where have you girls been?"

His voice was gritty and deep, straight from the garden. His German accent, still strong after all the years here, made him seem rougher and more brusque than he actually was.

"The gully," they replied in cheery unison.

"Did you see any snakes?"

"No, Opa."

"I hope you were careful. This hot weather brings them out."

"Yes, Opa, we were careful," they responded dutifully.

Then Jen reported, "We caught heaps of frogs."

The old man's back stiffened, and he moved closer to them. His eyes were stern and shadowed. His wrinkles tightened.

"Why?" It was a demand, firm and scary.

"Mum said we could. We've done it before."

Lara was glad that Jen did not feel afraid to speak out. She didn't seem to mind so much if Opa stopped smiling at them. Lara shifted uncomfortably on her bare feet.

Their grandfather bent down to them, his voice now earnest.

"You know they are endangered?"

"No." They looked down at the grass, and Lara tried counting how many ants she could see.

"It is not right for you to catch them. It is cruel to take them out of the water. They need the water to breathe."

"Yes, Opa."

"If you were a frog, you would not like to be caught and put in a jar with no air, and so much afraid?"

"No, Opa!"

"Well, then … "

Jen shuffled around, then stuck out her chin stubbornly. "But, Opa, we let them go!"

"Yes, we only keep them for a bit," Lara joined in. "We count how many we've got, and then we' let them go!"

"Mum said we were allowed to. We don't keep them in the jars for very long."

Opa was quiet. He never liked them catching anything and imprisoning it. One night Lara had awoken to a thick-furred spider poised above her pillow. Her Opa had calmly maneuvered it onto a tennis racket and carried it outside. It was a sacred, unspoken rule—every creature must be allowed to live where it belonged.

"It is good if you let them go. I am only sad if you hold them in the jars so long that they die slowly from no air." He straightened up and gave Jen the bag of leafy chard. "You take this to Oma. I think she needs it for our tea. And put your shoes on."

He reached out a hand and ruffled Lara's hair. Then he winked at them in a peacemaking gesture. But she knew that somehow they had wounded him, had broken the sacred rule.

2.

Lara loved to believe that she was Maria Von Trapp. She had the dress, she could sing all the songs from *The Sound of Music,* and she could twirl and not fall over as she ran across imaginary Alps on her grandparents' lawn. She could climb every mountain, ford every stream.

When Lara sang robustly about her favorite things, the bushland sang with her. She *was* Maria! One day Lara would escape to a place where she could talk with her mouth full and put her elbows on the table. She would no longer be forced to eat silverbeet, or keep her shoes on.

In different ways and for different reasons, Lara's grandparents had both come to this house from the Old World. Growing up among the first generation of her family in this new land, her grandmother had spoken German before learning English. She would have continued speaking only German, if the First World War had not interfered.

Lara's grandfather arrived later, a thin half-man on a ship that emptied its human cargo unsympathetically into a bright and bristling land. Here, not long enough after the Second World War, those who bore in their eyes another hemisphere were received with cool politeness. It was not their accents so much as their eyes—they held a silence that made others who had grown up here suddenly feel they needed to defend themselves. Tomas had discovered Lara's grandmother like a familiar face in this strange country.

After the last stone of their new home had been laid, and the last windowsill painted glossy white, the kitchen door swung open for Lara's grandfather to carry his bride across the threshold. She had then set to work filling the house with tokens of the land her husband had left behind. Tomas, the one who was truly in exile, would just smile at her, shake his head and disappear into his garden.

So it was that vases of dried flowers stood proudly on the homemade dresser, and the top of the piano. Wooden clocks ticked precisely on whitewashed walls, while alongside them hung pictures of alpine scenes and chalets with red geraniums clustered at their windows. Little wooden peasant figures formed a beautiful still life across the length of the mantle above the fireplace. Books with glowing foreign binding peered from the shelves, beckoning to Lara in a language she did not know, but from a world to which she felt irrevocably connected.

Lara was made to learn "Silent Night" in German and to sing it at Christmas time for their infirm and desperately homesick great-grandmother, who cried as Lara's high-pitched little voice crooned the words from a long-ago childhood. *Stille Nacht, heilige Nacht; Alles schläft; einsam wacht.*[2]

The house's interior was presided over principally by Lara's grandmother, her reign extending to the manicured front lawn and its obedient geraniums. Needless to say, the children preferred what lay outside the back door and across the creaking veranda, with its cobwebs and faded deck chairs. Here the rustling eucalyptus trees were stitched together with the joyous tracks of children and animals. Here, flanked proudly by a row of towering copper beeches, rambled the wild relative of their grandmother's imposing front yard; the distant cousin that growled and stalked and romped on the other side of the house.

This was their grandfather's garden. Secrets grew here, too, their grandfather's secrets, with small, dark leaves like pine needles, pricking the skin if you walked too close.

---

2   Silent night, holy night; All is calm, all is bright.

With crackling steps Lara walked amidst the trees, their leaves caroling softly in the wind. She found a smooth-topped boulder, crowded by undergrowth and yet with clear spaces between the tiny branches to view the wilderness. It was her favorite place to sit in solitude and watch the birds.

Often her Opa came with her. He too loved birds. But today, Lara was alone. Her binoculars, child-size, hung heavy around her neck. Under her arm were her notebook and pencil. She also had her worn, beloved reference manual, her name inside the hardcover in large, possessive handwriting. This book, like the binoculars, was a present from her grandfather.

Lara wriggled, then rested on her stone, focusing her field-glasses on the trees ahead. She placed her reference book on her lap. Lara tried to arrange everything so that she did not have to move; this way she would not disturb the birds, or make them afraid.

Now, this was the best part—the beginning. At first the trees, even though the wind was rippling them, were unyielding. But she knew to wait, and keep waiting … suddenly she would witness the virescent curtains shred, and with rapture Lara would watch a myriad of tiny lives dart and perch and wing. It was as if the birds shimmered into focus, and where there had been nothing, the trees revealed vivid, vibrant life.

She always thought she would stop and write down the species she observed as she went, but Lara was fused to the binoculars, drawn on by seeing more, and yet more. She was afraid that if she dropped her gaze for even a moment, she would miss the sight of a rare finch, or a wren bluer than she had ever seen before.

Lara spent an hour, two hours like this before she was exhausted and had to rest her eyes. She then scribbled frantic sketches of what she had seen, strange contortions of birds rendered by her child fingers, rough notes on color and shape, to show her Opa.

"Do you know, Lara," his soft, guttural voice like earth, "Some will live only days, perhaps weeks. Listen."

It seemed to Lara that she strained to hear their fragile, determined warbling.

"Child," Opa would repeat patiently, "Listen."

❧

Lara's mother stood in the doorway, smiling and holding postcards.

"Guess what arrived in the mail?"

Lara's father was in Germany this time, which meant exciting, colorful mail now and chocolates when he returned. Lara looked at hers. It had a cart and draft horses. The cart was filled with bright flowers and driven by a weather-beaten man wearing lederhosen.

Oma stood next to her. "Market day?" she wondered aloud.

The children would not show Opa—he possessed a keen distaste for postcards. He would growl and throw them down, then retreat to his workshop like a disgruntled fox.

The girls moved on and ran upstairs, tearing along the hall until they fell into their bedroom. Second-hand beds were covered with feather-stuffed quilts and toys; an odd assortment of chests, and a large antique wardrobe created a crowded, energetic atmosphere. The windows commanded a view of the extensive back garden and the small paddock beyond where sheep grazed and chickens scratched at the stubble.

On the wall above Lara's bed hung a wooden shadow box. In each delicate compartment sat an ornament, and

Lara contemplated them each night before she fell asleep: the tiny doll in German national dress, the miniature cowbell, the little wooden angels with their exquisitely carved wings no larger than Lara's fingernail. And then there were the ones she could not understand: a polished black stone, the mahogany violin peg, and a broken compass—and her favorite, the feather.

The girls quickly swapped postcards and laughed because a similar message was written on each one. Their father had signed the cards with a tiny scrawled picture, rather than his name. Each one was different—he had a repertoire—and they wanted to see who had got the crocodile.

"It's on mine!" Jen squealed.

Their mother called from the kitchen. Lara and Jen washed their hands for dinner, then hurried downstairs to the huge wooden table, where they waited for Opa to come in from the shed.

❦

Lara sat at the table with her sister, mother, and grandparents. A bowl of oranges served as a bright centerpiece. Opa muttered a perfunctory grace, then they ate from plates piled with slivers of corned beef, shriveled green blobs of home-grown silverbeet, and mashed potato.

"Must I eat the silverbeet?" Lara asked plaintively.

"Yes, Lara, you must," replied her mother, unfolding a cloth napkin and laying it across her lap.

"Why?"

"Because." She turned to Lara's grandmother to begin another conversation.

"Because why?" Lara insisted, and her mother sighed and glared at her.

"Don't be rude. Your grandmother has cooked this especially for you."

"No, she hasn't. She's cooked it for everyone."

The others were eating; their silverware sounded like little clipped bells.

"Opa grew this silverbeet in his own vegetable patch," Lara's mother responded, putting some on her fork as a deliberate demonstration. "You must be grateful to your grandfather for growing the silverbeet, and your grandmother for cooking it. And besides, there will be no dessert until you eat it."

As a child, Lara had both a respect for, and a fear of the vegetable patch. She much preferred the orchard, where in summer the trees burst with plums and apricots, and she could lie underneath them and eat until her stomach ached and cramped.

Sometimes she would sit in the warm, fragrant grass and watch her grandfather at work. He was always bent over, digging. He never looked up. He leaned toward the earth when he carried plants, moved his wheelbarrow, or hoed the ground. He was always bent, so he never saw her watching. If she wanted attention, she had to call out to him in her high, clear voice. He would look up, half-smile, and then bend again.

Lara sometimes wondered whether he was afraid of the sky—that postcard blue, an enormous postcard you could never tear up or throw to the floor; a relentless blue light that forced her grandfather to bow toward the earth, and tend those whispers that refused to give up their roots and die.

3.

There are said to be two sides to everything; yet two elements eternally joined are often in complete opposition. Lara had noticed this on many occasions: two disparate worlds, two places, two realities, coalescing to make a crazy third entity. Dawn intrigued her for this very reason, as did twilight. And then, of course, there was her grandfather.

"Opa, where are you going?" Lara looked up from her reading as he walked purposefully across the back lawn.

He paused and turned his head. "Rabbits," he muttered in disgust. "They are eating everything!"

Lara covered her smile with the motion of suddenly putting her bookmark in its place. *The Secret Garden* could wait, especially as this was her third reading of it. Opa seemed to make an exception to his principles when it came to rabbits. "They are not natives, they do not belong here! They are outlaws!" He would make such pronouncements while fingering the remnants of his lettuce plants, the glare in his otherwise steady eyes forbidding any argument. Lara would ponder his words, and wonder. Because Opa, she knew, was also from another place.

She looked up at him now, shading her eyes in the strong afternoon sun. "Can I come?"

Lara hopped up and followed him to the shed. She saw him carefully take the slender rifle down from its high, high hooks. She watched him slowly choose bullets from a small drawer much, much higher than any child's hand could reach. He was quiet, preparing to kill. Opa glowered and flexed his hands. Lara knew how much he detested the rabbits, the destroyers of his precious garden.

She followed him as he left the shed. Jen called out from a distance and hurtled down the path to fall in step with them. The three crossed the paddock and made their way to the large vegetable plot at the bottom of the orchard. Opa stopped, and motioned the children to do likewise. Then he turned to them.

"I will show you. This once. And," he added wryly, "perhaps do not tell your father when he returns." He raised one eyebrow at them and grimaced.

Later Lara remembered how strange it felt to not only hold a gun for the first time, but also to feel her Opa's hands, like thick leather gloves, coating her fingers. He explained what to do, then did it with her. For her. Before she realized what had happened, there was an explosion. She jerked backwards, and several meters away a rabbit dropped, now motionless, another shade of the grass. Lara trembled and clasped her hands together.

"My turn!" cried Jen, and when Opa ignored her, she darted in front of him and called again.

Opa froze. He drew himself up to his full and intimidating height. His eyes blazed at her like cold blue fires, and his voice was a cannon roaring.
"Don't you ever, EVER, stand in front of a gun!"

Jen crumpled like the rabbit.

"You foolish girl! Both of you, *go home now!*"

He was a giant framed in apple trees. Invincible, terrifying.

Jen picked herself up, and without a word grabbed Lara's hand. Together they ran, panting like pursued animals, back towards the house.

They heard two more shots, then silence.

It was autumn, and the evening air was cold. The house felt lonely and strange with only Jen and her mother for company. Lara's grandparents were out on a rare foray to visit an ill relative, and the place seemed hollow without them.

Through the window Lara watched a full moon rise and fan the trees and buffalo lawn with white. She listened to the purr and thump of a possum as it jumped from the roof to the top of the water tank. She heard the clinking of the last cleaned plates being put away in the kitchen, and then the television being switched on in an adjoining room. Her mother called up the stairs to Jen to turn off the light and go to sleep, then Lara listened to her getting comfortable in an armchair in front of the TV. Tonight Lara had been allowed the special treat of staying up that bit longer.

Orchestral music finally drew her from the window and into the lounge room doorway to stare at the screen. Her mother didn't hear her. She moved closer. And every night after that, Lara wished that she had stayed at her window watching the moon.

Because it was like this. On the TV screen in her grandparents' lounge room, a bulldozer methodically pushed emaciated people into a huge pit, like so many hundreds of sheaves of wheat that had become untied, and then fallen into and away from each other.

Lara wanted to be sick. They were real, and they were dead. They had eyes, breasts, arms. Lara felt herself dilate, then retract, as if her whole self was being sucked deep inside a tiny cave. She was seven years old and suddenly unable to move, to breathe, to think. Never in any book she had read, picture she had seen, story she had heard, had she absorbed anything that could prepare her for this. She was witnessing something that she could not bear.

And yet she could not close her eyes. It was like watching the birds. She could not close her eyes. Who were those people? Who was the man driving the bulldozer, and who were those men wearing uniforms, holding guns that never fired? Why didn't anyone stop them?

And the voice speaking over the images in strongly accented English, explaining why he was only following orders—

"Mum, is that Opa?"

Her mother's back shot up and her hand quickly

grabbed the remote control, which then clattered to the floor. Lara watched the panicked fingers fumble at the buttons, and suddenly she was viewing a toothpaste commercial.

"Oh Lara, are you still awake?"

It was an accusation. Lara started to cry. Her mother reached for her, but Lara pulled away.

"Who was that? Was that Opa?"

"No, no, darling."

"But it sounded like him!"

"That's just because he was German."

"Opa's not German!"

"Yes, darling, he is."

"But he can't be! He's here!"

"Yes, he came here a long time ago."

"When?"

"A long time ago. That was not Opa talking."

"What was he doing?"

"Opa?"

"Yes. No. That man."

"He was explaining what happened."

"What was it?"

Her mother said nothing, just pulled her daughter close.

"Were they—dead?" Lara's voice sounded shrill. Her throat felt like a splinter.

"Yes. A terrible man called Hitler killed them all. In a war that happened a long time ago."

"Why?"

"Because he hated them."

"Even the ladies? Were they ladies?"

"Come to bed, darling."

"Was Opa one of those men who made them fall in the hole?"

"No, darling." Her mother's voice choked slightly. "Oh Lara, you should not have seen that."

"Where was Opa?"

Her mother was silent. "I don't know. But he never did anything like that. I promise."

"But—"

"Lara, bed." Her mother took her hand and led her up the stairs, away from Hitler, away from the hole, and away from the man who sounded like Opa but wasn't.

"Can I ask him tomorrow?"

"Who?"

"Opa."

Her mother grasped Lara's shoulders, too hard.

"Never. You must never ask him."

Lara saw a face she did not know.

"Why?" It was a whisper. "You said he wasn't there?"

"Opa lost people he loved in the war. We must not make him sad."

"Why were you watching?"

"We need to know."

"Then why can't I ask him?"

"Because he wasn't there."

"Is that why he came here?"

"He came to meet Oma."

She was trembling. Then, quietly, "I am so sorry you saw that, darling. One day you will learn how brave Opa was. He is a good man."

"I know."

"And he needs us to love him."

"I do love him."

"I know. Now let's decide not to bother him with any questions."

"Yes."

"I love you."

"Yes."

Her mother held her for a moment, then tucked her into bed, and closed the door.

In Lara's dream it was night. And this became for her the recurring dream, the nightmare refrain that snarled from then
on through her childhood. And beyond. It was the quiet,
profound invasion.

In this dream, the darkness flared with torches, and harsh
voices punctured the silence. Lara watched herself awaken.
She saw herself panic, then calm, as if her mother's hand had
slid across her face. She woke the rest of the family.

In her dream there was a trapdoor. They slipped
through it, and then on into the dark trees enfolding the
house. Following a narrow wallaby track, they descended
into the gully that wound like a breath among cliffs steep
with eucalypti and red earth.

In the dream they moved smoothly, like water. Their
enemies were close behind them. Lara sensed the presence
of the caves above, their walls traced with ocher hands. She
began to climb, maneuvering around boulders and stubborn
trees that grew almost at right angles to the ground.

They reached a cave, its entrance hidden by prickling
Kangaroo Thorn. They crawled through into the shadows,
and Lara pressed herself against the earth; her heart was burning. The cave's mouth seemed to have torn the sky; its edges
were jagged, and the bright, staring stars hung at odd angles.

Lara woke at this moment—she always woke at this
moment, as their enemy scaled the cliff, while she and her
family had nothing but damp earth to protect them. The stars
would betray them; she knew their distant, cool voices would
whisper to the soldiers—but she always woke before they did.

She forced herself to sit up. Her eyes grasped the raft of
morning light, and she watched dust motes tangling with the
wan rays. As Lara's gaze traveled the lines of her sister's bed,

the window, and the ornaments framed above her, the dream lingered only a thin veil away; so near that a hand could easily pull her back through its folds. Sternly Lara reminded herself that they were safe, that armies would not invade Australia.

But the shadow endured. She was no longer Maria von Trapp. She was no longer the Brave Catcher of Frogs, Discoverer of Birds. She was only Lara, and she was hunted.

4.

Jen tumbled into the room to see if Lara was awake. Her sister was a quietly breathing mound, a swathe of sunlight had cut across her face and turned her hair red. Outside, the mid-summer day already shimmered with cicadas' song.

"Lara! Come on!"

Lara mumbled and turned over. Jen, now all of seven years old and no longer nervous of her sister's wrath, leapt nimbly onto the bedspread. She deftly squeezed a cold, wet washcloth over Lara's sleeping face. The effect was instant, and—for Jen—gratifying. Lara bolted upright, blinking the water out of her eyes, and gasped. Jen squealed with delight and jumped backwards to the door, just in case.

"Oma's made gingerbread and she's icing it now," she called across the room. "We can choose three pieces to take to the gully!"

Lara glowered and shook her head. "I'm all wet!"

Jen giggled and waved the washcloth like a flag. "Your fault for sleeping in and wasting the day!"

"You sound like Opa," Lara growled.

"So do you."

"Whose idea was the washcloth?"

"Mum's."

"What?!"

"Well, not exactly hers. Remember how she told us what she used to do to the other kids at school camps, when they had bunks?"

Lara sighed and pushed back the covers. She was too tired to fight back. She didn't want to talk about school, any school. She still felt worried that Mum and Dad might send both of them back there one day. She changed the subject.

"How many gingerbreads?"

"Three. Hurry, or she'll change her mind."

They could hear their mother and Oma chatting, and

Lara thought again how lucky they were to be able to stay here in the stone house. "I'm glad Dad works overseas."

"Don't you miss him?"

"Sure. Heaps. But I like being here."

Lara rummaged around for some socks her size, while Jen crossed the room to bounce up and down on her bed.

"You act like a four year old sometimes, look at you!"

Jen poked out her tongue, but settled cross-legged on the quilt. "How long do you think we'll stay this time?"

"Two months, I think."

"I heard Mum saying to Opa that it was six."

"Dad won't want to be away from us that long."

"That's what I said."

The two girls raced each other down the stairs, their hands sliding along the glossy banister. Lara marveled that her Opa had carved and planed it so smooth. It seemed to her that there was nothing Opa couldn't do.

❧

The gully opened to them as their feet found the path that lead them across the spur. The Spear Grass scratched, a magpie chortled from a drooping Sheoak, and faint clouds streaked the pale blue sky. Lara was just thinking again of the luxury of three pieces of gingerbread, when she heard a shout, and immediately turned around.

"It's Opa!" Jen tugged Lara in surprise. Lara narrowed her eyes in concern, but then realized that her grandfather was not waving with any urgency. The girls stopped, and waited for Opa to join them. They surveyed him curiously. He carried a rucksack, gripped a hiking stick and wore his thickest boots. He grinned from under his hat, and they returned the smile.

"Are you coming with us?" Lara asked hopefully.

In answer, he reached out to reposition the overall strap that had fallen off her shoulder. He ruffled Jen's hair.

"Did you fill your water bottles to the top?"

They nodded, then he led off. They followed him a little way across the brow of the hill.

The girls expected Opa to leave the path, and dip down towards the creek their usual way, but to their surprise he broke off through an opening between white-flowering Christmas Bush. They scrambled after him across some boulders, and on the other side lay a track they had never seen: it carved a tiny ditch through blue-green tussocks of Scented Iron Grass, and wound through Acacia trees, until it arrived at the base of the surrounding cliffs. There, it seemed to vanish.

Lara craned her neck to scan the rocky wall towering above them, and then wheeled around in excitement as it dawned on her where they were headed.

Opa met her eyes. "Yes, Lara," he replied to her unspoken question. "You are old enough. Today, we visit the caves."

He straightened up and rubbed the back of his neck as he, too, gazed up at the cliff face. "Good thing we don't have to climb that."

"How can we get up there?"

"You'll see. But before we do anything more ..."

He paused and swung his pack to the ground, and widened his shoulders in a stretch. Lara and Jen glanced up expectantly. He took a swig of water, and they followed suit. Then he squinted over their heads at the bright sky before finishing his thought.

"There were people here before we came. They lived here for many thousands of years.

"What happened to them?" asked Jen.

"Gone." He threw the word to the ground, and the girls did not press him. The silence held something ominous. He waited. A shadow passed over their feet, and Lara looked up to see a hawk gliding way above them.

"Today we will see where they lived. We will see their hand-prints on the cave wall. Perhaps you can still see where they had their fires." He looked pensively at Lara, then at Jen, before strapping his water bottle onto his belt. "Do not touch anything. These caves were sacred. We will not speak when we arrive. I will show you, and then we can go. You can eat when we come back down here."

Lara and Jen dutifully copied Opa in lifting up their day-packs to begin the next part of their trek.

The path was steep, and in places Lara had to pull herself up by holding onto exposed tree roots. She was panting, her skin heavy with sweat. She turned to heave Jen up to the very last rocky shelf.

They found themselves on a natural balcony of pressed red earth. Far below, on a railway line that snaked between the hills, a train whistle seared the hot, still afternoon. When Lara turned her eyes north, she could pick out the roof of the stone house. With delight she observed the postal van appear, a flash of white and red, and she wished for two postcards to arrive. Lara was beginning to be worried her father might have forgotten them.

Opa touched their shoulders. Behind them yawned the cave, its rough opening rimmed with thorns. Opa approached the entrance, turned once to gesture for the girls to drop their packs, and disappeared. He soon poked his head out and beckoned for Lara to join him. She burrowed inside, and took the flashlight Opa handed her.

At first she could see nothing. She was engulfed in an enormous shadow that she could feel on her face. It was hard to breathe; the cave was filled with damp, close air. In the flashlight's beam Lara picked out the cave walls, scalloped and intricate, as if someone had been moving slowly around the edge of the space with scissors.

She felt Opa's hand hold hers, and point the light towards the ground, several feet away. Lara noticed a small mound. She inched across the dirt floor and bent to examine the charred remains of wood and blackened stones. The fire pit looked more recent than several thousand years ago, and she turned to ask Opa, but he had rejoined Jen for a moment at the cave's entrance—she could see the brim of his hat shaped against the sky outside, and hear Jen's muffled protests. Lara knew her sister would be terrified of coming in here.

Lara swung the flashlight across the interior of the cave, and noticed the crushed shine of an empty beer can. Her breath rose angrily on seeing the trash, and she stooped to pick it up. At least she could remove it and leave this place— and its ancient people—some small token of respect.

Opa returned. "Jen is staying outside."

Lara held out the can to him. She sensed him recoil.

"It's terrible," she whispered, "I'm taking it with us."

He didn't reply, but lifted her hand again with the flashlight, this time training it on the wall ahead.

"Listen."

She knew he meant to say "look," but she did not correct him; it reminded her of the two of them watching birds. Lara peered where he indicated and noticed the faint handprints. They had been placed neatly together, fingers fanned out, their edges blurred with white. It seemed to Lara that whoever made the markings had tried to push through the cave wall to the other side. What had they tried to reach?

The two open palms were an invitation; she moved forward. To Lara, the shapes glowed rust-red, mystical portals to another time. Haltingly, she extended her own hand, to press it lightly against the outline. The fit was perfect—the prints could have been her own.

"Lara."

She stepped back.

"Do not touch them. Come back, now."

The sharp command in her Opa's voice startled her.

In the split second of blackness as she switched off her

flashlight, she was disoriented enough to wonder how long it would take before the invading soldiers of her nightmare discovered her here.

In the next few seconds she emerged into the sunlight, blinking as she had when Jen had spattered her face with water that morning. There were no soldiers, no stars—only the constant, parched sky.

Jen was sitting on the ground, drawing sulkily with a stick that kept breaking into smaller pieces. It cracked once more, and she threw it away.

"Can we go now?"

She really did sound four, Lara thought again. She looked at Opa. He did not seem cross at her for touching the painting.

"Have some water and then we will climb down another way, not so steep."

He waited while they drank. Lara glanced at his face. Her urge to touch the hand-prints had been overwhelming —she was unsure of how to share it with him, but he needed to know she had meant no disrespect. How could she explain the feeling that her skin on the painted stone might dissolve the wall?

Opa didn't look angry, just thoughtful.

They picked up their packs, and turned to go. Opa briefly locked eyes with Lara, and smiled gently. She moved shyly to his side, reached out and took his fingers in hers, as they retraced their footprints across the dust.

He understood, she was sure.

Back at the stone house they hugged Opa briefly and watched him withdraw into the shed. Lara and Jen loosened their packs and clomped across the back veranda. After a quick glance at each other, they raced to be first to touch the screen door—but as Lara's fingers reached it, the girls hesitated. They could hear someone crying.

"Stay here." Lara made Jen stand in the shadows while she crept forward. Leaning her face into the wire mesh, she could just barely see into the kitchen. Her mother stood in silhouette, against a rectangle of daylight in the doorway. Her shoulders were moving as if someone invisible were standing behind and shaking her, over and over. But there was nobody there.

Lara motioned to Jen, and they very quietly opened the screen door and slid through, remembering for the first and only time not to let it slam. The silhouette went quiet and shifted out of sight.

They stood there awkwardly, not sure what to do next.

"Let's go to her," whispered Jen.

"No."

"Why?"

Lara just shook her head and took Jen's hand. "Let's go outside."

"Do you think Dad's lost his job?"

"Maybe."

"And we won't have any money?"

"That won't matter."

"But we can't buy food then!" Jen began to cry.

"Opa grows most of our food, and we have chickens. Don't be silly."

"But you said—"

"I never said anything."

The two girls stared at each other, their faces sullen.

"I'm going in to ask her," Jen announced.

"No. Stay here."

"Why do we have to stay outside?"

There was a pause. Then Lara grabbed Jen and raced to

their tree swing that Opa had made. "You can go first," she offered, and Jen clambered up, still sniffling. "Push me really high, so I can see the gully," she ordered.

Lara obligingly pulled the large knot that Jen clung to, high over her head, before she let go with a roar of effort. Jen swung out and over the terraced herb garden, and sang as she could see the tops of the gully cliffs, then, "The sea!" she called happily.

Lara breathed hard, pushing all the anxiety out of her body. After ten swings Lara dropped her arms, exhausted.

She noticed Opa appear on the periphery of the garden. His shoulders were squared, as always, and his felt hat shaded his face. He stood still, observing them. Lara waved. She watched him walk towards them, and noticed that he looked at her and Jen with a gruff tenderness she did not often see in his face.

"You are getting stronger, Lara. Jen went high today,"

Jen grinned at him from the rope swing as she allowed the cord to slow. Then she remembered the silhouette in the kitchen. "What's Mum upset about?"

The rope slackened and she slithered onto the grass. Lara stood with her arms crossed in front of her. She noticed Opa was standing the same way. He reached out a hand and touched Jen's head.

"Oma is with her," he said softly. "It is best to leave them be." He held the gaze of each child, one at a time, before he continued. "Your mother is a brave and good woman. You are fortunate children."

He paused.

"Do you want me to swing you?"

"Yes!" Jen quickly scaled the rope and ensconced herself on the swing. Opa tilted Lara's chin with his finger. She noticed that black earth lined all the grooves, making his skin a contour map. "You first."

He turned to Jen. "Get down, little monkey, and let your big sister have a turn!"

Jen jumped down, and scurried to sit on a nearby rock.

Lara closed her eyes as her grandfather pushed her up and away, up to the trees, across the sky, over the caves. She felt like a hawk soaring. When her turn finally ended, she climbed down sadly to let Jen back onto the rope.

Opa did not seem to tire; he swung them until the sky turned the color of bottled apricots, and a cool wind caressed them from the gully. Only when they could no longer see their fingers curled on the rope, did they finally go inside.

❧

At the evening meal, they sat mute. Lara ate her silverbeet without complaint, frightened by her mother's face. Mum had always been a private person, but now she seemed closed, as if she could only see inwards. Oma bustled, sniffled and occasionally slammed plates of food down in front of them. There were gingerbread men for dessert, and Oma didn't even notice that the children took three and shoved more into their laps, for later. Even stranger, was that Opa pretended not to notice. Mum continued to stare into herself.

"Is Dad gone two months or six?"

Jen's question was a switch that immediately turned her mother's head, lit up her eyes, and caused her voice to emerge strained. "Jen, it seems as if he is not coming back at all."

Oma stood up and quickly put an arm around Mum's shoulders, while her daughter's face collapsed into her hands.

"Shhh," soothed Oma, as if Mum had fallen and grazed her knee, "Shhh."

"What do you mean?" Jen shrieked.

Lara's face went cold, and the tips of her fingers tingled. Could you get hypothermia from news like this? Did something like this make you so cold you could die?

"Did he write?" Lara asked in a small voice.

Oma nodded at her, while her mother's shoulders shook.

Oma glanced at her husband and gestured with her head. It meant "take these girls out, and leave me with mine."

Opa pushed back his chair and stood, motioning to the girls to join him.

"Come," he ordered, not unkindly.

The girls followed him, and together they went outside. The sky was soft and dark, the stars glistened. Around them the eucalyptus trees crackled their long curved leaves in the night wind. Opa took his grand-daughters' hands into his own, and stepped off the veranda.

"I can smell the moon," Jen breathed.

Opa squeezed her fingers, and Lara's too. Together they walked soundlessly across the grass, past the swing, past the herb garden. The moonlight made it easy to find the rock that Jen had perched on earlier, while Lara had swung out across the sky.

"Here." Opa lifted them up one at a time, so that they both faced him, at near his height. He remained on the ground.

Jen whimpered and rubbed her eyes. "Why isn't Dad coming back?"

Lara could still not do what she needed, to make her voice come out. Her neck and face were stone.

Opa reached out to stroke Lara's hair, as if he understood. In response, her eyes warmed and swelled, before tears slid down her cheeks.

"He was offered a good job there, the University is famous. It has made it very hard for him to say no."

But that wasn't the reason, Lara knew. The last postcards had not been signed with an animal. Something had happened to make him forget them.

Opa sighed and then leaned closer. Whether he was angry, they could not see in the dark, but there was a fierceness in his silence.

"He has decided to leave your mother. He has, it seems, met another lady. He wrote that he is in love with her, and will be staying now in England."

"Does he want a new family?" Lara asked faintly.

"I don't know. I don't understand how he could do this. But he has made up his mind. That is clear."

There was a pause, before he added softly. "But you girls and your mother will stay here while she works out what to do. We will look after you."

Jen slid down off the rock and ran back into the house, sobbing. The screen door slammed and from the garden they heard the frantic thumping of her feet on the stairs. Lara buried her head in her arms, and cried. Opa's arms landed on her shoulders with weight and warmth, as they pulled her tight to him. She shook under his embrace; he said nothing. When the sobs tapered off into erratic breaths, he held her tighter still.

"You will not be alone," he whispered. "Your father has left, but I will stay. I will do this for you and Jen. I am your Opa."

The Gift of Birds

At first Tomas walks without purpose. He does not notice the light rain dissolving the soot on his coat, nor does he hear the keening of dissatisfied gulls. He does wonder briefly at the arctic whiteness of their feathers, but his mind is too full to absorb much of what surrounds him.

Just because he feels he is drifting does not mean that he meanders. He strides. *False purpose,* he thinks once, then clenches a fist in his pocket. The rattle of a trawler engine cuts through the mist and damp. He follows the sound. When he finds its source, the putt-putting has turned to an uneasy roar. Tomas watches the stern disappear in an angry wake.

A homeless man shuffles across the periphery of his vision. There is an army of such men; they march in disjointed battalions through the post-war streets of this German town. Tomas observes the despairing rhythm of the man's walk. *Tempo Rubato.* A rhythm that fractures its own pulse. *Lamentando.* His body carves a lament. Tomas looks away; it is enough to bear the weight cradled under his coat.

He knows he must leave. He must escape this place where his only companion is the familiar cloud that descends on him daily, its gray and clammy hands tightening around his body, his heart. He aches now, like an old man, yet he is only thirty. So much terror has criss-crossed his path with venomous patterns that he cannot erase, has spurted from his own hands. He fears what he has been. Perhaps he is unforgivable.

Tomas lives in a defeated country. The buildings have crumbled, and many places have been flattened beyond recognition. Roads no longer take him where he wishes to go, but seem instead to direct him to ruins: wrecked houses, devastated people. Ragged figures pick carefully and uselessly through rubble. Dogs stand peevishly at street corners. An enormous silence has descended on this city, and on others like it, he is sure.

It is 1946. He is twenty-nine—no, he reminds himself, thirty. He thinks about his birthday, which falls at the beginning of each year. He burned a single candle and sang Bach in his head, that freezing January morning. Tomas recalls the emptiness, and the dirty glass window the wind was determined to crack.

His mother and father are dead. His hands shake. He is in constant pain. He wonders whether he has lost his soul, wonders whether that is what the ragged figures pick through the stones and mess to find, any soul—something that they can hold aloft and then perhaps find reason to hope. Tomas hates the despair on their faces when they dig and find nothing, and it makes him angry.

He turns now, down a street that still possesses several shops, although they are shut at this early hour, doors bolted, with *Closed* signs hung at awkward angles behind streaked glass. His feet mark out distance and time as he wanders past. He glimpses his reflection out of the corner of his eye. Mostly he tries hard not to see himself, with his thin shoulders and a back that seems permanently bent. If Tomas accidentally catches sight of himself—even if in a fleeting way—he perceives that he is just the same as the scavengers searching pitifully for their small tokens of life.

His sanity rests on the belief that he is different, that he must be to have survived, that he will not spend his remaining days on the earth picking restlessly through the debris of his past. He must build something new, or else he will cave in on himself. He will become a ruin. Yet, when his reflection shines at him from glass, he develops a sudden burning fear that he has already become one. *It is just the way I am walking from the cold,* he tells himself. *I am not the same. I can leave.* Tomas passes another window, another glimpse of himself.

Then he sees something else.

It rests delicately on the pavement, strangely pure and unsullied. It's a perfect feather. He stops and gazes at it. He cannot determine which bird it may have fallen from. It is pale brown, fringed with perfect, tiny lines like a soft breeze through pines. He picks it up, and it seems to sigh into his hand.

He does not have a working compass, but he knows that he must find somewhere new to go. Here is only death. Tomas puts the tender shape inside his pocket, and turns toward the city center.

For all its lightness, the feather warms his fingers, and he suddenly recognizes the beating of his heart.

Part Two: Courante

(n): A Baroque dance, generally the second movement in a suite. It originates from the French, literally "running," the feminine present participle of "courir." In Der Vollkommene Capellmeister (Hamburg, 1739), Johann Mattheson wrote that "there is something heartfelt, something longing and also gratifying, in this melody: clearly music on which hopes are built."

5.

Ten years before, she'd sat in exactly the same place. Then, it had been at her grandmother's funeral. Now it was her grandfather's. Her beloved Opa.

She had not really been present for her grandmother's funeral, although her feet were clipped into her best shoes, and she'd mouthed all the hymns. She had been focused intently on the contortions made by her throat, how the tiny muscles heaved, contracted, hardened. It was like holding a sponge in your fist and squeezing out the water until it is dry.

Now she was at her Opa's funeral, and all she could think about was whether there would be tuna sandwiches at the wake. In fact, she was thinking about those sandwiches quite desperately; they were the unlikely hand-rail that kept her from plunging overboard into grief.

The church felt barren, the decoration of the stained-glass windows ineffectual, like make-up on a tired old face. Lara imagined her own face, and wondered if she should have worn make-up. She was twenty-two, and although her fresh skin often made people think she was much younger, today she too felt old and strained.

Another loose curl fell across her eyes. It didn't seem to matter what Lara put in her thick hair, it tangled wildly and refused all efforts to tame it into submission. Like herself really, she thought, sitting here in her dark blue dress that only just hid her favorite pair of stripy socks and Blundstone work boots. But today, especially today, she wanted fiercely to be herself. She would resist becoming small, voiceless and gray, like those around her.

Her cardigan slipped off one narrow shoulder and hung in sympathy with the lock of hair. She heard her mother sigh next to her. Then the vicar leaned forward and gathered them in with his tired, sing-song voice.

"Our friend Thomas Miller was a man who cared for the beauties of nature. To see that, one has only to visit the block of bushland that was his home for so many years, as I had the privilege of doing on Saturday last, when I spoke with the bereaved family members, many of whom are gathered here today. They took me on a tour of the garden, which I can only describe as resplendent with care and attention to detail. Every plant was labeled, every path lined with stones that Mr Miller himself hewed from the ground.

"Years of planning and maintenance went into this garden. I am told that he was the greatest collector of native flora in the region. This summarizes so much of the man we all knew and loved. He was a quiet achiever. His passionate love for all things Australian, and indeed for all things pertaining to Australian flora, quite filled his life."

The vicar continued talking as if he had known her grandfather, which he had not. But who truly had? As Lara looked around at the mourners, she was struck with the fact that they were all friends of her mother there to support them, or relatives of her grandmother. Now that she thought about it, Lara did not know that Opa had ever spoken of having friends; certainly nobody outside the family, or beyond her mother's or Oma's circle of connections had ever spent time at the stone house. Was it possible that Opa had lived his life alone, but for them?

Lara had studied T.S. Eliot's poems, and she wondered if the image of the man everyone thought they knew was also hollow, filled with straw; that perhaps Opa's real self had existed somewhere out of their reach. Even here at his own funeral he stood off to one side, in shadow, while stories about him hovered center stage, delivered through the mouths of hired actors.

When she thought of the grandfather she loved, Lara realized her every memory of him seemed now to hold silence at its core—even the night he had gathered her hands and held her while she sobbed under the moon for the father she would never see again. Like mirrored glass, Opa had always reflected and never revealed—it seemed to her now that he had simply thrown back at Lara images of herself. In panic she wondered what else she thought she knew, that was not?

And then, without warning, Lara was four years old, holding her grandfather's hand; they were moving together toward his workshop under the stone house. The grass was uneven, and they took a shortcut over a low, rocky wall dividing the front lawn from the path that ran from the gate to the house. Lara stumbled, but her grandfather's hand halted her fall and lifted her again, so that little more happened than the spiky earth swerving almost to meet her chin and then dipping away from her, as if she were a swooping bird that had missed its prey. Her grandfather held her upright, his fist tight around her hand. The stumbling had got in the way of her question.

"Opa?"

"Yes?"

"Opa? What will happen when you are dead? Will the spiders take over your house?"

Her grandfather's leg hesitated at her side; a slight speed bump had jolted their smooth passage. Lara supposed he laughed and spoke matter-of-factly about why spiders would not conquer his personal terrain, even after he moved on. She clearly recalled her suspicion of the tiny creatures, their many miniature arms folded, watching from corners—always watching, ready to take advantage of any opportunity, wanting to own the house for themselves but biding their time.

The adult Lara gripped her fingers together; again, she needed to stop herself from falling.

She noticed her great aunt sitting on the far side of the church. Bertha, Oma's only sister, had appeared episodically over the years, to offer pastries and warm, knitted clothing. She was wrapped in a dark green shawl, and wore a slightly faded straw hat that made her seem from another time, although Lara knew it was a stubborn resistance to fashion that caused her to dress that way. Lara had always felt sorry for her great aunt, probably because of her name. Bertha Hilda—a name for an ox, Lara thought, not a woman.

The face under the hat looked bemused. Lara's attention was held by the profile etched against the whitewashed church wall; it looked different from the other mourners' faces. Lara waited for the old woman to shift or cough, or cover her mouth with a delicate handkerchief, like so many of the other older women were doing, but she remained perfectly still. Not a muscle tensed. No hint of a breeze even dared lift a scrap of her white hair; she was simply watching. And thinking, Lara realized. This wasn't shock—she seemed to be processing something.

Everyone stood, and the vicar announced the next hymn. Jen shot her an agitated glance, and pointed to the order of service. Lara's heart leapt. She stared down at the stark white paper in front of her. They had only two verses, before she would be called upon.

Lara smoothed down her dress and adjusted her woolen jacket. Out of habit she twisted the loose strand of hair around her finger, and then checked to be sure her earrings hadn't fallen out.

Then the past clutched at her, as if trying to hold her from moving ...

The kitchen. Lara and her mother. The space between them, as always, a deep and frustrating sea.

"What was Opa like when he was young?"

Lara was trying to extract the past from her mother, who guarded her childhood as closely as her own father had guarded his. But Lara was fourteen years old, still young enough to believe that if she hammered hard enough, all doors would open for her.

"Oh, he loved the outdoors, camping and exploring. He was very good-looking. He was outgoing, everybody liked him."

Like those ridiculous dating shows Lara and her friends

watched: *Thomas likes travel, water sports, and meeting people.*

"Why can't you tell me?"

Her mother lifted one eyebrow—a gesture that infuriated Lara—and she tried to control her frustration.

"Oh, he traveled."

Travel. Lara leaned forward. "Where did he travel?"

"Oh, around Europe, then he came here, of course."

"Where in Europe, exactly?"

"Not sure."

"When?"

"Forgotten."

"Why?"

"Oh Lara, don't ask so many questions."

And her mother stood, smiled lightly, and left the room. She always left the room. And Lara would remain, stranded, an island with silence eroding her like a tide.

Don't ask so many questions.

At the funeral, the hymn ended.

Lara, Jen, and two cousins walked nervously up to the coffin at the front of the church. They had not rehearsed, but only been told what to do. They each bent down and fastened one hand around a brass handle. Darting anxious looks at each other, they raised the coffin together. It was not heavy, which shocked Lara. It should have been full of Opa's strength.

The coffin lifted at a slight angle, and with disgust Lara felt the body slide and bump dully against her. Like a body filled with straw—a hollow, T. S. Eliot body—there was nothing warm in its husky slither across the wooden surface. Suddenly sickened, Lara realized that she carried the shell of a human being. It was so tragic that she almost moaned, but social convention kept her upright, her eyes straight ahead.

They carried the coffin with measured step—a strange reversal of a bridal walk down the aisle. It seemed years before the damp old church smell gave way to a mixture of fumes, fish and chips, and Spring blossoms, as they emerged onto the street. A black hearse waited, with what looked like security men or terribly serious real-estate agents, who took over the burden of the coffin, and slid it with well-practiced ease into the back of the car.

Lara and the others watched silently. The rest of the gathering poured steadily out of the church door, just as taken by the sudden bright daylight and sounds of passing traffic. It was reassuring; life moved all around them.

But not for Lara. The world had slipped into slow motion. Sound and light had dimmed, because now Opa was gone.

6.

There were tuna sandwiches at the wake, which was held in the living room of the old stone house. Lara grabbed one from a tray set out on one of the tables.

So many gatherings had occurred here, and after this last one, there would be silence. Even now, while people drifted through the rooms, the place throbbed soundlessly with the power of absence.

She was just taking a mouthful when someone tapped her lightly on the shoulder. Lara turned her head. Behind her stood the wiry, but now slightly wizened figure of Great Aunt Bertha, wrapped in the dark green shawl. Lara smiled fondly. In many ways this woman had filled a painfully empty space in their lives when their grandmother had left them.

Bertha had lived on her family's farm for most of her life. When she finally became too old to hoist sheep and cook dinners for ten people, she decided begrudgingly to move to where wide roads, plenty of shopping malls, and hospitals promised safety and community. She also believed that she was needed by her sister's grandchildren, regardless of what this meant for their mother. Bertha Hilda Brenner had slowly adapted to city life, albeit with a fair degree of grumbling, and a constant need to be out in her vegetable garden.

Lara was fifteen when her mother had first decided to step out on their own, leave the stone house and move to the city. Lara had found it hard, but not as impossible as she had imagined, to return to school. She was able to disappear into a music practice room as many lunchtimes as she needed to forget herself in playing her cello, and being a musician gave her a credibility amongst the other students that meant she was no longer a target.

It was odd going to sleep at night with the sound of traffic and sirens, rather than the growl of possums and croaking of night birds. It was strange and sad to now have Oma gone, and Opa a long, half-hour drive away.

Even more surreal was to leave the house each morning for school, and be confronted with the blur of fast-moving cars that were the principle feature of living on a busy main road. Lara tried to ignore the polluted panting that filled her airspace as she walked to the train each day. The road fervor persisted even on Saturdays, but on those mornings she could lie in bed and try to concentrate instead on the sound of the magpies that mercifully sang quite loud near her bedroom window.

On one of these weekend mornings a muddy, gasping truck braked at the top of the drive. Its dented bed was stacked with antique furniture, cooking implements, and an enormous black kiln. This vehicle could be conveying only one person, and Lara ran downstairs to fling open the front door. Great Aunt Bertha had arrived, complete with all her china-painting gear, flustered and ready as always for a cup of tea.

When Lara's mother left to go out for the afternoon, Great Aunt Bertha was given her first city assignment: to look after the Davies children and keep them out of mischief. The children were pressed into service to heave the kiln from the metal truck-bed and set it on the front porch.

"Cover it! Cover it!" cried an anxious Bertha, as the girls frantically gathered sticks and leaves to hide their great aunt's most treasured possession from the thieves that she was convinced cruised this leafy neighborhood, on the prowl for expensive china-painting equipment.

Afterwards, they sat in the living room while Bertha unpacked one box after another, searching in a mumbling, intensely focused fashion for her knitting. They could hear their great aunt from the next room, constantly huffing and resentfully kicking each box that refused to yield her wool and needles. The girls half-heartedly played Monopoly, and Jen cried when she lost the last station.

Lara saw the fox first. They rushed to the window, their voices raised with excitement. It was a thrilling moment—

immediately they were back on the bushland farm, calling for Opa, tearing off with sticks, their grandfather with his gun. Now here, sitting lethal and plump amidst the new, lush suburbs, was a fox!

Great Aunt Bertha flounced in. "What's all the commotion?" she yapped with annoyance. She peered out the window toward where Lara was pointing, drew a quick breath, then disappeared. Lara and Jen stared at each other, then raced out after her.

They were too late. There was Great Aunt Bertha, having thrown a blanket over the animal, now clubbing it viciously with a pick that had been lying on the back veranda. With a triumphant hoot, she whipped back the blanket, grasped the tail, and held the bloodied corpse in the air like a bargain at a department store sale.

"We finished 'im! Oh, yes, we did! Put the kettle on, girls!"

For a week, that fox hung on the Hills Hoist[3], and friends and neighbors were invited around for many ceremonial viewings—all over a cuppa, of course.

And now here was Great Aunt Bertha, frail but firing, a saucer trembling between arthritic fingers. A wisp of white hair hung between her eyes like pulled cotton.

"Didn't think much of that vicar."

Great Aunt Bertha tapped the table with one twisted finger. She noticed a crumb and flicked it onto the floor. "Don't think much of the food here, either."

She peered closely at Lara's tuna sandwich. "Haven't tried one of them, though."

"They're not bad, actually."

Lara watched the old woman bend toward the tray, then straighten up again.

"Lara, dear, fetch one for me? I can't see what's them, and what's jam tartlets!"

Great Aunt Bertha was never one to talk with her

---

3   A height-adjustable rotary clothes line

mouth full, so she spoke a couple of words between each bite. Her voice was as energetic, and her conversation as unconventional as always. Lara was grateful for distraction from the severe, silent grieving all around her.

Bertha shifted from offhand remarks about the food and décor, but her eyes continued to flicker around the room.

"He was a odd one, your grandfather … oh, yes, indeed. He never said much, now, did he? Eh? What's that?"

"He was very quiet."

Lara wasn't sure she wanted to talk about Opa with Bertha. Bertha had never liked him, she suspected. He always grumbled when she arrived at the door; Lara would slip away at her first opportunity, and scurry to the orchard, or the garden, to see where Opa had hidden himself.

Lara took another sandwich from the tray, and hoped her great aunt would go and talk to someone else.

"He's quiet now, that's for sure!"

Great Aunt Bertha wheezed with laughter, glancing around furtively to see if she had been overheard. Angry tears threatened to explode behind Lara's eyes.

The old woman leaned forward conspiratorially.

"If you want my opinion," she whispered loudly, "he was a bit strange in the head. Always was. I told your grandmother to leave him be, but she took no notice. He was so good-looking."

"What do you mean?" replied Lara sharply.

Bertha shut down, found another tuna sandwich, and waddled off to offer advice and condolences to Lara's mother.

Lara stood gripped in her own question. She hardly noticed when her sister came over and tugged at her sleeve.

"Isn't this just awful? It was bad enough at Oma's funeral, but this seems much worse—nobody's talking about him!"

Lara tuned back in to the room and to Jen's voice.

"Everyone's talking about what the vicar said," Jen continued, "and about Opa's garden, and about the copper beeches at the back. In fact, I think there is going to be a tour very soon."

"I felt the body slide in the coffin, Jen."

Her sister's eyes grew wide.

"It was like there was a scarecrow in there, not a person at all."

Jen brushed some crumbs off her sleeve, then looked up. "This whole day doesn't seem real," she muttered.

Lara looked at her keenly. "What do you mean?"

"Like I said, nobody's talking about him."

"Except that he loved the outdoors and was a passionate gardener."

"Exactly."

"What do you remember most about him?"

Jen thought for a moment. She refilled her cup from the nearby urn. "I will never forget when he taught you to fire a gun." Jen shivered at the memory. "We were never allowed to touch one again after that. And that was fine with me." She took a sip of her coffee. "He was always keen to see our school reports, to see how well we'd done. I never got as many A's as you did, and I always wondered whether he thought I was a bit stupid. Still, he would sit me on his knee and say, 'Work, work, work. The work is the way you will get what you want.'"

Lara was subdued. "But the swing, Jen. Remember how high he pushed us?"

"He loved us."

"Of course he did."

"He just never spoke much about it." Jen stopped, and looked at Lara. "Not to me, anyway."

Lara reached for Jen's hand, and they both remembered the day the screen door didn't slam, and the way they both went back outside. They had remained outside, of everything, from then on, it seemed. Some things change you forever.

Lara's mother came up to them. Her eyes were red.

"We're going on a tour of the garden and copper beeches. Will you girls come?"

Jen stared pointedly at Lara before replying to her mother. "All right, I'll go. As long as we can walk on ahead."

"That's fine, I'm sure everyone will understand. After all, it's … " She broke off, weeping under the cover of her hostess face. "I am now an orphan," she murmured.

7.

The two young women walked ahead of the relatives and friends. As she looked around her, Lara recalled the bedraggled, wiry sheep and the raucous excitement of chickens in the yard. The old corrugated-iron shed, where she had spent so many rich hours observing her grandfather as he worked, had been pulled down. It had been the place of daily activity, lingering odors of oils, paints, lanolin, and dust. Lara's throat caught, remembering those smells, and the feel of the warm iron handle as the enormous ridged door slid open to let her in.

Here on the bushland farm, everything had been discovered, drawn up, created, and reflected upon in that shed. There was always a way to fix things. Precious items were brought there to be doctored and righted by her Opa's weathered hands. Sometimes the objects expired from their wounds, but very rarely.

Every tool hanging on the wall had been meticulously labeled and stenciled—if Opa removed a hammer, then its shadow remained in its proper place. There was a myriad of tiny drawers, each holding a different size of nail or screw. There were clearly marked containers of nuts, bolts, washers, even rubber bands and the ends of pencils.

Her grandfather worked quietly, solidly; he seemed an extension of what he held in his hands. Lara learned that this old man loved to inspect objects from every angle—he seemed to need to know something completely before he contemplated its repair. Eventually he would draw in his breath, his shoulders dropping a little. He turned to find a small tube of glue, a wrench, or whatever else was needed. Tool in hand, he would bend so near to the object that she could no longer see his face under his wide-brimmed hat. Perhaps a few minutes, perhaps an hour or so later, he would straighten his back and pronounce—not verbally but in his eyes and the full stature of his body—that the item was finished, repaired, brought back to life. It was always a grand, if quiet, moment.

As a child, Lara had loved to pretend she was a wandering gypsy, without family or way in the world. She had needed the right shoes for this: earthy, clumping clogs made of wood. She remembered eagerly requesting that her Opa make her some. It took him a whole morning in the shed, tracing over solid bits of wood, then sawing around their shape, and fastening straps over the ends to hold her toes. When he had finished, Opa smiled and said, "You cannot possibly walk in these."

This had made her cross—as if he knew anything about wandering the world, of camping like a gypsy, living without possessions and having adventures.

Lara's throat tightened once more. She knew she still had those clogs somewhere. She looked down at her feet, encased in her faithful Blundstone boots. She could wear these anywhere. With a spot of polish they were even good enough for a funeral, Lara thought sadly.

Jen grabbed her and pointed skyward. They were just entering the copper avenue of trees. Staring upward revealed what looked like layers of a colorful cake—frothy cloud, a line of fresh blue, and then the glowing, textured mass of beech leaves.

Lara was about to ask Jen what she had seen, but then she didn't need to. The hawk swept gracefully into her line of vision, curving and cutting across the air above them. It was enjoying a wind current that swayed it like a soft, feathered flag. Lara and Jen drank in the hawk's flight, imagining. Then it vanished, distilled into wind and cloud.

The young women turned and walked pensively through the archway of enormous trees, feeling with every step the closeness and safety of the protective foliage. They walked without speaking, not because there was nothing to say, but because there was too much.

They could hear the chatter of the rest of the party behind them. They turned once or twice to see their mother, in black but with overly bright eyes and a chirpy voice, explaining the special features of the garden.

"It used to be so much larger, you know. We had to subdivide when my mother … moved out."

"Didn't she miss all this?" asked a perfumed friend, with just the right balance of sympathy and nonchalance in her voice. At that point they all stopped, and took in the wide sweep of beautiful garden and the wild patch of bushland that now—instead of reaching out toward the gully—lay in a meek strip at the back and side of the landscaped grounds. The abundance of native flora, the dart of tiny finches, and the insistent, scraping sound of eager wattle birds were all focused upon, were suddenly the joyful features of the day.

"Life goes on," murmured someone, lifted by the effusive growth all around them. A magpie, encouraged by the respectful silence, lifted its refined face to the top leaves of a silver-gum, and sang with heartfelt pleasure at the day.

Lara felt tears spring to her eyes, and was momentarily hurtled to many years ago—she lay back and gazed up through the leaves in the orchard, wondering at the trembling shapes they made against the blue above her head. And here, with the magpie calling, she could hear her Opa whistling serenely, like a peaceful bird—the dull thud and scratch of his shovel creating rhythms that melded effortlessly with her breathing.

Lara remembered she and Jen as children, following Opa down to the furthermost corner of his land, where the native cherry trees grew. The grass was feathery and dry, and the ends tickled them with warm, rustling fingers. Opa hummed contentedly, carrying a saw on his right shoulder. Small white butterflies spun out of their way, while bees zigzagged through the summer air.

It was early afternoon, and the scrub smelled hot—warmed eucalyptus and dry earth. Their feet crunched sun-baked leaves, and the sky was pale and parched above their heads. They finally reached the native cherry trees, with their weeping branches and leaves that drooped like deep green hair.

Opa let Lara and Jen choose branches, then he sawed determinedly until the wood snapped. He breathed heavily. Dark patches of sweat formed on his khaki shirt. The children watched the pile of sweet-smelling, leafy arms grow larger.

When enough had been collected to fill the corner of the living room, Lara and Jen ran up the thin bushland track to call for their father, and together the two men heaved the branches back toward the house.

Lara realized that must have been their final Christmas together, and that she could no longer recall her father's face. Her mind could only find Opa's.

Later that evening, Oma had found the old boxes filled with sparkling fiberglass spheres, tiny wooden angels in small hoops, delicate pine snowflakes looped with crimson thread, and foam balls speared with hundreds of glowing sequins. The Christmas tree, made of native cherry branches, drooped with the weight of so much color and light. It remained for a month as a welcomed guest, its sharp and piny fragrance permeating the house. They gathered in this room, enjoying the scent, the colors, and each other. At these times it was good to be together in the old stone house.

For her grandfather, although Lara could not know this, the past retreated for a season, hibernating beneath the laughter and the silent sparkling of the little spheres circling the tree's dark leaves.

8.

The magpie continued to sing in the silver-gum, and the funeral guests remained with Lara's mother, listening.

Jen and Lara made their way back to the house.

Once inside, she left Jen, and moved numbly across the carpet, breathing the scent of dried flowers. She put her hand on the banister, swung her body around it with well-practiced ease, and climbed until she arrived at the middle window on the stairway landing. She could see the row of copper beeches, the herb garden, and the magpie that sat watchman-like on a graceful ballerina arm of the silver-gum.

She heard a creak behind her and looked around. There stood Great Aunt Bertha, looking slightly sheepish, and holding a half-drunk cup of tea.

"Nice view," she croaked.

Lara softened. Bertha was very like Lara's Oma in some respects, but she differed in one important way. She was not a romantic, as she often reminded them—especially on her birthday, when Lara's family took her out to tea and gave her presents. *Not sentimental either, not like that grandmother of yours.*

Lara turned back to the window, moving to allow her great aunt room to join her, as she surveyed the garden and the figures strolling among the trees.

The two of them listened to the ticking of the old clock in a downstairs room. Each tap of time sent more dust into the air.

"Now I suppose we can finally sell the house," Lara murmured.

"And about time, too." Bertha tugged on Lara's sleeve. "I have something for you."

The old woman shifted immediately from the window, and began climbing the rest of the stairs. She heaved and creaked like the wood beneath her feet.

Lara followed. She knew instinctively where they were going. Her grandmother's final words, she knew, rested in a large wooden chest in the gallery, and to get there meant climbing stairs that no longer quite held together, that cried out when you trod their surfaces. Lara could put her fingers in her ears, she supposed, but that meant she would not be able to hold the rail, and the rail was as important to her climb as were the tuna sandwiches at the wake.

Great Aunt Bertha clambered up the final steps and arrived at the gallery that ran along the upper part of the house. After all these years, Lara could still feel the excitement of running up here to plan and scheme with Jen, to plot adventures, plays and secret excursions. It seemed that Lara's childhood self tore past her, and nearly knocked her off her feet.

Bertha halted, and Lara saw they had come to the Camphor-wood Chest—a large, intricately carved trunk that over the years had held fabric, books, and linen. The last thing her grandmother had done before going into the hospital for good was to reorganize the chest and fill it with items wrapped in old towels … her last words.

They had all let Oma do whatever she wanted that day. Lara's grandfather had spent all that morning in the garden. Later, when he drove her away in his shiny old car, without speaking a word, Oma's eyes had been fixed on the windshield; she both refused to look back, and resisted looking toward their destination. Lara still wondered what she had seen. Her grandmother spent the rest of her days in a hospital bed, draped in sheets, like a half-hidden carving.

Lara pressed her fingers very tightly into the wooden railing and rubbed the surface viciously for a few moments. Great Aunt Bertha sneezed. Then, muttering, she reached out with both sturdy arms to undo the brass clasps on either side of the chest. She flipped the lid backwards, and a puff of fragrance emanated from inside the trunk. It made them both cough, and then cry—the scent reminded them of her and of him, and of other griefs rolled together, and then suddenly Lara was crying about the body bumping the side of the coffin and the fact that the spiders could come now if they wanted.

Bertha cried in a messy, awkward way; trying to shovel the tears back into her eyes. Lara and her great aunt didn't hold each other, they just stood and inhaled the sadness that both of them had been resisting for much of the day. They cried until they no longer knew what they were crying about.

After a time, Bertha patted Lara on the arm, and Lara's body gradually ceased trembling. Once again she was aware of the clock downstairs, ticking as it had always done. Around her, the wooden railing, the floorboards, and the Camphor-wood Chest glowed amber with afternoon light.

"It's in here somewhere … " Her great aunt scrabbled among the aging piles of cloth. This went on for a few minutes. "It's in here somewhere," she said again, and then straightened up.

In her hands she held a large lump of pink terry toweling. Lara wasn't quite sure what to say, but she couldn't help smiling at the incongruity of the material. Moth-eaten silk would somehow have seemed more appropriate, and it certainly wouldn't have been pink.

Bertha hurried her into one of the upstairs rooms. The one she chose was empty of furniture. The wallpaper was stained with the damp, and curtains hung limp in a dormer window. Bertha looked at Lara stolidly for what seemed like a long time.

"She kept these for years. I know she wanted you to have them. She said you always stared at them so much when you were a little girl."

Lara had taken only her bed, books and her clothes when she had moved away from home—and her cello. Everything else had been stored in the attic of her mother's home. The inner-city flat she shared with her fellow music student was tiny. If you didn't clear up the dishes at the end of a meal, then that was it—you couldn't get into the kitchen. Lara wondered suddenly where she might put this beautiful, fragile collection of belongings wrapped in the dull pink towel.

Bertha shuffled on her feet, and for a moment her face contorted. Lara placed her hand on Bertha's arm, concerned.

"Are you alright?"

"There's something else."

She waited, but Bertha just wrestled her hands with each other.

"Please tell me."

"There's something I found, and I needed to give it to you. To someone. It's in there … with everything else."

"What is it?"

"I don't know, but I know it's something, well, something about before he came here."

Lara turned cold. "Before he came to Australia?"

"I suppose so, I suppose so. You'll see."

"Should I look now?"

"No, no. Not here." Bertha sounded frantic. "Go home."

"Where did you find it, whatever it is?"

"I'll tell you now, then I never want to talk about it again. It's out of my hands, and I don't want to know. I wouldn't tell your mother either."

"Did Oma have it?"

"She never said anything, and she was my sister." Here Bertha's voice crumpled. "I would say she never saw it, or—"

"Or?" Lara barely spoke. She felt trapped in the forward motion of this moment.

"Or, God save me, she might never have married him."

Lara had the sensation that she had slipped away from her body, and fragmented, like the dust motes that drifted about the room.

"I was cleaning out your Oma's things. It was stuck down behind a drawer. I don't think she ever knew."

"Why on earth were you pulling out drawers?"

"It was jammed! I thought something of hers might have been down there!"

Lara wanted to be three years old and cry out, "I hate you!" and for that to feel better, as if simply hitting out would bring everything back into order. But she could not hate her great aunt, who looked so defeated.

"I wish I had never found it." Bertha pulled at the sides of her shawl, and moved away.

She didn't even notice the old woman's uneven steps as she retreated down the stairs. Then slowly, Lara became aware of the musty breath of the dormer room. The sun-faded curtains shifted. She sensed the changing light, and stepped back through the doorway.

She realized that if she were going to move on, she could not unveil these things in this house. When had it happened, she wondered. When was the moment that her imagination ceased its habitual leap to this stone house at the mention of home? Was it today, when Bertha spoke of the strange object, and Lara disintegrated? Could someone enter a state of exile that swiftly? Or perhaps it had been ever since the recurring dream, the nightmare refrain—those human sheaves, untied and falling.

Lara remembered the breasts of one woman, flapping like empty, bleached bags in a cold wind, as she was pushed over the steep edge of the pit. She had borne children, perhaps written poetry, caught a train, drank coffee. The bodies falling with her had built houses, used stethoscopes, fought and dreamed. For Lara, the sheaves would always be falling.

After her mother had tucked her into bed that night all those years ago, Lara had needed desperately to know two things that no one could tell her: who was Opa? And, where was God?

She had felt betrayed. She still did.

Lara remembered that she had got up early the next

morning, eaten her breakfast, and watched birds. She had tried to forget what she had witnessed. Years later, Lara thought she had succeeded.

Now, as she stood holding the mysterious bundle in her hands, she lived again the parting of leaves as she sat on her rock as a child. Lara heard again their fragile, insistent singing. And once more, as she stood in the shadows of the deserted upper room, she heard her Opa's voice whispering beside her: *Listen.*

Lara wondered how to get down to her car unnoticed. Finally she decided that boldness was the only way, and she trod firmly down the stairs, through the throng of mourners, and out the kitchen door.

The front garden was full of birds. The geraniums along the border formed a throbbing red chorus that joined with the mass of finches, magpies, wrens, and wattle birds. Rufus Whistlers called to each other, their singing so full and robust, that she could not even hear the trickling of the water fountain in the middle of the lawn. Were they welcoming her? Or singing a farewell?

Lara moved across the grass, swayed by the joyous music. She did not even say goodbye—just switched on the ignition, heard her little Renault chug into life beneath her, and drove away. She didn't turn her head to watch her family home slip behind the ridge in the road.

Although it was years since she had moved away, Lara was finally leaving.

He stands in the line of people waiting to see the immigration officials, who sit in small rooms at the end of the corridor. Those in the queue appear frayed by solitude, faces and clothes slightly torn at the edges. A bulb on a thin wire hangs from the center of the ceiling, coating everything with sallow light. It is the color of despair.

Under his feet, the boards are scuffed and dented. In the corners of the walls, the paint peels and bubbles, privy to tiny earthquakes that the humans who work and wait here do not notice.

Occasionally somebody crosses the corridor, not even glancing in the direction of those who wait. It would be impossible, Tomas thinks, not to at least *feel* the presence of the queue, humming as it does in a blurry, constant fashion like the building's poor heating system. A secretary appears briefly. Paper flutters in her hand, and high heels carry her firmly out of the way. A man in a gray suit darts across the contained horizon of the corridor. Neither he, nor the secretary raises their eyes.

Tomas notices many doors in this hall, and imagines that each one opens into a burrow where the officials are industrious rats, scratching at typewriters and squeaking busily at each other through telephones. He imagines he can hear them, gnawing on tiny sandwiches, creating their nests of yellowed paper, chewed pencils, and important documents.

He still has the feather—it is now a year since he found it on the streets of the city. He has passed another birthday alone with a single candle and the ragged January snow. To Tomas it feels as if every day he has come here, and every time he hopes they will let him leave.

He has a brochure of where he wants to go. It sits folded in a pocket, next to the feather. Together they make his compass. Tomas has been working at whatever he can—clearing streets, selling vegetables, mending shoes—to save the money he needs for his passage. Now he has it: a tightly rolled bundle inside a sock, stuffed into a hollow tree where only he knows.

Tomas waits, humming under his breath and watching those far ahead of him disappear one by one into the small rooms. They come out again with different faces: some droop, some glimmer, and some stare straight ahead.

You need money and also permission. You need a medical certificate. You need skills, a fair amount of work left in you. You need contacts, if possible.

He wants another chance at life, as they all do who come here to beg from bureaucracy. They have seen the signs that read *Skilled Immigrants Needed* and have done everything and anything to seem skilled, to collect the necessary funds, to contact those they once knew who live there, far across the sea.

It seems another year, but his name is called, and Tomas crosses under the dull lighting to enter the door at the end of the corridor.

Maybe this time.

9.

Sometimes, the past is a shell curled against the ear, its muted storms calling across a thin, white corridor. Sometimes, Lara feels like there's something hiding at the back of family functions, some vital cog that, if turned, has the capacity to shift everything, even destroy it. She doesn't know when she first realized the presence of this feeling, but she can remember a time when she didn't.

It is a very early memory of her grandmother holding her and showing her off to friends. Lara had been eating a frankfurter, and she spat the skin out in her grandmother's face. She can remember being quite unconscious of what anyone else thought, while also registering Oma's shock and disapproval—Lara had let something out that should have been digested quietly and never seen.

When they met for coffee last Tuesday, her mother talked very carefully about Lara's music studies and the plans to finally sell the stone house. Lara wanted so much to talk to her about the funeral, Great Aunt Bertha, and what she had been given, but there was no opening. She was stuck. So was her mother. They were both grieving in their own way.

As they had sat at their corner table, unsure of how to meet with each other, Lara found herself returning to the day Oma went into hospital. The car that held her had moved, but somehow Oma had not. It was as if she had turned to sepia, become a photograph—two-dimensional, fixed in time. Lara, eleven years old at the time, had stood next to her mother, solemnly and absurdly waving. She had wondered whether Oma was going somewhere good after all, because this is what you did when people went on vacation—they packed their bags and dressed up, and you waved to them as they drove away.

That day had been silent, and she never heard her grandmother speak again—although, once, Lara heard her sing.

She had returned to the hospital ward to collect a forgotten toy, anxious her family—poised to leave at the glass doors in the lobby—would not wait for her as promised. At the threshold of Oma's room, she paused, uncertain of how to enter without disturbing her.

It was then that she heard it: a breathy voice—thin and diluted by pain. Lara gazed at her Oma's open eyes, fixed on a patch of chiffon sky framed in a far window. Lara's heart contracted, and she was three years old again and lying in Oma's arms by an open fire while her grandmother sang to her, as if they were the only two people in the world.

Little Mister Baggy Britches, I love you!

Lara could still hear the soft croak of her voice.

… If you'll be my Sunday fellow, I'll patch you in purple and pink and in yellow, and folks will say as they lean on the old Zee wall …

Oma never explained where Zee was, but Lara knew it was somewhere far away from her and close in Oma's memory.

… Lila's been patching her Jakob till he's got no britches at all! Ja, ja, ja, till he's got no britches at all. Lila's been patching her Jakob till he's got no britches at all.

The gentle, swaying tune mocked the room's straight lines and white walls, and Jakob's rainbow britches scorned the plain hospital gown Oma wore.

Lara left the toy in the room. Oma must have been singing it a lullaby. Her grandmother was both somewhere close and far away, and her voice sang to her grandchild from the land of Zee.

She stared at Oma's face for what was to be the last time, then tiptoed away with her insides tightening.

For some reason, Lara felt the same today.

She had telephoned her mother again yesterday, and now they were sitting opposite each other—in a different café this time. Lara wanted to try again. They were crammed next to tall windows that granted them a generous view of the busy street. They found themselves flicking their eyes back and forth so that they could take in the colorful passersby, and also each other.

The waitress arrived with their coffees, and she too was drawn to the outside world. She was staring at a young man putting coins in a meter, and spilled Lara's latte. They all laughed—the waitress's was a rather embarrassed giggle—and she retreated quickly to find a cloth and another coffee.

Lara was glad this had happened; it meant the air had been warmed, and they both relaxed. The young man glanced at the window, but could not see them; his eyes were stopped by the glass. He put his hands in his jacket pockets and moved away.

Lara turned her eyes back to the table, and watched her mother straighten the sage green scarf around her neck. Neither of them had talked yet about the funeral. Lara certainly hadn't said anything about Aunt Bertha's gift that now sat watching the mountains from her bedside table. She was not good at subtlety—never had been—so she began with a cough, and asked outright,

"Did Opa ever talk to you about the war?"

Her mother stirred her coffee vigorously. Lara half-expected her at any moment to stand up and leave—but instead she simply lifted one eyebrow, and shifted her weight on the wooden chair. Lara felt again like a tiny island.

"I just want to know some more. There is such a … silence about it all. He refused to let me interview him for history class—several times."

"I think what he actually said was that there was nothing to say—his story was too dull, and you should interview someone else."

Lara knew her bottom lip was sticking out stubbornly, because Mum was smiling at it.

"So maybe you should just believe him."

"Why?" Lara tried to lift her mother's face with her

eyes, to make the "why" a sharp lever to force some response; she craved even the slightest hint that her mother might also want to know the truth.

Lara paused and glanced outside. A woman and her dog meandered past—they were both wearing yellow sweaters. Now would have been the perfect moment. She could simply produce the tiny cosmos with which Bertha had burdened her. But then she would need to sit by and witness her mother fracture and dissolve, as she herself had done the afternoon of Opa's funeral.

Lara wondered suddenly if sometimes there was something more precious than truth, and that was keeping those you loved, whole. Her anger didn't quite dissipate, but it fell back somewhere deep inside herself.

She knew then that she was on her own in this. She was sure of it. She realized too that she wanted to be on her own with this, she just hadn't been aware of it until right now. If Lara couldn't find the answers in her mother, she would need to find another way.

Her mind took a photograph of the moment—the late morning sun in a small square on their table, the droplets of coffee on the polished wooden surface, the chipped nail on her mother's left hand.

Don't ask so many questions. Just sit there quietly and finish your silverbeet.

But she wouldn't. Not this time.

10.

When Lara first arrived home after the funeral, her key refused to turn in the lock. She was impatient to get to the top of the shared concrete stairway, and into her own space. Lara hadn't said goodbye to anyone, and expected a phone call later that evening after the wake was over.

She kicked the thick glass—the door jolted, but the key wouldn't slip into place. In desperation she even prayed, and for some reason the lock then shifted. This bothered her, too, but she brushed aside the feeling and mounted the stairs two at a time, as she always did. Lara's roommate was out, which was good. It was an extremely small flat, and she wanted to be alone as she unwrapped her strange present.

It took two seconds to cross the living room, push open the bedroom door, and fall into the tiny space that belonged to her. She closed the door. Finally, peace.

Lara was facing a large window from which she could see corrugated iron rooftops adorned with sleeping cats. The houses formed awkward silhouettes, fringed with television aerials, that hacked at the sky for miles. Then the sprawl stopped, and there, sudden as moonlight, were the mountains: opaque, glimmering, softly textured as clouds.

Lara had always loved the mountains. They whispered of adventures in the gully, of times when life seemed so much less complicated and she really believed that she could do anything, even fly.

I miss Opa.

She cried again.

Lara allowed her breathing to become regular, then placid, and smoothed out the covers on her bed. She sat on them cross-legged and placed the pink parcel in front of her. She began to unfold the terry-toweling; Lara knew what it would be … and yes, the exquisite shadowbox she discovered inside smelled just as the wooden peasant figures on the mantelpiece had—of fragrant wood and smoke and dried flowers.

The scent made her cry all over again. Oma and Opa were dead. The house would be sold, and everything was going to change. Lara didn't just feel sad, but in transit—stranded in the dark at a railway station that she didn't recognize, without even a watch to tell the time.

Her eyes returned to the shadow box. Lara lifted one ornament at a time from its small cubic space. There was a tiny porcelain horse with a chipped tail, its head held proudly aloft.

There was a piece of extravagant lace; it lay in her palm like a stray wisp of cloud. The fabric was delicate, creamy, and papery—part of her grandmother's wedding gown. It felt like a crumbling letter from another world. Then there was a miniature cowbell, with a faded painting of a gentian flower on its thin side. Finally, her fingers caressed a diminutive wooden doll, brown wool twisted in sweet braids atop her round, smiling face.

There were other objects here that Lara recognized. She had contemplated them so many times, yet only now did they stir questions in her mind.

A violin peg of black mahogany.

A smooth black stone.

A broken compass.

A piece of resin.

An old postcard, the writing on the back so ruined by water that she could not read it.

A feather.

Somehow Lara didn't even want to pick them up. She only rested her gaze on them, pondering their stories.

And then she remembered—Bertha's dark pronouncement in the upstairs room. What was it that she had found?

Lara plied open each fold in the toweling, and finally saw it; Bertha must have hurriedly tossed it in with the other items as she re-wrapped the gift.

It was a small enameled button, with a pin in the back to attach it to clothing. It was mildly concave, black and slightly tarnished. On the front, two white lightning bolts were depicted in static parallel: the runic symbol of the *Schutzstaffel,* or Nazi elite division—responsible for everything from Hitler's personal protection and secret intelligence, to the *Einsatzgruppen,* or mobile death squads, and the administration of concentration camps. She picked it up, gingerly.

What Lara held in her hands was, unmistakably, an SS lapel pin. And it had belonged to her grandfather.

Memory

"John loves to play football."
Schon lofs tool play foortborl.
"John hates to play soccer."
Schon herts tool play zokker.
"John loves to eat cake."
Schon luffs tool eat cerk.
"*John hates to eat sauerkraut, wiener schnitzel, and dumplings.*"

Language class. Day one. Day sixteen. Day one thousand and three. Each day is the same. Each sentence is completely divorced from the real. Each sentence serves to outlaw me and my past. I hate much of my past, but it is my past, and therefore part of me.

Am I then an outlaw in this country?

I wonder about this as I finger my pencil.

I love a sunburnt country. A land of sweeping plains. Of rugged mountain ranges. Of droughts and flooding rains. I love her far horizons, I love her cruel seas. Her beauty and her terror—the wide brown land for me.[4]

Yes, I know her seas are cruel, filled with malicious fish that kill you as you swim, that stalk you when you are floating, that hire cars and cruise inland at night to taunt you and steal your sleep.

Is this the land for me?

I wonder.

I sit in this class, a thirty-two-year-old man behind a desk made for a twelve-year-old. I watch the teacher as she smiles blandly at us with her taut and shiny welcome, the way her teeth form two straight rows. Her vowels swing in a strange fashion. I have heard English, but not like this, not

---

4   "I Love a Sunburnt Country." by Dorothea MacKellar.

Australian English. The beginnings and ends of words I can grasp, but from one end to the other the sounds teeter, sway, and bend so that they feel slippery to my ear. The tone is bright and hard, like Antipodean sunlight; it is a light that exposes everything and burns me; yet I am grateful to be here, I remind myself, and switch my pencil to the other hand.

I remember the brochure. I threw it away as I walked down the gangplank, because I realized that I didn't want live through pictures anymore. My own heart would be my reference point, not someone else's photographs. I think of my brochure, soaking up the salt water and disintegrating, crushed by waves and becoming part of the ocean.

I have not been concentrating, and I am about to be asked how to walk into a shop and purchase a pound of tomatoes. The lady smiles fixedly at me. She is trying to be friendly and calm. I stare blankly back at her, wondering how her teeth can be so straight and white. Maybe they are fake—but, at such a young age?

I do not know how to ask for a pound of tomatoes. I do not want a pound of tomatoes. I hate tomatoes. I hate shops.

I smile and shake my head. *Not today,* I think. *Please don't ask me today. Maybe tomorrow I will like tomatoes.*

Part Three: Gavotte

(n): A Baroque dance of French peasant origin, which evolved into an elegant dance, often with simple rhythms. It has a homophonic texture, in which two or more parts move together in harmony. The relationship between the parts creates chords—as distinct from "polyphony," in which the parts move with rhythmic independence.

Memory

I climb through a hole in the building—only it is more like a wound, bleeding rubble and plaster. Outside, the street is a cacophony of gunshot percussion, a bizarre nightmare orchestra. On this side of the wall, the space holds its breath and waits for the next explosion.

I struggle to my feet and lean against a broken wooden closet in the bombed-out room. Light spills onto the floor. I shut my eyes and hear my own breathing—rasping, tight from running and from my body's traumatic thrust into this place of shelter. It is my worst moment. I do not know where the others are, or even if they are alive. I know only that I am here, and it is now. I am starting to cough from dust and … that familiar smell.

I open my eyes. Along one wall are rows of hooks, and I can now see broken strings and the violence of ripped, raw wood. Glass forms a glistening crust on the floor, overlaid here and there with tools and faded paper packets.

The scent comes pungent and sharp to me now: linseed and resin, I am sure.

I notice a single violin, dangling opposite me as if from gallows. My heart pounds. The rifle feels cold in my hand. There is suddenly silence—perhaps a dial has been turned. Silence. Not even breath. Does my father appear in the door? Can I hear the tutor scribbling from down the hallway? Can I hear the click and patter of my mother knitting? Where am I? Who am I?

And who owned that violin?

I step towards it, reaching out my hand, then trip on a shard of wood at my feet and fall forward. I steady myself against a workbench, but the vibration rocks the instrument. It descends to the floor in stages, like a scale.

There is a crack as the violin catches on the sharp edge of a glass panel. Then it is lying broken at my feet, as if shot.

From nowhere pour violent tears—but it is not nowhere, just a place that has for so long been burrowed deep inside me that I have forgotten it exists. I am frantic. The violin must live! I lift and stroke it, this small animal, wounded and helpless in my arms. It groans in my grip, and a miniature black peg drops onto my boot and bounces through a crack in the boards. I sink to my knees and weep, cradling the wooden body. The resin soaks into my nostrils and skin, and I cannot stop my sobbing. I rock to and fro like a metronome, my face wet and ashamed.

The pale light washes over my skin; I shut my eyes, and feel terrified of going home.

11.

Germany

Spring, 1930

Tomas was born in a small village where a wide, rutted road emptied itself of travelers by tipping them into the town square. On every other day, a colorful market flourished here on the cobblestones, where humans and geese crossed paths, and hands grasped for vegetables brought in from surrounding farms.

Over many hundreds of years, myriad worn lanes had twisted outward from the market square, finally petering into farmland and forest. The village dwellings had also expanded—little by little acquiring gables and thatches, wood stacks and extra chimneys. Women swept, shopped and gossiped, their heads wrapped in scarves, aprons tied around ample waists. Men hammered, built, mended shoes, and worked the surrounding fields. The church bells chimed out the hours, the sun and moon marked the days, and the years went by unnoticed.

To the south of the square a furrowed lane hoisted its way up a steep incline, then ran straight past the only building in Zweibach that could boast three stories: a modern structure possessing rows of sparkling clean windows and an impressive balcony. From this height, one could see the far city whose towers, like beckoning fingers, captured the longing stares of village children—promising adventures they couldn't put into words because they hadn't known them, but on clear days made their insides churn: *one day, to leave.*

This was the schoolhouse, and within its walls boys and girls from the surrounding villages and farms came to learn how to write, count, and speak their conjugated verbs in time with the other children. They learned that it is good to be clean, bad to be barefoot, and most important to spell correctly and stand when an adult enters the room. From here they first saw the city.

It was here that Tomas met Gustav.

It had been an adventurous Friday morning. Frau Henkel was probably still writing carefully on the board, chalk screeching under her slow, methodical hand: *aaaaabbbbc-ccccddddd*. What nonsense that you had to learn to write in unreadable cursive, with a pen that was difficult to hold! Much more fun to flick ink at the timid girl in the next row of desks, or smuggle a slice of dark bread from your pocket and take furtive bites, pondering the quickest and easiest way to leave the room without being noticed.

It was lucky that Frau Henkel was so focused on the board, as it gave the boys a chance to slip into the space beneath their desks, and then head toward the edge of the classroom.

With student solidarity as their cover, Gustav and Tomas edged around the imposing wooden door and then leaned heavily into the wall on the other side, waiting to be caught and dragged back into the room to suffer a cane smashed across their hands.

But it didn't happen. They grinned at each other in happy disbelief.

The two boys reached involuntarily for each other's fingers, glanced at one another conspiratorially, and then bolted down the hall like soldiers breaking through enemy lines.

The Headmaster's familiar tread pulled them upright—in a strategic flurry, Gustav pushed Tomas roughly into the janitor's closet. Tomas collected a mouthful of broom and stifled a cough. Gustav grabbed his arm hard. The pain distracted him for a moment, but it was long enough, and they heard the creak of floorboards recede.

Gustav pushed open the door gently—just a crack. *"Komm!"* he whispered, and the two boys fell out of the cupboard and raced through the side door of the school building. They popped out like corks; round and rolling on the soft summer ground. The sky radiated its brilliant blue across their faces, and the sun called out to them in joyous camaraderie.

In their knickerbockers, too-tight shirts and woolen coats, the boys scampered across the walled pen that was the Zweibach School grounds. They crawled through a gap at ground level, and lay for a moment, eyes blinking as if they had just escaped from a cave. Gustav whooped loud and long and then leaped on top of Tomas, wrestling him before he had a chance to uncurl.

"Why … you!" Tomas protested as he tried to grasp his friend in a headlock and then fell back, laughing. "Let's get out of here before someone sees us."

Tomas was always the more careful one. He benefited from associating with the more reckless Gustav, who had a happy disregard for anything but what was on his mind at any particular moment—right now this was sunshine, the smell of a long summer break just around the corner, and the knowledge that the swimming hole was only a short run from where they stood.

Gustav was a stocky boy, thick-shouldered yet quick on his feet, and with the darting, impulsive movements of a tiny bird. His brown eyes sparkled as if his agile mind were constantly conceiving games—which was often true—and the smattering of freckles across his slightly upturned nose made him appear even cheekier than he actually was. Gustav received more than his fair share of the cane, and he blamed his speckled, cheery nose.

Tomas was thirteen, but was far more boy than man. He had the gangling limbs of a stick insect, a rather refined face, and serious gray eyes that caused him to avoid punishment, as much as Gustav's appearance seemed to invite it. The two were inseparable, and completely united in the adventures and diverse schemes that colored their otherwise quiet village lives.

The sounds of horses and women's voices spurred them into a gleeful dash across the grass. They ducked under overhanging oak branches, and slapped the ancient pines with their hands as they passed. They had barely enough breath left to scramble up the rocky incline that fell open to a clearing.

From here the countryside swept outward and away, toward the distant white points that were the foothills of the German Alps. Beyond those frozen peaks lay Austria, Switzerland, and the rest of the vast world that one day—the boys had vowed—they would explore together. They had already designed a raft to take them down mountain rivers, and had managed to find half a map of Europe.

For a moment, the two explorers held their breath in wonder at the view before them. They always did this; they were passing into a very special place whose threshold demanded reverential silence.

It was, however, only a moment. The two tumbled down the slope like puppies, stripped off their heavy woolen clothing, and jumped into a wide, smooth pond. The water was deep and fresh, fed by two streams that flowed from the mountains and gave the village its name.

The ripples from the boys' landing surged out toward the grassy bank as they duck-dived and opened their eyes under the water. The shock of the cold made them both blink furiously for a few seconds, but then they were free to inspect the waving reeds, the small gray fish the color of the horizon, and the mysterious shapes below them.

Tomas swiveled onto his back like a seal, staring up at the sky rimmed with trees. He listened to the twin streams cackling, and the ripples he had created with his own body slap against the rocks edging the pond. He watched a hawk soar overhead, and counted seventeen ducks flying together in a beautiful V formation on their way to a far lake.

Soon all the birds would come back from the places to which they had escaped during the long winter months, and he would greet their arrival with excitement. Birds were the real explorers. They saw the earth as no one else did, from far above. They could even dive through clouds, as he was diving through water. Where did they go, he wondered, when autumn passed its frosty hands over the land and sky, delivering colored leaves and freezing nights? He longed to climb aboard a feathered back, snuggle into warm down and be transported to the other side of the world.

A frog landed on his face—Tomas spluttered and yelled. Gustav grinned at him from a safe distance, but Tomas grabbed some weeds from under the water and lunged at his friend. They pursued each other, until Tomas finally caught Gustav by the foot and pulled him underwater. He rubbed the weeds in Gustav's hair and held him down long enough to teach him a lesson. Gustav bobbed up choking and smiling, a bit of weed hanging out of his mouth.

"Revenge!" crowed Tomas.

"The frog was unbeatable!" Gustav retorted, and he lurched at Tomas, pushing him roughly under the water. Tomas glimpsed darting fish, and spied a beautiful stone that quivered like a shadow on a bed of gravel and dirt. He scooped it up and, when he arrived in the fresh air, stroked over to the grassy bank.

"Look!" He proffered the stone.

His friend waded out after him, and the two sat side by side, taking turns fingering the rock. It was shiny, and drying rapidly in the sunshine. It was perfectly round, like a small loaf of black bread, or the eye of a bird, grown large and monstrous. They rubbed its surface with their chilled pink fingers.

"It's colder out than in. I'm going back," chirped Gustav. He sprang up and leapt into the water.

"Hey!" he called to Tomas, "I'm going to find more of those stones!"

He swam over to the rockier side of the swimming hole, took a breath, and disappeared. A few moments later he emerged, hair plastered over his face.

"Find any more?" yelled Tomas.

"No, but I need to go deeper! That one you found over there was one of a kind—those sorts of rocks are not normally so near the bank. See you!" he called, and duck dived.

This time the surface of the water was smooth for a long time. Tomas knew his friend was a strong swimmer. He was slightly older and—although Tomas never would have admitted it—quite a bit stronger.

Tomas rolled over onto his belly and rested his chin on the grass. He watched tiny insects step nimbly across the dirt. He marveled as an ant carried a burden more than twice its size. Tomas drilled shallow holes into the ground with a stick, and watched the ant maneuver its way through them, dipping down and clambering out the other side.

He grew bored, and pushed himself upright to stare at the water again. There was no sign of Gustav. The pond was still. Tomas supposed Gustav had climbed out and was hiding, waiting to jump out and grab him. He was glad he was no longer lying down.

Tomas got up and wandered over to the rocks. He climbed onto one and felt its warm skin against his. He settled there for a few moments, enjoying being enveloped by the heat. Then he glanced around. Gustav was nowhere in sight.

"Hey, Gustav!"

Silence. Nothing stirred.

"Hey, Gustav! Come on! Where are you hiding?"

There was no movement. A fearful churning began in his stomach as he stared down at the water that suddenly looked very forbidding. He remembered the Headmaster's face when they had been caught two weeks ago, wet and dripping, on their way back to school.

Tomas launched himself back into the pond and dived. It was deeper than he had been aware, because he had never before searched for someone underwater. He blinked and moved his hands like fins to propel himself downward. Then he saw Gustav, limp and white, his legs caught under a shelf of rock and weeds strung about his face like ropey hair.

If Tomas had believed he could actually scream underwater, he would have. Instead, a peculiar calm overtook him, and he reached out and shoveled at his friend's foot until it pried loose. It was bleeding and twisted. Gustav floated before him like a strange, pale fish. Tomas grabbed his friend and pulled him to the surface.

The boy's body was heavy and inert, and it was hard for Tomas to heave them both across to the bank. Tears clouding his eyes, he tugged at Gustav's arms and rolled him onto the grass. His own heart felt hard, like a stone in a slingshot, ready to be fired and angry enough to kill.

"Gustav!" he bellowed and whacked the older boy's back, pummeling the skin until it reddened. Something like a belch emanated from the boy's mouth, and a flood of water hit the ground with a sickening rush. Tomas wanted to vomit. Gustav spluttered, and his eyes rolled open. Tomas walloped him some more, and something like dark weeds spilled from between Gustav's teeth.

Tomas turned him onto his back, and peered down at his face. His eyes were open and slowly focusing. Gustav coughed hard and tried to sit up, but could only flip his arms vaguely.

"Gustav?" Tomas whispered.

"I ... "

"Are you alive? Are you all right?"

"I couldn't ... "

"Couldn't what? Please tell me!"

" ... couldn't find any stones," he whispered, and the faintest flicker of a grin passed across his face. More tears burst from Tomas's eyes, and he turned away quickly to find some clothing to cover Gustav's shivering body. He piled nearly everything they had worn onto Gustav, tucking it under his body, and then he threw himself on top to add more warmth.

They stayed like that until the sun started to fall toward the distant Alps, and shadows stretched across the water to the rocks on the other side.

Tomas sat up on his heels, shaking with cold and shock. With difficulty, Gustav hoisted himself up too, and looked for a long time at Tomas's face.

"I think we need food," he said unevenly, "and I don't want to go home now. Mama will be so angry with me for being wet and missing school."

"We need to go home eventually."

"No we don't. We can stay out here. We can light a fire. There is some bread in my pocket, and there are berries in among those trees. We can go home tomorrow, when they will all be so worried about us that they will forget we ran away from school."

Gustav's reasoning seemed logical and convincing, and the prospect of really being like explorers, feeding on berries and sleeping outside near a fire, was compelling—it would be good practice for their future.

Tomas peered closely at his friend's mouth to see if his teeth were still chattering. He was relieved to find they were not. Even his skin had begun to look healthier, or maybe it was the sunset.

Gustav poked out his tongue. He had to untangle himself from the layers of clothing to stand, and as he did so he dressed himself properly. It warmed him to put on his thick socks and boots, even more to pull the woolen sweater over his damp head. He was unsteady on his feet, but made up for this with the bravado of his smile.

"Come on, then! Supper time!"

Tomas looked to see where the sun was. "You find some berries, and I'll make a fire."

Animals and insects began to croak and crackle, supported by the sweet, sharp calls of night birds. Tomas had some tinder and flint hidden in a tree just behind the swimming hole. It was part of his secret explorer's stash: a candle, his map, a compass that didn't have its glass anymore, and a knife. He didn't want Gustav to see them—it was that secret.

He meandered in the general direction of the hollow, collecting kindling as he went. He was grateful for the dryness of the day, as there were plenty of leaves on the ground to help get the fire started. He checked over his shoulder every so often to reassure himself that he was not in Gustav's view.

Tomas traveled in a broad, circular path, gradually moving closer to his tree. Then he straightened up cautiously, watchful. As he thrust his hand into the hollow in the trunk, the same thrill passed through his heart, as always. One day he would move beyond his village where nothing unexpected ever happened, where it was already decided how everyone's life would be. One day he would reach the outer edges of his small world, and walk triumphantly over the threshold into … whatever it was that was out there. This stash was proof. The knife, the compass—it was all a deposit toward what would happen one day if he wanted it enough.

Tomas heard his friend calling him, and he promptly pulled out the required items. He stuffed the bark back in front of the hollow, and darted back toward their temporary camp.

The Alps were already dark and ominous, like spies in the shadows. There was just enough light to dig a small hollow in the earth, and arrange around it some river stones. Tomas filled the hollow with leaves and pine needles, and went to work on his flint. Gustav sat nearby, watching intently. He knew better than to ask where the flint was from. He knew that Tomas had a secret hiding place, but loved him enough not to demand that it be shared. His job was to gasp admiringly when the flint was lit, and then move in closer to help pile on the sticks.

As the stars became brighter, so did the flames from the tiny fire. There were plenty of pine cones and fallen branches; nobody else ever camped out here. It was a clear night, so all they had to do was lie close to the little blaze, their thick clothes forming a protective layer between their skin and the cold ground.

Gustav pierced his bread with a long, thin stick and dangled it dangerously over the flames. It was soon blackened, smoky, and warm. One slice of bread and four unripe berries between them did not fill their stomachs, but it made them feel adventurous and slightly heroic. They had not mentioned the incident.

Gustav picked up the stone Tomas had found earlier. He smoothed it in his hands and rubbed it against his cheek.

"It feels wonderful. Feel!" he commanded the other boy.

When Tomas closed his fingers around it, the stone lay perfectly encased. He opened his fist and suddenly passed the rock back to Gustav.

"You can have it," he offered.

Gustav said nothing, but he took the stone and held it tight.

"My chest hurts." Gustav flipped himself over so that he could stare up at the sky. "They say that when you are on the other side of the world, the stars are all upside down."

"Really?" Tomas lay fully on his back to get the best view of the array of stars in their glittering dance. It always amazed him that there were so many thousands, millions of them, and yet they didn't look crowded. Each star had its place, and all together they made a beautiful, shimmering cloud.

"Yes, someone told me once—someone who knew."

"Who?" Tomas was listening intently. Did his friend really know someone who had traveled to the other side of the world?

"Oh," said Gustav vaguely, "just someone. A cousin or something. He fought in the war. He knows lots of things. And his face was funny."

"What do you mean?"

"It was, well, it sounds horrible to laugh at it, but it was funny. It was weird and horrible and funny all at the same time."

Gustav rolled over again to face the fire. Tomas remained silent, listening.

"He didn't have a nose."

This was too horrible to contemplate; nonetheless, Tomas realized he had to think about it, to try and understand. Then he found himself holding a hand over his mouth and giggling—but not inside. Inside, it frightened him.

"What do you mean, he didn't have a nose? What happened to it?"

It was suddenly so funny that they couldn't bear it. There was a pause, and then their mouths cracked wide open, and loud, bubbling laughter exploded from their fire-warmed faces. The two boys rolled, ached, and beat the turf with their arms as their breath rasped.

"Stop!" Gustav panted. "I told you my chest was already hurting!"

This made them laugh even harder, until they were crying. Then Gustav remembered his swollen foot, and his sobbing intensified. Tomas wasn't quite sure what to do, so he quickly piled more pine cones onto the fire. He didn't know whether to look at his friend, who had now turned away and was shaking. He rearranged the warm stones around the edge of the fire. He tried to count them. He wished for more bread, or for a bowl of hot dumplings and broth. He thought of anything other than the ghostly white shape of his friend drifting before him in the murky water.

The snuffles subsided, and Gustav turned again toward the fire, then fell back onto the ground to stare once more at the sky.

"My foot hurts."

Tomas tried to say something, but found himself watching ants instead. The fire cracked and spat. Sap hissed from the end of a twig, and an ant crawled frantically into it, wilting instantly.

Gustav spoke hoarsely. "If you ever, ever tell anyone that I cried, then I won't ever come swimming with you again, and I'll tell the other boys at school about your secret place."

Tomas jolted his head up, fear dilating his pupils. He didn't know what frightened him more—losing his secret or suddenly realizing that he and Gustav were not one boy, that one could walk away from the other.

"But you don't know where it is!" His voice came out as an undignified squeak.

Gustav refused to meet his gaze, but his profile was stiff and desperate. "Do so! And anyway, I can find out, can't I? There can't be that many hollow trees here."

The boys each picked up sticks and drove furious tunnels into the sides of the coals. Tomas's stick snapped, and roughly he threw one end into the fire.

"I won't tell anyone," he muttered, angry that he was thought capable of such base betrayal. He stared up at his friend briefly, then dropped his eyes. "Anyway, I cried, too. A bit."

Gustav's profile lost its marble hardness.

"Just a small bit," he elaborated. "When I thought you were dead."

Their eyes met across the glow, and the rift was quickly filled with grins and the shared fire.

"My cousin, the one without a … "

They were off again, and the story never got finished; but the man with the flattened face and twisted skin stared at Tomas in his dreams that night. In fact, he swam after him through an enormous underwater sky, where the stars were stones, and Gustav was a piece of weed that floated way above his head.

Memory

I strain my eyes at the porthole, hoping for a glimpse of light. The moon has shifted, and now hovers delicately on the horizon, pale and almost self-effacing. I sit up and narrowly avoid scraping my head on the boards of the bunk above me. I decide to stand and urge the morning to come.

I have lost count of the days; I simply live the same hour over and over, only sometimes it is dark and sometimes I am in daylight.

The ship heaves. I am thrown off balance and steady myself with an arm. My hand accidentally lands on a sleeper's overhanging limb, and I start at the sudden contact with another human. I mumble an apology, which the sleeper ignores or does not hear, and maneuver my way to the door. It creaks, bangs, and then I am outside in the cramped corridor. I suddenly feel I will be sick in the stale air, and I move as quickly as I can toward the deck.

After a time I emerge into the cold, stepping gingerly over sleeping bodies wrapped in blankets; I wonder if my presence is sensed in their dreams as I pass. My hands grasp the railing of the ship, and I breathe deeply. The nausea ceases, as it always does once I am here and the fresh sea wind hits my face.

I can no longer see the moon, and to my relief the sky is starting to evanesce, its edge now a lip of blue. I feel my old life disappear with the last stars. It is strange, I think, that the day has become my rest. Around me the sleepers on the deck stir, and I hear the first sounds of morning awakening on the ship.

12.

"What are you going to do when you leave Zweibach?"

"Leave? We need to finish school first."

"Yes, but then?"

Gustav was interrogating his friend. The fire was stocked with pine cones, sap fizzled into the flames, and above them the stars whispered. A cool breeze swung from the top branches of the fir trees, making a mysterious hushing sound.

The two boys lay close together for warmth, as the ground around them grew damper. Their eyes were dry and stretched with tiredness, but neither of them wanted to sleep. They had made a pact to stay up all night and watch the dawn come. Although they were not saying it to each other, they felt that they would rather be awake in case any night animals come to inspect them. An owl had hooted earlier, close by, and they had watched two bats flit across the clearing. Little rustlings and the scuttling of mysterious, furry somethings kept them alert and chattering.

"How old will I be?" Tomas was always a stickler for facts, precision, and boundaries, yet he was not constrained by them. Rather, they indicated to him where he needed to cross in order to escape.

"As old as me." Gustav dug him in the side with his fist.

"No I won't! I'm younger than you."

Gustav punched him back. "No, you're not."

The physical dialogue continued. "Yes, I am."

"Just answer my question!"

They were too exhausted to play-fight for long, so their hands moved back to the warm crevices under their arms. Tomas held his mouth and throat tight so that he didn't yawn, and his voice came out funny.

"We'll be exploring, won't we? We've already designed our raft. We've got a map."

Gustav laughed. "Half a map—a piece of Holland, and most of France. There's more to the world than that."

"We'll find the other half of the map. Anyway, at least what we've got gives us a start. Zweibach's on it."

"All right, so we leave and go exploring. How will we find food?"

Gustav seemed to Tomas to be deliberately aggravating. Tomas decided he was not going to be baited, and he was certainly not going to let his friend's retorts stop him from feeling passionate about his plans. He took a deep breath and continued his defense.

"That's what we've got to get better at," he conceded. "All right, so trying to find the berries didn't go well this time, but what we need is to discover what foods we *can* eat from the wild—herbs and things. We can raid farms for fruit, and maybe do odd jobs around the place for bread and milk. We'll be fine. We can get so good at exploring that we can travel to places nobody has ever heard of. In fact," his voice rose with excitement, "we will be paid by rich people to travel *for* them! We can take big ships and planes to far-off places, then come back and tell them what we have discovered about the world! We can draw maps, and write down all the plants and animals we see. We can discover things, Gustav!"

His friend began to join in his enthusiasm, despite the cold and the fact that only hours ago he had almost drowned. "Hey, they will study us in school!"

They both started laughing. They imagined the face of Frau Henkel, much older and more wrinkled, holding with shocked silence the Newly Improved Geography Textbook for German Students. They imagined her voice sounding their praises as heroes, and the wide-eyed reception of the pupils: *Yes, boys and girls, they went to this school, and I was fortunate to be their teacher.*

Memory

I do not like to think on the last time I saw him. We argued, then we fought as if we were again thirteen years old, yet with the bitterness and dark vigor of men. Over a ticket, a concert—I cannot remember clearly, but I will write to him and explain.

I will tell him it was seeing us changed so much that made me angry—I did not want the concert ticket, I no longer wanted to listen to an orchestra playing. And I wanted to kill. Not him, but those who had done this to us. But how can you murder war, and how do you choose what to destroy when what you must kill has no form?

I was angry that he refused to come with me on this boat. We clashed in cold silence; first the concert, and now this. Our friendship teetered, and I felt desperate. I waved my pass for the ship's passage in front of him. I cajoled, I begged, I threatened. *This is our raft,* I tried to tell him, but he just shook his head and looked sad.

Yes, I must write to him.

13.

When dawn came, the two boys were asleep. Their faces were as pale as the overcast sky: a flat, metallic gray. The dew had wet the grass around them. The fire was now a mound of blackened wood and stones. There was no sound; the water's surface spread taut and unperturbed.

In his dreams Tomas was aware that his back ached. His head and eyes felt heavy, as if they were sinking; he tried to hold onto sleep, but the combination of light, cold, and sore muscles finally made him give in.

Tomas wanted to be home. He opened one eye at a time, squinting. He lay still, surprised by the quiet around him. Then he heard it, the first bird. It twittered in an impulsive fashion, then chortled like water forcing its way out of a pipe. This was the signal, for all around him, as the first rays of sun were breaking through the cloud cover, the trees exploded in song.

Tomas sat up and groaned, and his neck refused to relax. He rubbed it with his hand as he tried to see the birds. It was incredible that they could create so much sound, and yet seem invisible. He stared out across the water and watched the sunlight restore some sheen to its surface. Sunrise. The dew began to sparkle, and the clouds looked softer and less intimidating.

He shook Gustav. "Wake up!"

Gustav mumbled and flipped up his hand, keeping his eyes shut.

"Sit up or you'll miss it!" urged Tomas, and he grabbed a stick and poked Gustav several times.

Gustav rolled over, then clambered to a sitting position. "What?"

His eyes were red-rimmed and held a glassy, faraway stare.

They could see the sun now, above the distant mountains. It dissolved the steel of the sky and poured warmth like liquid over their skin. It was beautiful, like soup, like a warm bath. The birds called madly to each other.

Gustav rubbed his eyes and tried to focus around him.

"We didn't do it."

"What?"

"We didn't stay up all night. I wonder when we fell asleep?" Gustav shook his head and wiped his dew-wet hands on his trousers.

"Don't know," Tomas replied absently, "but isn't this wonderful!"

"I'm hungry."

"Listen to the birds!"

"I'm starving! I could eat birds!"

"Look at the sun."

"No thanks. Let's go home."

Tomas stood up and stretched. Gustav joined him, and they walked to the edge of the water. The strength of the sun's heat told them that the day would be another warm one. They knew, however, that they wouldn't be swimming.

"Saturday," Gustav offered.

"Market. Household chores. Trouble," Tomas replied.
They stayed by the edge of the water, unsure of what more to say. Then by silent agreement, they turned and walked—backs to the sun—in the direction of the village. The movement reminded them of the soreness in their legs, but it also pumped energy into their bodies, despite the remaining ache in Gustav's chest and foot.

They trudged along in silence, Gustav limping. They were enjoying the heat on their backs, but felt their stomachs churn in a mixture of hunger and nervousness. They decided to avoid the schoolhouse, and instead they followed the stone wall along the edge of the village.

The boys turned down a narrow lane bordered by rendered houses that sagged with years. This lane would take them by the town square, toward their homes. With all the movement and chaos of market day, they hoped to slip unnoticed through the village and home to bed. Both boys knew how to enter their houses by rickety windows. If they could convince their parents that they had come home late at night, perhaps that might lessen the punishment. It seemed a vain hope.

When they neared the first collection of houses that ran in a bank along the square, disappointment surged through them. There were market stalls being assembled and carts of vegetables and goods being unloaded, but they also saw groups of men and women, gesturing and talking anxiously.

Instead of walking straight into the crowd of people, the boys changed direction, and moved stealthily over to the wall of the nearest house. It was solid, lined with an enormous woodpile, and the thatched roof hung low toward the ground. The boys, in their scraggly brown clothes, were well camouflaged. They crept forwards, trying to decipher the adult voices.

"They must have drowned in the river!" a woman sobbed.

A gruff male voice answered her. "We checked it this morning at dawn. No bodies. No sign of anyone having been there."

"Poor boys! Poor boys!" wailed another voice.

Their ears picked up a flurry of sound further away, a heated argument between a female and two male voices. Someone was yelling at Frau Henkel.

"What do you mean they just *left*! What were you doing? Where are your professional standards!"

They heard the snuffling sobs of their schoolteacher, and knew they were going to be in for it.

"Whether the boys are found or not, you are leaving! I will not have such carelessness in the classroom!"

"An oversight, Sir! Please, little Anna was ill, and there was so much to write on the board—"

"We have standards! For twenty years now, many of our students have gone on to study at the University. Negligence will not be tolerated!"

"I have given ten years of service! Where will I go?"

"You should have thought of that, Frau Henkel, when you neglected your duties yesterday."

The boys craned their necks to listen further. Beyond their hiding place by the woodpile, a wooden table held mounds of fresh apples. This distracted them for a moment. Nearby, two farmers heaved heavy burlap sacks from a cart, obviously listening to the villagers. The boys heard one of them whisper, "About time that Jewish cow was told where to go!"

Tomas hated it when he heard that sort of talk—but it was not uncommon to find support for the National Socialists in Zweibach. To Tomas's father, and therefore to him, the National Socialists were little better than thugs; Tomas couldn't understand why so many he knew had voted for them.

Tomas recognized the farmer who had spoken; his accent was Polish. Hanna, his one daughter, sat at the desk between Gustav and the window. She had a ruddy complexion, and her hands were always scratched and roughened. She was pleasant enough, but not very bright. Tomas remembered her having to stand in the corner and wear the dunce's cap several times for her lack of accuracy in spelling and arithmetic. She was constantly being told to wash her face and hands.

Frau Henkel was always concerned that every child was clean. Fingernails were inspected regularly. Tomas was made to write out lines one afternoon—*I will clean my nails and hands*—over and over, so that even in his sleep that night he had been writing those words. He remembered with a guilty conscience how he had wanted to pick up an ink pen and scratch *I will clean my nails and hands* all over the teacher's smug face, her arms, her hands and her nails—make her so dirty with lines that she would be marked forever. However, his excellent result on the geography test had quickly dispelled this image. He wondered if it were different for Hanna, who never came to school clean, or received high marks on her tests.

He was dragged back to the present by an insistent tugging on his sleeve.

"Is Frau Henkel Jewish?" whispered Gustav to Tomas.

"Must be."

"You'd never know."

"What do you mean?"

"She looks just like us."

"What do you mean, she looks just like us? Why shouldn't she?"

"You know—they often look a bit different. Kind of pointy-looking … their noses."

"You and noses!"

"I'm being serious."

"I've never met anyone who looks like you said."

"Look harder. What's his name? Feldmann! You can tell with him."

"Johannes?"

"You know, the way his nose kind of juts out."

"Have you ever asked him?"

"What? If he's Jewish?"

"Yes."

"No, but Mama says they close up their shop every Friday evening. It annoys her that she can't buy bread from them on Saturday mornings. And Hans says—"

"Hans?" broke in Tomas bitterly. "Hans Ecker? What does he know?"

Hans was the schoolyard tyrant, and his father seemed to have even the Headmaster at his beck and call.

"Everything," grumbled Gustav. "His father leads that youth group—you know, the one Hans is part of, they keep handing out all those leaflets on Hitler. Haven't you seen him dressed up and leading them all marching in the square?" Gustav bent close to Tomas's ear and barely whispered, "My father said that Herr Ecker took it on *himself* to make sure everyone voted 'properly' in the last election."

The boys were startled by a voice very nearby, and melted back into the woodpile. Someone strode past, but unfortunately for the boys, this time their camouflage wasn't good enough. That someone was Gustav's father. He stopped, swiveled around to stare at them, and then let out a roar. What he said was unintelligible, but his actions were absolutely clear. He hauled the two boys out from behind the woodpile, and dragged them by their collars into the square.

"Look!" he called, angry and loud. The crowd turned. White faces, frightened faces; for a moment they all looked like they were underwater. Everything moved in slow motion, even the voices slowed to a deep, incoherent murmur.

Tomas was aware of Frau Henkel's tear-stained face, thin and panicked. A gray shawl was wrapped around her bony shoulders. She looked tired and defeated. He suddenly felt guilty. Tomas looked away, but not before he caught sight of Hans and his father, standing just behind the Headmaster.

Tomas could see Gustav's booted foot scuffing at the cobblestones. He did not dare look at his father's face. The hum of words moved around him like a cloud, and Hans was forgotten.

Later he would recall being grasped territorially by his mother and shaken roughly, her tears on his hair and cheek; then his father, grim and silent, taking the thin switch from its hook behind the kitchen door, and running it through his workshop-worn hands. Tomas would hear many times—as if in a dream—the hiss of sliced air, feel the shock of the pain on his backside, the impossible heat of his skin, and wonder at the scream that seemed to come from somewhere beyond him.

Then the most awful punishment—spending time with Gustav forbidden, a hired tutor and extra lessons during the summer. Tomas would begin learning Latin and Greek to prepare for secondary school—perhaps even a scholarship; his father was determined that, poor as they were, his son would attend university and enter a respectable profession.

It was all too horrible. Tomas shivered as he thought of enduring school until he was nineteen, let alone the extra preparation now, when he hadn't even finished at the *Grund-schule*.[5] After all, Gustav's father wasn't making Gustav learn dead languages!

---

5   Elementary school.

14.

Tomas had not seen Gustav for two long weeks. At school they were forbidden to sit next to each other.

The Headmaster had been teaching their classes until a replacement could be found for Frau Henkel. He would stride in each morning with his enormous black gown billowing around him, his forehead brooding and eyes suspicious. Classes were very quiet, except when the children obediently recited their grammar or sums. The cane was displayed menacingly above the blackboard; the children averted their gaze from it, lest they become distracted, and fail to complete their mathematics problems accurately.

A night came when Tomas decided it had to end. He sat upright in his bed, eyes wide open, staring out at the moon. He imagined his hollow in the tree—he had not been able to check his knife and map for what felt like a year. There were only three weeks left of school, and then he would be forced to begin lessons with the tutor. His father was determined to see his son educated, as he himself had never been. Tomas knew his father's dream was that one day his son would be a professional man—a doctor, or a lawyer—anything, it seemed, but a luthier. Tomas didn't see what was so wonderful about being a lawyer. He loved absorbing new information, but he also knew that explorers learned as they traveled, which was how he planned to learn about the world. Until then, he was more than happy to work in his father's music shop.

Tomas sighed. He fiddled with his quilt and shifted restlessly. He tucked his hands under his head and stared up at the ceiling. It was split by huge old beams of dark wood that stretched like strong, protective arms over his bed. He examined the beams and then, in his mind's eye, journeyed through the tranquil house below him.

He imagined the workshop, smelling of wood, resin and oils, with the instruments hanging on the walls in placid expectancy. Tomas sung a Bach tune softly to himself, the one he always hummed when he pondered the violins and cellos lining the walls of his father's shop. He enjoyed the challenge of getting all the triads exactly in tune, which was difficult when they followed each other so rapidly. He loved the way the melody made him ache for something that he couldn't articulate.

His father played this piece on the cello. He had tried many times to encourage his son on the instrument—any instrument, in fact—but had been unsuccessful. Tomas was outdoors at every opportunity, tracing lines and paths across the land, charting his journeys and secret places. But he did love music, and he would settle himself on the big wooden bench in the kitchen, to listen enraptured as his father placed lines of melody in the air, mapping sound as Tomas mapped the hills, fields and forests around his home. He felt close to his parents when the fire was crackling, his mother was sewing, and his father was playing the cello.

Yes, he would not mind at all if he were to one day become a luthier like his father.

Something clicked against the glass of his window. He was out of his bed in an instant, and deftly hoisted open the sash. The moon was large and full, bathing everything with colorless light; it was like staring at a black-and-white film. He could see Gustav down below, jumping up and down to keep warm. He looked like a small Charlie Chaplin.

Tomas slithered into his day clothing, clambered across the branch of the huge tree next to his window, and swung himself down to the ground.

Gustav grinned in the darkness. "Fancy a stroll?"

The two of them set off through the cold, free air.

It was wonderful. They chatted as they walked, but in whispers.

"I don't know how long until we can be friends again," said Gustav, "but I know that if we do well in our studies, that's going to help. Then we can find work, and get out of this place!"

"It will be years," Tomas replied mournfully. "My father is determined for me to go to university. That would mean going to the school in the city. He wants me to get a scholarship."

Gustav grimaced. "I don't care," he announced. "I'm getting out of here the first chance I get. I'm going to make lots of money and be famous, and everyone will want me to open their public buildings and bridges. Then they will all be sorry they ever did this to us."

They fell silent. A twig cracked under their feet.

Memory

I lie here in the dark, hearing again Gustav's boyish defiance. *They will all be sorry they ever did this to us.*

Above me a man snores, the sound like a fragmented wave that has somehow come aboard and now crawls restlessly around our cabin. I, too, am restless. I feel the ocean swell beneath me; I tense involuntarily and then relax my limbs into its rhythm.

My papers are in my pocket. I slip my hand into it and feel their creased, soft surface in my fingers. I must sleep, but I cannot. It is the moon, playing on the corners and shapes in this room with its distilled light. The sea breathes outside my porthole. I remember.

15.

For the next three weeks until the school year finished, Gustav and Tomas were strangers by day, and best friends at night. Twice they even made it to the swimming hole, where they sat on the rocks at its rim, gazed at the moon, and planned their futures. Sometimes while they were doing this, Gustav took their stone from his pocket and Tomas had his turn to finger it quietly, marveling all over again at its smoothness. These secret times made the days more bearable.

Finally the bell sounded for the last time that school year. The Headmaster cleaned out his desk, and all the children ran home, laughing and happy. The warmer weather hovered over them, lightening their mood and putting a reckless generosity into their hearts.

The boys were finally told they could spend time with each other again, and they were ecstatic.

"But only in the late afternoons," Tomas's father insisted, his eyes stern. "In the mornings you will continue with your lessons, and in the afternoons you must help me in the shop. Then you may play."

This was better, so much better than the past weeks.

The tutor arrived—he was a tall, thin man from Leipzig, which was a comfortable train journey from Zweibach. He brought with him a university seriousness, the pale, academic look of a learned man who spent many hours absorbed in his books, away from sunlight.

Tomas watched him walk cautiously up to the front door in the fresh summer morning. His suit had been pressed carefully, and his hair combed back. One thin, white hand clasped a suitcase; the other arm was wrapped around a pile of leather-bound books.

Tomas opened the door before the man even raised his head to locate the doorknob. The man smiled, surprised.

He had a gentle face. His eyes gleamed for a moment, then resumed their vague gaze.

"Good morning. Master Tomas, I presume?"

Tomas had never been addressed in such a grand manner, and he wasn't sure quite what to say. He stared at the man and then replied shyly, "I'm Tomas. Would you like to see my father?"

The man nodded, and the boy led him through the dark hall, turning left to enter the back way into the shop. The air was sharp with the smell of linseed. The walls were hung with pieces of wood of varying sizes. Tools, smooth and sanded half-bodies of instruments in progress, cases yet to be finished, were set out in orderly rows. Tomas also knew that strings lay in shining whorls behind the counter, each carefully wrapped and labeled with fine script.

Tomas's father was bent over his workbench. He made and sold violins, cellos, bows, bridges, and cases, and he repaired and reconditioned instruments that had lost their sound or beauty. He had an excellent reputation as a mender and maker of fine instruments, and customers came to him even from the big cities and towns. Tomas marveled again that his father should think that being a doctor or a lawyer was more important.

The thin man bowed his head politely, and introduced himself. "My name is Tomas Solberg. I believe that today is the date you desired that I commence my employment."

Tomas was intrigued—this man shared his first name. The boy stared at the tutor with a mixture of respect and curiosity.

Herr Solberg smiled at him. "There are two of us. Tomas. Didymus."

"I beg your pardon?" asked the boy politely.

"Didymus. Greek for twin. Tomas is … the Aramaic form, I believe. So you see," he gently inclined his head as if addressing a fellow gentleman, "of course it is natural that there are two of us!"

Tomas's father straightened up and wiped his wide hands on his leather apron. They shone with a fine coating of oil. His eyes widened in amusement and respect at the young man's way with words.

"You're very welcome," Herr Müller replied. "Come through, and my wife will fix you something to eat."

The three of them filed out of the shop-front and down the corridor to a spacious, homely kitchen. Sausages hung from the rafters, along with strings of onions and bunches of dried herbs.

Tomas's mother turned from adding wood to the stove. She looked startled for a moment, and then she smiled. "Please sit down, Herr Solberg. I will find you some breakfast."

The young man set down his suitcase and books, then sat—or rather perched himself with the delicacy of a bird— on a wooden chair. Tomas's summer had begun and, with it, a new manner of exploration.

Memory

How strange is time. One moment expands to fill a room, while others gather in absurdly tiny particles like dust, brushed into corners and never seen. Through it all, like a river, runs the feeling that had I done this or seen that, then perhaps the decision I made that day would have been different.

But I have stepped onto this boat to begin a new life, not to live the old one again. And yet ... the past seems to hover around me, barely touching my skin and clothes and hair.

16.

"You must take more care, Tomas," murmured the tutor as he scanned the boy's latest piece of translation.

Tomas fidgeted in his chair. Outside the sunshine beckoned, and he heard the church bells chime eleven. Today, his father had impulsively given Tomas the whole afternoon to spend as he pleased—surely he would be allowed to leave soon.

Herr Solberg focused on the paper in front of him, and clicked his tongue absently. Tomas stared at the side of the young man's face, wondering whether his skin was so pale because he had been born like that, or if it was the amount of time he spent indoors. Then he found himself analyzing the shape of his nose. *It's just like anyone else's,* he thought, and was secretly quite pleased that Gustav hadn't been right about something.

The tutor turned to the boy and looked at him carefully. Tomas colored slightly, but the man didn't seem to notice.

"Can you see the mistake you have made?"

"No," grumbled his student.

There was a pause. Tomas kicked the chair leg with his foot.

"What tense did you begin the passage with?"

"Past simple."

"Good, and so you should have. But here?" he tapped the page a few sentences down with one long, refined finger.

Tomas peered closely. He frowned and tried to shut out the sunshine, and concentrate instead on the scrawl in front of him.

"I've changed tense?" he asked finally, his voice unsure.

"Yes."

"Into what?"

"You tell me," Mr Solberg continued patiently.

Tomas knew by now that his tutor would wait until he arrived at the answer, even if a whole quarter of an hour passed while he tried to figure out the problem. Sometimes his tutor's patience irritated Tomas, and he wasn't sure exactly why. He wondered why this man didn't yell at him the way Frau Henkel and all his other teachers had. Tomas looked again at what he had written.

"Tell me, and then you can go," said the man gently.

Suddenly Tomas's face lit up, in spite of the fact he was largely uninterested in the task. "I've gone into present tense?"

"Yes."

"So it doesn't make sense anymore."

"Correct."

"Do I have to fix it now?" He tried not to sound too plaintive, but the tutor was not deceived.

Herr Solberg pursed his lips firmly but didn't insist. "By tomorrow. You have had enough for today, I can see."

The young man sighed, took off his glasses and rubbed his forehead.

"You look like you've had enough, too," replied Tomas impetuously. He blushed. "Sorry, Sir."

The tutor smiled. "I have many things to think about, and sometimes they make me tired."

Tomas was curious. "Like what things?"

"Things you will also need to ponder one day, although hopefully not too soon."

"What things?" he asked again.

"Your father has not engaged my services so that I can weigh you down with politics, but that you may improve your grammar and Latin and enter a university."

Tomas was not put off. He leaned forward conspiratorially. "Do you mean the National Socialists?" He almost whispered the name.

The tutor looked at him evenly, and Tomas continued. "My father hates them and says they'll only ruin us—if they ever get the power they want."

"And does your father think they will?"

"He says it's all bluff, that up North they will never tolerate such a ... a word like 'beseal' or something."

"Imbecile?"

Tomas grinned triumphantly. "Yes, that's it! That's what he calls him!"

The tutor's face grew grave for a moment. He twisted the pen in his hand. "Then your father has to be careful, Tomas."

"Why?"

"Not everyone thinks as he does, and those who disagree with him are very powerful people."

Tomas cocked his head to one side. "You mean those men in the brown clothes? I saw them in Leipzig when I went with Father to get a tool repaired. Oh, but we don't have any of those in our village. They are only in the city." He paused, thoughtful, and then he perked up again. "I've never seen them around here."

Then he remembered Hans, and what Gustav had told him, that terrible morning by the woodpile. He went quiet.

The tutor looked at Tomas for a few moments, then placed the pen down and leaned back in his chair. "But enough of this. It is your summer break—go outside and make what you can of your boyhood!" He chuckled at his own words. "I sound like an old man," he mused as he closed the books.

They stood up, and Tomas made for the door. At the last moment, however, he turned with a question that at the beginning of the summer he would never have dreamed of asking.

"Would ... would you like to come swimming?"

The tutor paused and looked almost shy. "Where do you go swimming?"

"It's a secret. I'll have to blindfold you some of the way. But do you want to come?"

The young man shuffled his things for a moment, looking down at his hands. Tomas wondered whether he had perhaps been a bit forward.

Then the tutor raised his head. "Yes, I will come." He looked uncomfortable for a moment. "I … I don't have a costume."

Tomas looked bemused for a moment, trying to think what the tutor meant, then he realized and grinned. "Just wear something you can swim in! Or," he added, "get in the water like we do!"

"We?"

"Gustav and me!"

"You mean there will be others there?"

"Just him and me. And you, if you want to come. He's my best friend." Tomas had a sudden thought: *my twin.* He paused, then glanced at his teacher mischievously. "He knows all about you."

Tomas darted off, calling over his shoulder, "I'll meet you at the end of the lane in five minutes!"

The tutor gathered up his books and papers, humming happily to himself.

He met them at the end of the lane, as promised. He looked exactly the same as he did at Tomas's lessons, except that he wore no tie. Tomas and Gustav glanced briefly at each other, wondering whether he would actually swim in his suit. They said nothing, however, but led the way between stocky stone walls to where the meadow ended, and trees clustered together under the hot sun.

It was the edge of the village, and a track wound through and between some fields and copses. They didn't pass the schoolhouse when they approached the swimming hole from this direction, which was just as well—the boys didn't want any reminders of where they would have to be every day in only two weeks.

The trees thickened into a forest, their branches billowing and locking together. Birds piped, and the shade was cool and green. The boys grinned, then stopped, and Tomas drew out a piece of cloth. The tutor stared, surprised.

"I thought you were teasing me about the blindfold!" he exclaimed, somewhat startled.

Tomas smoothed the material, and came over to him. "It's a precaution. This is our very secret place, and nobody knows about it but us. We're nearly there. It's all right," he added when he saw that the tutor was actually nervous, "It isn't a trick, or anything,"

Then the man relaxed, and even smiled slightly. The tutor suddenly looked much more his actual age. He shrugged his shoulders nonchalantly. "All right. This afternoon I am not your teacher." He paused, searching for some more words. "This afternoon I am your honored guest."

This attitude instantly melted any remaining awkwardness among the three. Tomas wrapped the cloth around the man's eyes. The boys then took one hand each, and led him gently through the remaining forest, being careful to instruct him as to when to bend his head or step sideways. They all crawled until they arrived at the end of a tunnel the boys had cut into the undergrowth.

Tomas triumphantly removed the scarf. They had arrived at what was the most spectacular entrance to their secret place. Before them stretched the glistening, gently slapping water. On the far side of the pond, the rocks glowed with moss in dappled light. The grassy bank rimmed the water like a velvet cloth, through which tiny star daisies poked their delicate white heads. The streams alternately chuckled and soughed like wind in pine trees. The sun seemed to gather them in with blazing, welcoming arms. The tutor's eyes glistened, but the boys had already raced around to the other bank, stripped off their clothes, and dive-bombed into the water.

"Come on!" they yelled in raucous unison, splashing and tussling and laughing.

The young man looked around him shyly, then slowly took off his coat and shirt, shoes and socks. He carefully rolled up his trousers and walked to the water's edge.

Then something happened. As soon as his skin felt the fresh, cold water, as soon as the sunlight warmed his face, as soon as the sweet air brushed his chest, the learned man dropped from him into his pile of clothes on the bank.

The tutor straightened up and, with a broad smile, looked every bit the young university student that he actually was. He plunged into the water, Latin and politics and fear dissolving around him, and he forgot for one summer afternoon in Zweibach that a decade of democracy was fading, times were changing—and that he was a Jew.

Part Four: Sarabande

(n): One of the most ancient court dances of the 16th century, it was originally a lively and passionate dance, and was eventually banned in Spain. The Sarabande then evolved into a grave, slow processional dance, during which couples paraded forward for four steps, and then back for four steps in an endless variety of patterns.

Memory

I distrust moonlight. It is so careful, soft-footed, and cruel. The moon makes night like a padded room where I can throw my thoughts around but can't kill them—where all the hard walls are yielding. I believe that my thoughts know this, and creep out of the hidden recesses of my brain to play and scamper in frustrating safety.

I am becoming accustomed to the movement of the boat. It is even beginning to feel normal. I will probably lose my ability to walk on solid land, and be doomed to spend the rest of my life on the water, always journeying and never arriving.

I am thankful for the rare privilege of a porthole in my cabin—our cabin, to be more accurate, as I share it with others, whom I presume are sleeping. I am fortunate enough to have my section of the bunk just underneath the porthole, so if I sit up, I can watch the sky outside; the porthole is my eye.

Go away, thoughts! Be repelled by the smell of garlic, sweat and bored, restless sleepers—and leave.

I turn over. I think I am asleep. I dream. I bathe in a stream in Germany. There are pine trees, elms. We swim, and Gustav almost drowns. We try to catch fish, and end up catching stones instead. We? They. I feel no connection with them, yet this is part of my past. *Please, no dreams.* We line up stones and give each one a name and a story, a fantastical narrative about how our lives will be.

I need to know what date this is, how old we are … it feels like we are ten, twenty—but then we have been doing this for so long, even after we grew up and went to university, and then to war.

Every warm night we both swim, I know, wherever we are, and the stone falls again into our hands.

17.

Autumn, 1930

The school year had started again, and the summer had entered its slow, inexorable transformation into autumn chill. Tomas, now fourteen, walked toward the schoolhouse with Gustav.

A new teacher had been appointed, Frau Henkel was only a memory, and the boys were to begin preparing for their scholarship examinations. Study had become more serious. The beckoning fingers of distant spires had now become the hands of a clock, ticking away the time they had to spend in this imposing building, the time left to them to be boys—and they felt it. All the children felt it. Life was changing.

The schoolyard blazed with action, and exploded with sound. Girls screamed as boys pulled their hair and stole their skipping ropes, other girls twittered secrets to each other under the huge, patient oak at one end of the grounds, and grubby boys tore around the obstacle course of the busy yard, chasing and running and fighting.

It was recess. The sun was crisp, and early falling leaves crunched beneath their feet. Tomas and Gustav leaned against the brick wall, trying to absorb as much radiant heat into their bodies as they could before going back inside to resume their lessons. They closed their eyes against the sharp sunlight, enjoying the friendly quietude that rested between them.

The first hint Tomas had of Hans's presence was the shadow that fell across his face. Gustav stiffened beside him. For some reason Tomas kept his eyes shut, as if it made him invisible—if he stayed quite still, perhaps the preying Hans would move on, thinking Tomas only a shadow on the bricks.

Gustav moved a little closer, and nudged him with his pointy elbow, and Tomas opened his eyes. He saw not only Hans, but Hans and fellow conspirators—his faithful, ever-heckling mob from the back row of their classroom.

Tomas had no idea whether Hans had chosen his gang for their size or their stupidity, or both. But they weren't all muscular brutes—two smaller boys trotted loyally alongside their leader like dachshunds. Then there was the angular, well-dressed Wilhelm, reveling in his father's high position on the village council.

Tomas and Gustav discussed it sometimes. Regardless of height or size, the group was a collection of idiots, they reasoned. Why else would they find such pleasure in the senseless taunting of their fellows? Gustav and Tomas never talked about them unless they were on the way to their swimming hole, or on one of their night walks around the village. Only then did they feel strong enough to face what terrified them most, deep down: being caught and tormented by Hans Ecker and his henchmen.

"Idiot!"

Hans pushed Tomas roughly, as he tried not to meet the bigger boy's gaze. The ring of followers snickered, and edged closer. Tomas wondered at their boldness in the small school-yard, when at any time a teacher could stride past on the way from one part of the school to another. It wasn't as if he and Gustav were in a lonely, unfrequented area of the grounds.

The more he pondered it, the more it bothered him. This was not a secluded lane or remote byway; he and Gustav conscientiously avoided such routes, especially to and from school. But it was morning, bright daylight, and they were surrounded by children in the open air.

Gustav and Tomas glanced at each other. As if at a secret signal—although this had never been rehearsed—they both ducked under Hans's arm and bolted. They ran in tandem across the school-yard. Perhaps it was their practice at escaping school, but they moved smoothly and didn't need to speak.

The mob were surprised for only a moment, and then chased after them as a body. Other students parted quickly for them, and watched the attackers chase the pair through the yard. This was not a large space, however, and it was only a few minutes before Gustav and Tomas were encircled by sneering faces and bare, tense forearms that pulsed like snakes.

The two boys had not quite made it to the break in the hedge, although they could see it from where they stood: a rift in the leaves that glimmered with the green and blue of a field, and free autumn sky. Gustav and Tomas stood back to back, holding each other upright, and turned their faces away.

Instinctively they clenched their fists, and Tomas felt all the muscles in his body tighten. His heart was pounding, and he knew he must be red in the face. Beside him, Gustav's breathing rasped.

Every part of Tomas yearned to run, but he remained immobilized. Was it his imagination, or had the whole of Zweibach suddenly become mute? He heard Gustav's voice sounding strangely high and far away.

"What do you want with us? Why us? What have we done?"

Hans mocked them by appearing to take Gustav's question seriously. He stared up at the sky for a moment, tapped his chin like a caricature of a judge, and then turned to his right hand man.

"What *have* they done?"

Wilhelm grinned maliciously, and joined the game. "Why, what *haven't* they done? I counted at least three answers given in class today that were designed to make us look like we had not done our homework."

There was a silence, undercut by sniggers that hovered in the air like a cloud of sinister insects.

"There you go ... *designed*," murmured Hans, shaking his head at them sadly. He narrowed his eyes, and his whole face blended into one angry, pointed mask. "You show no compassion toward your poor classmates when you take your work that seriously."

Then he suddenly became bored with playing the grown-up and snarled at them. "Idiots!"

The boys around him snarled too, like a pack of dogs, or a menacing Greek chorus. The insects hummed more loudly—ominous, threatening, waiting to devour.

Tomas and Gustav moved closer together. Hans once again shoved Tomas roughly, but he remained upright. Another boy pushed him, and then let his fist fly at Tomas's face. He ducked and lost his balance, which caused a triumphant response in the assailants. They kicked Tomas while he tried to lift himself up from the gravel; he scraped the skin on his hands and legs in the process, and watched dots of blood burst forth on his muddied skin. He felt the dull thud of a thick shoe in his ribs, and he collapsed again, a small moan escaping his lips. He tasted schoolyard earth on his tongue.

Gustav bent to help him, and was hit across the back with a branch, then kicked viciously in the calves. He fell on top of Tomas, while jeers and booted swipes rained down upon them. They writhed helplessly in the dirt.

"Tell that to your father," spat Hans in Tomas's ear.

There was an angry, authoritative hollering, and a black-clad figure swept purposefully across the school-yard.

Tomas and Gustav clambered awkwardly to their feet. In spite of their pain and shock, they tried somewhat pathetically to smooth down their hair and adjust their shirts. Somehow, Hans was no longer there.

A freckle-faced boy was hauled off, and everyone else ordered to present themselves to the Headmaster for what they knew would be the obligatory caning. Another teacher arrived, and marched them all single-file to the row of metal faucets, where they were made to clean up in cringingly cold water. Other students filed by on their way to class, eying Tomas, Gustav and the other boys with furtive, sidelong glances.

As they waited in a line outside the Headmaster's office, each boy tried in his own way to deal with the whimpering and occasional yell that darted out from under the wooden door. Hair had been wetted, smoothed, and parted on the side as if their mothers had suddenly appeared and set about making them more presentable. Each boy knew that a hair out of place, a crease in a shirt, or a scuffed shoe could result in even more time spent prostrate under the swinging, vengeful switch.

Tomas stood last in the queue. He watched as, one by one, the boys moved through the door and returned to the hallway, their faces metamorphosed from white and resolute, to tear-streaked and sullen. Each stared fixedly ahead, wishing themselves six feet tall and armed with a booming voice—and perhaps a gun.

Again, Tomas noticed that Hans was not there.

As the last of the perpetrators filed past him with a subdued glare in his direction, Tomas realized that only he and Gustav remained. The door creaked again, and he watched his friend disappear behind it. There was a moment of silence, one yelp, and then Gustav re-appeared. The door closed behind him, dull and forbidding.

He turned quickly to Tomas. "He knows it wasn't our fault," he whispered, as he ducked past.

Tomas knew Gustav would not wait for him, but enter the classroom and join in the translation of a Latin story about brave centurions.

When this is done, I must forget what has just happened, Tomas thought. He knew that otherwise terror would become permanently implanted in him, rising every time he approached the school, and he did not want to be a prisoner of fear.

The door opened. The Headmaster beckoned Tomas in with a menacing curl of his finger. Tomas obeyed, and the latch slipped into place behind him. He looked around the room, moving only his eyes.

One narrow window allowed a slender shaft of sunlight to enter, giving the room an almost monastic atmosphere. A heavy desk sat firmly in the center as if it had grown there, its surface scratched red leather, piled with papers at various stages of yellowing. An inkwell perched at the left of the desk, with a shiny dark fountain pen resting beside it. A row of towering mahogany shelves lined two of the walls, and on one of the shelves stood a blurred sepia photograph. With shock, Tomas saw that it was a photograph of the Headmaster and a woman, and that he was smiling. He could not draw his eyes away from the photo—that is, until the Headmaster cleared his throat and ordered Tomas to lean across the solid wooden chair in front of him.

It was over quickly. The Headmaster's hand jerked expertly at Tomas's trousers, and the cane hissed against his skin, forcing his whole body to jolt slightly up and forwards. This was repeated two more times. Tomas pulled up his trousers. His breath heaved and his eyes prickled. He was sure that Gustav had only been caned once.

The Headmaster said nothing, but played with the weapon in his hands. He pursed his lips together, narrowing his eyes at the boy. The man then turned and clicked the cane into its customary position on the wall beside the window. He paused to glance outside and rub his chin. For a moment he looked disconcertingly like Hans. Tomas waited uncomfortably. He did not dare look at the photo again.

"Sit," ordered the Headmaster in a firm voice, without turning from the window.

Tomas gulped in surprise, and then in pain as he sat promptly on the wooden chair. He stared at the Headmaster's back, wondering what all this could be about.

"Your friend—Gustav—said nothing, even when I asked him what had happened. I now ask you."

Tomas wondered why Gustav had not spoken. He swallowed hard, and his mind raced. If Hans should find out—what then?

"Tomas Müller," the Headmaster snapped, "Answer my question, or I will have to use the cane once more."

"I … I … they … Hans … "

"Hans Ecker?" barked the Headmaster. "What has Hans to do with this? He was not even there!"

Tomas looked down at the carpet. It was a dull red with a line of tiny navy blue flowers coursing through it.

"I beg your pardon, but he was, Sir."

"The Geography Master did not see him."

"He was not there when the teacher came, but he was the one who started it, Sir."

"I refuse to believe it. Are you lying to me?"

"No."

"What did you say?"

"No, Headmaster, Sir."

Tomas suddenly remembered something that had occurred before the summer break had even begun. One afternoon, Tomas had been about to step inside the workshop, but was stopped short as he overheard his father saying something to a customer—a man whose voice Tomas hadn't recognized—about the dismissal of Frau Henkel. Tomas had heard the word "shameful," which in his memory his father repeated over and over. He could see in his mind's eye his father's oiled, work-worn hands wiping his leather apron in time with the words, a deep frown on his face.

At the time, Tomas had supposed that his father was blaming him, but now he knew for certain that there was something else that had compelled his father's anger. He recalled Hans and Herr Ecker witnessing Frau Henkel's dismissal, and the way they had stood at the Headmaster's right hand that early summer morning in the town square. In some way—Tomas knew instinctively—Hans was involved.

Now, in the Headmaster's office, all Tomas wanted to do was run, but he remained glued to his chair, as he had remained glued to the ground at Hans' taunting. There was a long silence. Tomas scoured the surface of the carpet, tracing the path of the miniature blue flowers.

The Headmaster sighed.

"Well then, you may go. I want no more trouble from you two boys. You caused enough last year, and it must not continue. There is always a price to pay for making trouble. Others have paid it, and so will you if you insist on behaving in this manner. Get to class immediately!"

Tomas thought again of Frau Henkel and how tired and gray she had looked that morning in the square. Again he felt a stab of guilt.

Tomas stood up and edged toward the door. The Headmaster did not move. The boy heaved at the polished handle and slipped outside.

He realized that nothing would be done about Hans, nothing discussed. Hans would never know what Tomas had said.

Tomas shivered as he realized that Hans possessed power he had not previously guessed at, a power he couldn't even fathom. He knew now that Hans would always win, every time.

I pivot on one foot and with a few more steps have completed another circuit of the deck. I feel invigorated, even purposeful. Finally I come to a stop. I must sit down. I find a pile of rope and perch there, glancing up at the sky. Now that I have stopped moving, I feel the spring chill. I pull my coat closer around myself.

I watch another man arrive at the railing in front of me. He has broad, strong shoulders, and his boots are worn thin at the soles. The man turns, acknowledges my presence, and settles near me on the coils of rope.

"Another clear day … it is good."

He offers conversation casually, as if we are already friends. I have met, for the first time, the one who will become my only ship brother on this journey.

"Yes," I reply, "another day means we are closer."

"It is good for those who spend their nights on the deck." He pauses, thinking, then adds, "They are the suffering ones."

I nod. "For those, too, who are stifled at nights in the cabins below."

"Yes, yes. It is good for us, too." The man rubs the sole of one shoe absentmindedly, and gazes up at the sky.

"You also are there?" I ask.

"Yes. There are many of us! Why do you sound surprised?"

"I thought that by this time I would know everyone there by sight."

I must look bemused because the man laughs—a loud, free sound, and I find myself warmed by it. It is a long time since I have heard laughter like that.

"Have you ever been where we are headed?" I feel bold enough to ask this question, although it is breaking etiquette: one offers one's story, it is never demanded. There are many on board who are trying to remake themselves in readiness for the new land, and do not want to be known for who they were.

"Never," says the man confidently, then chuckles. "Other places, yes, but not there."

"It might sound strange, but I am not looking for adventure. I want to settle. We have all had our fill of flight, I think."

"Ah, yes," responds the man thoughtfully. "Flight."

Just then an albatross passes close to the railing. Its wings are huge, like sailcloth. Its beak is a great hooked claw, and it swoops silently by before catching an updraft and soaring away. The man with the worn shoes follows the bird with his eyes, his hand held up to block some of the sun's glare.

"They say it's bad luck to see an albatross at sea," I say.

The man shakes his head impatiently.

"Ah! Who's 'they,' I'd like to know. There is a perfectly good scientific reason for seeing an albatross where we are." He harrumphs to himself and shifts his weight on the coils of rope. "But it sails as we do, on winds and chance. I only hope we can navigate the tides of our future as competently."

"You seem to know something about birds."

"I have spent many years studying them, and it must be said that I find myself, perhaps quite naturally, making comparisons between birds and my everyday life."

I shrug. "What is everyday life?"

The man guffaws and slaps his side. "Yes, indeed! What is everyday life anymore? Still, we must hope that once again we will have an everyday life. Here ... " He reaches into his pocket and pulls out a tattered bundle of papers. "Remember this?"

He shows me a postcard of a town center. An ornate water fountain sparkles in the sunlight, and tram cars rumble past. Women in tailored coats shop for vegetables, and two men talk jovially on the corner. The trees are full of leaves.

My own village appears to me.

"My town." The man sighs, then grins, shrugging his shoulders. "And may it be so again. I brought this with me so that I could remember my home for what it was. I think ..."

He rubs his beard. "I think the fountain is still there. Well, it is here, certainly!" He taps his head with a smile.

The man has begun to sift through the memories in his pocket. He pulls out a photograph and holds it in front of him so I can see it.

"Who is that?"

"Ah!" Another sigh. "We spoke of birds, but she, my friend, is the most delicate, the most beautiful of all God's creatures." He pauses. "My wife."

"She is not with you?" I ask softly.

"She waits in a faraway place … " His voice trails off. The man stares back up at the sky, now a sharp blue. He seems to be gathering information; he reads the space above us, his eyes scanning until he discovers what he wants to see. The albatross has returned. The man raises his hand in a salute.

"Good travels, friend!" he calls, as the bird moves away to skim the distant waves. Once again I feel the early morning chill, and I shiver.

18.

"So, who do you think will be next?"

Gustav rolled over on the carpet of dead leaves they had collected for warmth. They could see the swimming hole from where they lay in the autumn sunlight, but the air was far too brisk for the water to be tempting.

Gustav and Tomas had been trying to work out which poor student would be the next in the long line of victims of Hans and his gang. The two boys had successfully avoided the notorious school-yard bullies over the past few weeks, but others had not—their wounds had given them away, as had their shrinking demeanor, both in class and in the corridor. Only the girls had been exempted. How long this would last the boys could only guess, as their school was small, and the list of possible victims finite—unless, Tomas pointed out, Hans began all over again at the start of his list.

"He's a monster," declared Tomas.

"Not human," agreed Gustav. "The way he sneers at you while he's enjoying watching you squirm—I wonder whether he's always been like that."

"I don't know. He has as long as I can remember."

"Really? Come on, we've known him basically since he was born. Do you really think he was *born* nasty?"

"I haven't ever thought about it. I wonder whether some people just *are*—or maybe his parents are mean, too."

"They seem nice enough. My mother always has a chat with his mother whenever they meet, and comes home saying how friendly she is. She just won't believe me about Hans—she can't believe that such a lovely woman could give birth to a boy like I've described."

"It's strange. Maybe he ate something bad when he was small."

They chuckled then, and started to wonder what it could have been. Their list of foods became more and more disgusting until finally, as they got to rotting wild pig, they both sat up suddenly.

"What's that?" Gustav whispered.

"What?"

"That sound!"

"What sound?"

"Would you stop copying everything I say?"

Tomas bit back his response and glared at his friend.

"Shhhh!" Gustav grabbed his arm. "Behind that tree."

Since they were in a forest, Tomas simply waited for his friend to point. Gustav leaned on Tomas's shoulder far more heavily than was necessary to help himself up, then froze. Tomas heard it too—a sharp, high-pitched whimper.

The two boys advanced stealthily. The cry intensified; they were getting close. They each took opposite sides of the tree, moving their bodies carefully around its trunk.

Tomas and Gustav saw the animal at exactly the same time. The frightened dog lay trembling at the base of the tree, its leg twisted and bleeding. It was quite small, and had reddish-brown fur, like a fox's. It had a thin stump of a tail and eyes that were bloodshot with fatigue and pain.

Tomas lowered himself gently to the mossy ground. The dog saw him and started growling, but could not move to defend itself. Tomas murmured soothingly, staying completely still. Gustav watched patiently—he knew his friend had a way with wild creatures—but his heart was beating with excitement. He wondered if perhaps they could train this animal. Tomas was thinking the same, and suddenly in his dreams of future exploration, a small brown dog was at their side on the raft as they journeyed down the river, sniffing the air and warning them of danger, catching rabbits for their dinner, and protecting the boys during their nights in the forest.

Tomas talked softly and reassuringly to the dog for a long quarter of an hour before he moved closer; it slowly calmed down. After half an hour, Tomas was almost next to it, and after an hour the animal allowed Tomas to rest his hand lovingly on its head. It then fell asleep from sheer exhaustion.

"What do we do?" whispered Gustav, who was now sitting next to them.

"It needs water, and somewhere warm and safe to heal. We need to clean up this wound, too, and see if we can tie up the leg in a splint or something."

"Where can we take it?"

"Take it?" Tomas was so absorbed in imagining all three of them hunting together that he was not listening to his friend.

"It won't be safe here," Gustav insisted, "and it's going to get dark soon."

They thought for a moment. Then Tomas spoke decisively. "We'll take it to my home. Father will know what to do."

The firmness in Tomas's voice brooked no argument, and the boys then prepared the wounded creature for transport. They took off their sweaters, and carefully wrapped the dog in one of them, while the other they used as a stretcher. Between them they were able to lift the animal carefully off the ground, and carry it across the moss to the field. It lifted its head once, then flopped back onto the woolen litter, relieved to be cared for at last.

When they arrived home, it was Tomas's mother who took charge of its care, clucking and fussing as if it were a child. She warmed some milk and stew, which the boys fed it bit by bit while she washed the wound with rags dipped in warm, salty water.

"It doesn't look too bad," she murmured between dabs, and the boys glanced hopefully at one another.

The dog gulped down a bit of stew and all the milk, and lapped greedily at the water they offered. Then it fell asleep on its bed of clean straw, giving Tomas's father the opportunity he needed to bind its leg.

It was getting very late when they finally finished their collective nursing, and Tomas's father looked up at Gustav.

"Your parents will be wondering where you are. I'll walk you home."

Gustav's face fell—he was jealous of Tomas getting to have the dog near him, when it had been he who had heard it whimper first. Besides, the Müllers were having something for supper that smelled extremely good from where he was standing, and behind them the fire roared and chuckled. He knew where he wanted to be.

Tomas's mother smiled fondly. He felt hopeful and raised his eyes to Tomas's father, who laughed suddenly and warmly.

"You all prepare for supper, and I will wander over and let your folks know you'll be home in the morning!"

Gustav and Tomas almost cheered, but grinned respectfully instead. Tomas's mother bustled them into the main room, while she made the final preparations for their meal.

That night, after the last of supper was cleared away and the clock ticked in a relaxed, cozy way, Tomas's father took out his cello, rosined his bow, and sat down. Tomas loved the sound of the chair creaking, the faint plinking of strings as his father tapped them, and the scratching sound as he searched for his favorite hole in the floor for the end pin.

Gustav and Tomas settled as near to the fire as they could without being burned. Their noses and cheeks turned rosy. His father sighed contentedly, and then began a Bach Sarabande.

After several bars, Gustav turned to Tomas. "I want to learn to play that," he announced determinedly.

Tomas looked at him in surprise.

Herr Müller waited until he had finished playing the first section and then turned his head. "What do you want to play?"

"That," replied Gustav, pointing at the music propped on the stand.

Tomas hit him and laughed. "The world's first music-stand maestro!" he chuckled.

"The *cello*!" Gustav kicked him, but stopped when he saw the frown from Tomas's mother.

"The cello?" repeated Tomas's father.

"Yes!"

Mother looked across from her mending. Father straightened up.

"It is a lot of work." He glanced knowingly at Tomas. "Ask your friend."

Tomas grimaced. He had tried to blot the hours of squeaking strings and his father's frustrated coaching from his memory. "A lot of work. I gave up. It was too hard."

This made Gustav even more determined. The challenge was on.

19.

Spring, 1931

The relationship between Tomas and Gustav's families eased. The boys' schooling was very important to both of them, and the disruptions the friendship had apparently created to this vital component of their lives had made the last year and a half troublesome.

Now, however, things were different. Gustav appeared with a swag of sheet music under his arm three days a week, and Tomas's father disappeared with him into a corner of the workshop near the window. He taught the boy—painstakingly at first—where his fingers should go, and how to hold the bow steady without squeezing the life from it.

Finally the sounds changed from cats scratching at glass to full notes, then to several notes at a time. Tomas listened as he did chores, or worked on his homework at the big table. He listened as the runs became clearer, then as dynamics and expression started to flow into the notes.

One day whole pieces began to filter in through the door. Tomas was impressed. Gustav was either stubborn or talented, although he could not bring himself to admit the latter within his friend's hearing.

The small brown dog, limping but happy, padded around their feet and would sit at the door of the workshop, waiting to greet Gustav when he came through the house for something to eat before going home. Gustav always appeared tired but glowing, and Tomas wondered at the change in his friend. Sometimes he grumbled about it—he worried that all this music might turn Gustav's mind from their planned world explorations. And there was something else, something he did not want to admit to himself, something that whispered to him at night as he lay in his bed.

He knew, deep inside, that he loved the music that surrounded him in his home. Listening to Gustav learning had awakened a desire in Tomas to feel the notes that he hummed so often in his mind flow out through his fingers. He tried to remember the heaviness of practice hours, to remind himself how difficult it was to stay seated for so long, to focus on tiny movements of elbows, arms, and fingers—but the urge quickened within him. Only pride kept him from admitting this to himself, let alone to his father.

One afternoon he was outside with Dog (they still hadn't agreed on an official name). Between them, he and Gustav had been trying to train the animal so he would be ready to come with them on the raft. Dog could now come when called, if they had food in their hands. He had learned to sit motionless when they commanded "Hush!" and they had plans to teach him to catch rabbits.

Today the sun was bright, and Tomas's homework was finished. Gustav was practicing in the workshop, and Tomas felt irritated that his friend put playing the cello before taking Dog out for training, so he had stalked rather loudly out of the house. He called out to his mother to let her know where he was headed, so that she would not worry about his whereabouts, and he made sure that his voice was loud enough also for Gustav to hear.

He took Dog down to the pond and tied him to a piece of board that he then set floating out on the water. Tomas jerked the wood around with a rope until the animal had to try hard to stay on—Dog didn't seem to like the activity. Occasionally he whined and patted the water with his paw, but Tomas was a determined, if stubborn teacher. This afternoon he wasn't in a cheerful mood, and poor Dog could gain no sympathy as he floated precariously on his flimsy raft.

Tomas was trying very hard to be patient, but lately Gustav had been so absorbed in his practice that the two boys had not spent any time out in the forest together. He was starting to feel resentful, and blamed Gustav for the fact that Dog was falling behind in his practice. At this rate, Tomas muttered to himself, Dog wouldn't progress to rabbit-catching before the summer, and then what would they eat?

There was a sad bark, and Tomas looked up. His thoughts had taken up more time than he realized, and he saw with pleasure that Dog had actually managed to stay on the board for much longer than usual without panicking. He applauded his student, who wagged his tail at the attention. This was all very encouraging, but—mused Tomas jealously—Gustav was not there to see it.

Suddenly he heard a crackle of undergrowth, followed by a sharp voice. He turned around. Hans appeared, bursting through the bushes on the far side of the swimming hole. How on earth had he found the tunnel? With shock Tomas realized that the gang must have been spying on them. His heart beat hard twice, then froze. Hans was promptly followed by two other boys; even at this distance, Tomas noticed their eyes alight with a nasty glint. He burned with fierce anger—this was *his* place, his and Gustav's, and Hans had no right here.

Dog growled. The bullies whooped and tore around the pond. He now barked frantically, as the raft wobbled and threatened to overturn. In a moment Hans was upon Tomas, wrestling the rope out of his hands. Tomas yelled savagely and grabbed Hans with all his might, but in vain. The rope jerked, Dog fell noisily into the water, and Tomas was being beaten by three boys, all bigger than he was. He didn't know whether Dog could swim, but hoped desperately that the crippled animal would not come to his aid.

"Stay back!" he called as he tried to repel Hans' grip around his head.

There was a messy splashing and panting, and then Dog was at his side, growling fiercely and bravely. Tomas heard a yelp as one of the boys booted the animal away.

"Don't you dare hit him!" he spluttered furiously. Hans laughed, as the creature whimpered. Tomas yelled as a blow from one of Hans' henchmen landed in his stomach, and he doubled over. In spite of his injury, the animal went berserk and tore into the boys, biting and ripping whatever he could. It was, however, a losing battle. The others grabbed sticks and collectively drove Dog and Tomas into deeper and deeper pain and incapacity.

Are we going to die? Tomas wondered between blows. His vision swam, and all the sounds of pain and victory and blood-singing fused around him. He thought he saw Gustav's face for a moment, but then it disappeared. Dog was whining, and hot tears rushed to Tomas's eyes. He was fighting for all he was worth but getting nowhere. It was like a terrible dream, so much worse than that day at school. Then he sucked in his breath—was this what the attack was about? Surely they wouldn't seek revenge now? Or were he and Gustav right, and had Hans begun once again at the top of his list?

Tomas couldn't tell if the fight lasted five minutes or five hours, but then he heard an unmistakable deep roar that made him cry out with relief. There was a flurry of arms, legs and screams, and then Tomas was aware of a giant cane whistling through the air around him.

He collapsed at the water's edge, exhausted and unable to move. Dog lay near him, his tongue lolling out of his mouth, and his back leg rigid. Gustav knelt beside him and spoke in his ear, "Are you all right?" but Tomas just groaned.

His father had Hans by the scruff of the neck and was whacking him about the face. The other boys had fled, cowards that they were. Finally Tomas's father threw Hans onto the grass. The bully lay there, dazed. He would be hauled off later to receive a much overdue beating from his own father.

Gustav lifted Tomas's head onto a pillow made from his sweater. It seemed a strange return to last summer, only there were no stars, and no glittering fire.

Tomas swallowed his tears. "Dog … " was all he could manage between swollen lips.

Gustav didn't say anything but patted Tomas awkwardly. Tomas noticed that Gustav looked as though he was crying. He cursed Hans under his breath.

His father lifted Tomas and carried him through the trees. It was a long walk to the village. Gustav followed behind them sniffling. *Where was Dog?* Tomas wondered.

The rest of the afternoon was a blur. His mother nursed him as she had nursed Dog the day they had brought him home. Gustav disappeared back to his own house, and Tomas was aware of someone arriving at the front door and leaving again.

He felt hollow, as if he were a dark cave. He knew that Dog was dead, and he knew, somewhere deep inside, that now there would be no raft.

The man with the beard passes me again, and I call out to him. I am sitting once more on the coils of rope, my morning walk completed. The air is fresh, the way that only air at sea can be, biting and demanding. It mocks my threadbare coat.

"You are brave to sit in this wind," the man says, remaining standing while he slaps his arms at his sides.

Around us the ship creaks and the swell pounds. For miles in every direction, the water wavers and starts.

"The albatross … " I begin, uncertain of what my real question is.

"Ah yes, our friend from the other day. You have seen him again?"

"No."

"He will reappear, maybe. Our ship throws a lot of food, and the birds will gather. It is something to watch for. I recommend it. Shearwaters, petrels … " He stamps his feet from the cold.

"All seabirds look the same to me," I confess.

The man stiffens. He moves closer to me, his voice urgent. "The same? The same? No! I am afraid you are very much mistaken, friend." His arms cease their slapping. "They are as different as any two people on this ship, even within the same species. The variations in the gray, the brown, the white … the shapes of their tails, their wingspans, how they need to fly, the shapes of their beaks, their patterns of migration … " He pauses, his eyes alight, then continues.

"Why, the albatross, for example, has a wonderful sense of smell, and even possesses a special gland for filtering out the enormous amounts of salt from the water it drinks on its long flights! He is prepared for months at sea, whereas we— "The man breathes excitedly, his words tumbling.

I smile apologetically. "You are indeed passionate in your study and knowledge—please excuse my ignorance."

The man pauses for breath, and his arms are still. His eyes assume a faraway look.

"Storm petrels," he continues, almost reverently, "so common to everyday fishermen, but they are named after a great man."

I wait, absorbed.

"They are named for Saint Peter, because—with the help of Christ—he too was able to walk on the water, even in the midst of storms."

20.

Winter, 1931

The last of the birds departed in a steady journey south-wards, and winter wound its way around their home, whitening ground and sky. A dull grief lay inside Tomas.

One late afternoon while his father was away, he strayed aimlessly into the workshop. The kitchen sounds were dimmed, and the hush of wood and falling snow pressed gently against him. It was a form of peace; he felt calmer just being there by himself.

The wan light through the windows draped itself over the wooden instruments. Suddenly, as Tomas was contemplating the tools resting on the workbench, the setting sun ripped through the cloud outside and illuminated the shop like a flame for one tremendous, glowing second.

Tomas held his breath. A wooden cello, lying on its side near the bench, and away from the cold glass of the window, appeared golden and melting. Tomas was alone, supper was some time away, and all his chores were complete. He could not resist. He went to the instrument, clasped its neck and, supporting the wooden shoulders gently, lifted it upright.

It was amazing, the way it all came back to him—holding and releasing the end pin, the creaking of his body on the edge of the chair, and the tiny screwing of the metal point into a hole in the floorboards. Before he realized what he was doing, his fingers held a lightly rosined bow. He drew it like a wobbling breath across the D string, his index finger pressing into the mahogany. Surprisingly the note sounded in tune, although he was putting hardly any pressure on the string, out of fear of being heard. The sound scraped at his ears, making him wince.

He tried again, pressing more firmly this time. He felt the connection, the minute resistance of rosined horsehair on gut, the odd sensation of the bow both pulling and pushing at the string. The sound emerged, warm and almost fragrant. He smiled. His finger muscles had lain inactive for a long time, but he lumbered through a run of notes that had been moving in his head all day like a river current. How was it that he remembered more than he had thought possible? In a few minutes his hands gained confidence, although his wrists and fingers ached and his un-callused fingertips smarted.

He wasn't sure when the music started to unfold, but he began to create a line of notes. The melody developed, forming itself under his fingers. He found himself playing about Dog, about the sadness of knowing that winter was here and that a dream had perished. His breathing quickened, his fingers became suppler, falling into familiar patterns and shapes.

From another world he heard his mother's voice calling him, and then he heard footsteps, but heavier than hers. Still he kept playing. Where did the notes come from? How could they sound like honey, like warm sun, when his limbs creaked like rusty door hinges? But he could not stop, not until the last note was reached.

He sat breathing heavily but contentedly. It had grown dark, except for a rectangle of gold behind him. The rectangle filled with the shape of his father. The man moved quietly toward him, and Tomas felt a warm, heavy hand on his shoulder. There were no words, but Tomas felt as though their hearts were holding hands.

21.

Summer, 1932

The train pulled up at the station, emitting bursts of smoke and groaning steel. The thin man from Leipzig alighted, and as his foot touched the platform he felt a new energy stir in his limbs. He had arrived at a place of fond memories, relieved to have left behind the upheaval of his own city.

He wondered when arriving in Zweibach had first felt like a homecoming. He found himself anticipating the generous, respectful welcome that never changed, whether he had been a Masters student or—as he was now—undertaking his doctorate. Somehow this summer job had become a tender refrain in his life, and he treasured it.

The tutor collected his cases and strode out through a iron gateway held together by a tangled Honeysuckle vine. A sleepy guard sat stroking a cat in the early afternoon sun. The young man turned onto an uneven road, passed a row of cottages crisscrossed with rotting Fachwerk[6], then halted— confused. Had he really forgotten the way? He put down his cases for a moment on the undulating cobbles, and glanced around to get his bearings.

The sound of shouting caught his attention. He realized that he was very near the town square, so he picked up his bags and walked a bit further to see what was going on. He stopped at a shaded archway, and inspected the scene in front of him.

A vigorous column of boys marched past, dressed in brown uniforms. They were brandishing a flag and cheering—themselves, it seemed. Villagers who had been moving industriously about their tasks had stopped to stare—some of them waving—at the boys' homespun parade. In spite of the noise and movement, there prevailed an odd background silence; the young group appeared to march through a still life painting. The tutor was aware of his heart beating very fast, as

---

6   Timber framing.

if it too were marching, but for a very different cause. He felt a surge of sadness tinged with fear. *Even here.* For of course he recognized them; had they not been wearing their uniforms, he would have known them by their hard faces, the taut arrogant lift of their chins, the focus in their eyes.

With relief, Tomas Solberg remembered the way to the Müllers' home, and that he did not have to go through the square to reach it. He turned and walked at a deliberately moderate pace up the lane. He refused to run. He would not be what they wanted him to be—afraid.

It was with great relief that the tutor arrived at the Müllers'. He was welcomed in and given time to set down his things in the small back room that had been his home for three summers now. Times had gone well. Tomas's academic results had continued to improve, even with his now passionate study of music. His father seemed sure, with one more summer of coaching, that his son would excel in his final certificate and receive a place at the University.

The tutor refolded his clothes and laid them carefully in the drawers of the wooden chest. He straightened his tie, which had become slightly disheveled during the journey, and hung his coat on a hook on the back of the door. He placed his pile of books on a desk below the window, and smiled at the little pot of geraniums that cheered the otherwise barren sill. The sadness at seeing the Hitler Youth parade rose once more in his chest. He left the room and returned to his hosts.

In the kitchen, sausages and herbs still hung from the rafters. Frau Müller stood on a wooden chair, pulling a biscuit tin down from a high shelf. Herr Müller leaned casually against the doorway, wiping his hands on a cloth before taking off his leather apron.

The tutor almost failed to see Tomas, who was ensconced on a stool under the kitchen window. The boy—although "boy" didn't quite seem to fit anymore, the tutor realized as he took in the lanky sixteen-year-old's appearance—met his eyes and smiled. Tomas then dropped his gaze and continued his task. Herr Müller held out his hand, and Herr Solberg gasped slightly as the strong fingers grabbed his and shook his hand like a bear shakes a fish it has caught.

"Welcome again, Herr Solberg. Please sit as my wife makes us tea."

The tutor sat obediently, and returned Frau Müller's greeting.

"So, what's new?" Herr Müller asked jovially as they made themselves comfortable at the table.

Things are getting worse, he thought, then wondered whether they wished to know. The seriousness in his face caused Herr Müller to frown.

"Upheaval," the young man finally replied. He searched for the right words to continue. "An upheaval of ideas. But not just that. Everybody is affected, it seems. Even those one would have regarded as reasonable people."

Frau Müller poured tea and laid out biscuits on a large plate. Tomas sat in his corner of the kitchen, ostensibly peeling potatoes for their evening meal, but his ears were so tuned to the conversation that he barely realized that the knife lay motionless in his hand. He dropped a potato with a thud and reddened as the three adults glanced at him. He lowered his head and tried to be invisible, peeling slowly and methodically. They turned away, and the conversation continued.

"They say he will get into power, somehow. Certainly support for him seems to be growing, if the parades are anything to go by." The tutor sipped his tea and absently tapped one finger rhythmically on the side of the cup.

"Well, you won't see any of that here."

There was an uncomfortable silence. The tutor shifted on his chair.

"With all due respect, I beg to differ," he replied. He then related his stumbling upon the small but determined parade he had witnessed on the way.

Herr Müller waved his hand nonchalantly and picked up a biscuit. "Boys!" he asserted between bites. "Mere boys!"

"Boys who will one day be men."

"Yes, but hopefully by then this madness will be over, and Germany will be in decent hands." There was another silence. Then his father turned to Tomas, who had wondered whether or not they had forgotten he was there. "What do you know of all this parade business, son?"

Tomas stopped peeling potatoes. "There is a membership of the Hitler Youth at school, you can tell who they are. They misbehave in class, and are always out doing things in town, training or something. There are a quite a few who've left their youth groups and joined."

He paused, seeing the worried look on his parents' faces, then grinned. "Don't worry. Gustav and I stay out of their way."

Tomas's father made a sound of disgust. "Hypocrites, all of them. I hope you continue to stay out of it all."

"I will, Father."

Frau Müller topped up their tea. "Tomas has never been interested in that kind of thing." She smiled reassuringly, and glanced at her son with fondness. "He's always too busy exploring—and playing his music. We never could persuade him to join any sort of youth group, although there are quite a few he could have chosen. He and Gustav create plenty of activities for themselves."

"Who wants to hike in a large, noisy group? Better to travel light and with as few friends as possible," Tomas asserted. He was proud of the way Gustav and he could fend for themselves on their explorations around the area. They had come a long way since their impulsive night by the swimming hole—they had even learned how to catch and skin rabbits.

Tomas's father wagged his finger playfully.

"Activities that will be curtailed somewhat, now that Herr Solberg is here." He pushed the plate of biscuits toward the tutor, who politely declined. "Well, as long as you are well and your studies are progressing, what more can one ask? Anyway, as I said before, all this is a storm in a teacup. Everyone likes fads, it seems, and this is just another one."

Herr Müller was so determined that the tutor fell silent. How could he make this man understand? Hatred surfaced frequently now in unexpected places, fear crept readily into people's eyes. He knew two friends of his father who had already made plans to leave.

As for Herr Solberg, he had made the decision to bide his time and see. In one year he would complete his PhD, and be eligible for a post at the University. Then he would be in a position to afford to leave, if he needed to. He hoped the cynics and pessimists were not proved right.

He raised his eyes to Herr Müller. "Yes," he replied with a lightness he did not believe. "A fad. It, like all others, will pass."

22.

The summer progressed uneventfully. Tomas studied with Herr Solberg every morning, then helped his father in the early afternoons. As he poured over grammar, history, and classic texts, he listened to Gustav playing the cello in a light-filled corner of the workshop. He longed to have time for his own practice. The notes flowed into his mind, the syntax and phrasing melding until sometimes he felt that he and Gustav were on the same river of learning, borne by currents of rhythm and sound.

He admired his friend for the tenacity with which he had approached the instrument, and he noticed that in their lessons Tomas's father stopped Gustav less and less. He actually sounded very good, and Tomas enjoyed listening to him play. He wondered whether either of them would continue the cello once school finished, when—as his mother said—life got serious. For Tomas, the thought of not playing was inconceivable, it was too much a part of him now, and he smiled to himself when he recollected his boyhood resistance to the instrument.

Unlike previous summers, Tomas was allowed to use the afternoons as he wished on most days, as long as he did his chores and spent one full afternoon each week helping his father in the shop. He and Gustav swam and hiked, and elaborated on the maps they were creating of their town and the surrounding area. They explored the forests near their home and tried—mostly successfully—to stay out of the way of the occasional group of brown-shirted youngsters who trespassed onto their territory with their war games and raucous campfire songs.

Tomas and Gustav both knew it would be their last summer as schoolboys. University loomed, and Tomas felt more resigned than ever to his future. His father was determined, and Tomas loved him too much to deliberately disappoint him.

Soon the leaves began to turn again, as another summer drew to an end. Tonight they had even lit a fire. It was late, an owl called outside, and the hearth glowed rich umber. The tutor was still studying and scribbling, and light from his room filtered gently down the hallway. Tomas's father had long since returned his cello to its case, and now sat back contented in his chair, his fingertips pressed together and his eyes half-closed. Tomas, too, was almost asleep. Only the sound of his mother's knitting needles could be heard above the sigh of the coals, clacking through the room like a tiny train.

Suddenly there was a loud crash and splintering of glass, followed by shouts and the sounds of running feet. The tutor appeared at the door, clothed in his dressing gown and even paler than usual. The knitting-needle train stopped, and Tomas's father leapt to his feet. "Stay here, all of you," he called sharply, and in a moment was out the door.

Tomas's mother stood up and quickly checked that the front door was bolted. There was a cry from Tomas's father, and despite his instructions to stay put, Tomas ran into the workshop. By lantern light he could clearly see the devastation. Several bricks had been thrown through the window, smashing instruments and sending glass like chaff across the workbenches and floor. The cool night air had rushed in, and paint had been smeared on the remaining windows. Even backwards Tomas could read what it said, and he gasped in shock. *Töten die jüdische Ratte.*[7]

His father stood amongst the debris, shaking his head in disbelief. "Here? In our village?" he kept repeating, all the while moving his hands up and down as if conducting, or trying to work out what object to pick up first. "Go back and tell your mother and Herr Solberg not to come in here." He dropped his hands, then one formed a fist inside the other.

7   Kill the Jewish rat.

"Especially Herr Solberg. He must not come in here."

Tomas nodded, and ran back to the room where the others stood motionless and worried. He attempted to reassure them.

"It's all right. Someone threw a stone at the window. Drunk, probably. Father says don't worry, and we can go to bed. He'll fix it all up."

He knew they didn't believe him, but his mother nodded, and the tutor, his hands shaking, excused himself and returned to his room.

❧

The next day Tomas knocked on his tutor's door, ready to begin lessons. "Yes," came the response, and Tomas pushed open the door.

The man stood in front of a round mirror. He had packed his bags. His coat, freshly brushed and ready to be worn, lay over the back of a chair.

"Aren't we doing our lessons today?" asked Tomas, nonplussed. There were the suitcases, closed and waiting at the foot of the bed. He suddenly wondered in panic whether Herr Solberg had seen the words written on the glass windows, but surely not—he had heard his father go to bed very late last night and was certain everything had been dealt with.

"I am no longer welcome here," the tutor murmured, as polite as ever, wrapping his tie with practiced fingers.

Books lay stacked and bound next to the suitcases. It was very early in the morning, but Herr Solberg was determined to catch the first train back to Leipzig. Tomas felt a heavy grief forming in his heart. *They are only boys,* he thought, knowing instinctively who had caused the destruction, *and yet they can do this to a grown man?*

He sat down on the chair with his chin cupped in his hands. The tutor seemed so calm, and yet—was it Tomas's imagination, or were the man's fingers trembling?

"My grammar has improved, hasn't it?" he said to break the awkward stillness of the room.

Herr Solberg's hands poised for a moment between deft movements.

"Yes, Tomas. I can pride myself that under my tutelage these—is it four years?" His eyes shimmered, and he blinked rapidly for the smallest of moments before his expression settled again. "You have progressed extremely well."

"Will I get to university?"

Tomas was half hoping that the tutor would say no, so he might have some excuse for not continuing his studies—not that he knew what he would do instead. At one time he had wanted to work in his father's shop, but now … In some part of him, Tomas still wanted to prove to his father that he could achieve something more.

"If you continue your scholarly preparation with diligence."

Tomas watched his tutor make the final adjustment to his tie. The man reached toward the chair that Tomas was sitting on, and Tomas realized with embarrassment that he had been leaning against his coat. He mumbled an apology, which the tutor didn't seem to register. One thin hand collected the garment, and then Herr Solberg was dressed for his journey.

"Yes, Tomas," said the tutor gently, "I think you will be admitted to the University. And who knows?" he added with a levity neither of them felt. "I might be your professor!"

Tomas stood up. "Does my father know that you are leaving?"

"He will understand. Please—please pass on my apologies for making such a hasty return to Leipzig and … my heartfelt thanks for all that they have done."

He smiled—rather sadly, Tomas thought.

"The hospitality in your home is exceptional."

Tomas didn't know what to say, so he picked up a suitcase and followed the tutor to the door.

The man paused at the threshold of the kitchen. Tomas noticed that Herr Solberg's eyes were misted, and his hand shook slightly. Tomas's own throat hardened, so that he had to cough to relax it.

The tutor spoke, keeping his eyes on the room they were leaving—the herbs in fragrant sheaves, the braids of garlic, the teapot on the shelf.

"Tomas," he said softly, "May God watch over your family."

Tomas didn't reply. His hand felt damp around the suitcase handle.

"Tomas," the tutor repeated, "You could perhaps tell your parents that for many summers they have been my … "

He could not finish the sentence, but Tomas knew what Herr Solberg had been about to say. He simply nodded, and the silence seemed to seal a bond between them. The student and his teacher began their last slow walk together, down the cobbled lane to the station.

The whistle blew loud and long, the train huffed furiously, and with a great clattering of metal, drew out of the station. The tutor sat inside his compartment, staring blankly out the window. He watched Zweibach fade into fields and clusters of farmhouses. The morning sun gleamed, and cows raised their heads sleepily at the noise rushing past them.

He produced a book from his pocket and gazed absently at its pages, unaware that long after the train had disappeared from Zweibach, a young man stood on the station platform, tears clouding his heart.

"Come," whispers a hoarse voice next to my ear.
A rough hand pulls at my shoulders, and I see that the man who loves birds stoops over me. I am aware of moonlight streaming in from the porthole, and I blink my eyes. I am amazed that I have been sleeping at all.

The man's voice is restless, and I swing myself out of my bunk. Keeping my coat around me, I follow him across the tossing sea of sleepers until we reach the bow of the ship.

The ocean cascades below us, and our ship crashes into the hollows of the enormous swell. High above us the full moon blinks dully, like the eye of a swollen fish. Light the color of onions encrusts the waves. At intervals scraps of cloud filter the moon, and I see that the sky is whipped to as much movement as the water. I feel peculiarly still in contrast.

The man says nothing, but then grips my arm with such force that I lose breath for a moment.

"There, there!" he whispers, the cold air making his voice rasp.

I stare up at the moon. Dark shapes hover on its surface, yet they move forward—many shapes, necks outstretched and wings blurred. They cross the moon like a line of music, then melt into the universe. We watch as the last shapes flutter and dissolve, then the night migration has passed us. We are once again alone on the desolate sea.

How do they know? The question rises again in my mind, and I contemplate the mystery.

The man sighs and turns to me. "Beautiful, no? One great compensation for the length of our travel." He turns back to the sea. "Did you realize that birds may even be conscious of the Coriolis force?" He shakes his head in wonder.

I frown into the dark. "I'm sorry?"

"The force created as the earth spins on its axis. Birds can sense the tiniest changes in gravity, apparently. So much study yet to be done." The man slaps his arms against his sides. "Well, I'm off to bed. Good night!" He strides away.

I almost follow, but tonight it seems the birds have raised memories in their wake, and I need to see if they, too, will melt into the sky and finally leave me alone.

Part Five: Menuet 1

(n): A slow, ceremonious and graceful ballroom dance for two in triple time, from the French word for "fine, delicate." The first Menuet was often followed by a second one; this second Menuet provided some form of contrast, by means of a different key and orchestration. In some countries, the Menuet also kept some of the musical elements found in folk dance.

23.
Autumn, 1934

"This is crazy!" Gustav protested, as he and Tomas were swept along with the crowd down Reichstrasse. They were now freshman students at Leipzig University. Gustav's freckled face was as cheery and mischievous as ever, making him popular with the other (especially female) students. Tomas had grown into a tall, athletic young man. His face was just as earnest, and his gray eyes still held their look of serious contemplation; to his frustration and Gustav's endless delight, Tomas's intensity tended to scare off, rather than attract the young women they had been meeting here. Even so, Tomas possessed a warm, if rare, smile that could just as suddenly turn him into a very charming, handsome fellow. But now, both he and Gustav were scowling as they were jostled from all sides by a frantic, driving crowd. Around them the sea of faces held ecstatic expressions, and the air was thick with passion and the sound of marching bands.

A small child, hoisted by her mother into a better viewing position, swiped Gustav's arm with a lollipop dripping with saliva.

"Ach! Disgusting!" Gustav pressed against Tomas. "It's only an army, we—"

They caught their breath as they saw Hans march past. They were instantly quiet, aware of the sweat that prickled under their coats.

"He wasn't even conscripted," whispered Gustav.

Tomas felt shocked at the vague sense of admiration that settled over him as the soldiers marched past. They were so focused, so sure of what they wanted, whereas he felt aimless, detached, drifting through his life. His university classes created a routine, but they were not enough to convince him of his direction. Besides, all the best professors had gradually left, and even the courses had been changing.

The drums made his brain and blood pulsate, and something in him longed to be joined with the rhythmic thudding of shiny boots that never seemed to end. The urge both invigorated and shamed him, as half of him was swept forward down Reichstrasse, while the rest of him looked on in horror.

"Hey—are you all right?"

Tomas felt his friend prod at his arm, and he answered without turning his head.

"Yes, yes, fine. Let's get out of here, though, shall we?"

He and Gustav pushed their way through the crowd, which like a current seemed to keep forcing them toward the parade.

"It's a conspiracy!" muttered Gustav. Tomas just clamped his lips together. What was happening to him? Why had they even come here?

Finally they were able to extricate themselves from the seething onlookers, and they broke into a fast stride down a side street. Most of the shops were closed, but they stumbled upon one bakery that had its *Welcome* sign hanging on the door. An elderly woman stood at the counter, distractedly re-arranging cakes behind the glass. The bright sound of military music fractured the air like gunfire, and they watched the woman's brow wrinkle even more deeply.

"Are you open?" asked Gustav politely.

The lady started, then beamed. "Of course. One parade won't close us down." Her eyes fell on Tomas, and for some reason she smiled even more broadly. "Even such a grand affair as we're having today!"

Why is she treating me like this? Tomas wondered. Her demeanor disturbed him. Gustav seemed to be unaware, and ordered for the two of them as he always did. They sat down at the window and waited for their cake and coffee, as the old woman chattered. Suddenly she did not seem distracted.

"Fine weather we're having for it, although I daresay at an order from Herr Hitler even the clouds would *Sieg Heil.*"

"You must be joking," snapped Gustav, then apologized.

Tomas reddened. The woman moved tactfully back behind the counter, and Gustav looked keenly at his friend.

"What's going on?"

"What do you mean?"

"You've gone red—a first."

"I have not."

"Well, we could have a childish argument, but why not just tell me?"

Tomas felt more uncomfortable under his friend's gaze than he did under the eye of the Headmaster all those years ago.

"It's a powerful feeling out there," Tomas replied, as casually as he could.

Their order arrived and, with a final glance at two men, the old woman bustled off to wipe down tables.

"As long as it's out there." Gustav took a large bite of his cake.

"Didn't you feel it?"

"Yes, but so what? That's what the parades are designed to do."

"So, why did we go today?"

"Because classes were canceled, and everyone else was."

"Is that all?"

"I suppose."

"Come on, Gustav! We could have gone anywhere else. Admit it, you were as curious as I was."

Gustav laughed, and bits of cake sprayed onto the table. "All right, I admit it," he replied. "But that's as far as it goes. You're not going to find me joining them, it doesn't matter how many colored flags you fly in my face, or statistics you give me. They fake all the numbers anyway, apparently."

The music had faded completely, and with a sense of relief Tomas felt his old perspective returning.

"You're right. I don't know what came over me today. It was strange seeing Hans again."

"No it wasn't!" Gustav shot back.

They both fell silent. The street outside began to fill again with people, and the wave of voices curtailed any further conversation.

24.

Autumn, 1935

As Tomas turned the corner of a cobbled street in the student quarter of Leipzig, he collided with a man heading in the opposite direction, a gentleman whose hat tumbled to the pavement. As a thin hand stretched to retrieve it, Tomas noticed the frayed edges of the coat, then the pale and familiar face. Tomas drew a breath.

"Herr Solberg?"

The tutor darted an anxious glance around the street, and the two stepped into a doorway.

"Tomas?" He smiled tentatively, then asked, "You are ambling the student quarter for a reason?"

"Yes," Tomas replied warmly, "I am studying Liberal Arts."

"Not so very liberal these days, I'm afraid," Herr Solberg murmured wryly, raising one eyebrow.

Tomas considered the tutor's words. He had watched, ashamed, as anti-Jewish signs had begun to appear in shop windows, even in places he had considered immune—several cafés and a bookshop where he spent hours whenever he could. It had been a while since Tomas had read the newspapers, although it was nearly impossible to escape the barrage of radio announcements and propaganda. Strangely, nothing seemed to have changed very much outwardly in his day-to-day life. The streets bustled, old women gossiped on trams, and he still had exams to complete. Yet he had not expected student life to be so supportive of the new regime, and it made him feel confused, even angry.

"The course has changed," Tomas added, "even over a year." He noticed the drawn look in his tutor's face.

"I am, unfortunately, all too aware of that."

"Are you at the University?" Tomas asked shyly. "I had hoped that … "

"You might be in one of my classes?" Herr Solberg

finished for him, then grimaced. "Our leader was swift to make particular changes." There was an awkward silence before he continued, his voice low. "I was made … how do they put it? 'Redundant.' Falling student numbers, or some such reason; although I must say that certain members of faculty wrote letters of protest to the administration, which was brave of them. Still, what the Führer does, he simply does, yes?"

Tomas nodded again. He didn't know quite what to say. "Can you go somewhere else?" he asked hopefully.

"I am making arrangements, although it is harder for those of us in Humanities." The tutor smiled humorlessly. "Perhaps I should have been a master of physics rather than ancient languages. Still," he shrugged, "we will see. I certainly do not regret my choice." He paused. "Your music?"

Tomas looked at the ground. "Father wants me to complete my degree, although he pays for me to continue lessons with a teacher here."

"And you?" The tutor asked gently.

"Oh, I want to be a musician." His eyes narrowed in determination. "I want to play in the Berliner Philharmonic."

"You think you are good enough?"

"My teacher thinks so. I practice more hours than I study, but Father doesn't realize that." He laughed, then fell quiet. Then it all spilled out. "I don't belong here. It's all so fake. Did you know they just canceled classes the other day for another military parade? And that's not all. We have to have huge sports days, and we're given higher grades for attending camps than for class papers. I'm sick of it all already. And Father doesn't understand. He's sure it all can't be happening."

"Yes, he never believed Hitler would make it into power."

"He doesn't believe it's happened. In some ways I think my father is the craziest one of the lot. But anyway. " He petered out, suddenly tired. "I don't know what to do."

The tutor looked at him levelly for a moment. "If you have a gift, Tomas, follow it. I think—" he stroked the brim of his hat for a moment, and then continued, "—things will only get worse here. But perhaps further north they have held on to a semblance of sanity. Here, however … " He gestured vaguely at the street. "I don't understand it. I love this city, but now … "

The church bells clanged, and Tomas realized that the afternoon was starting to darken. He held out his hand. "It was good to see you. I hope you can get a job somewhere." His eyes lit up. "America, maybe?"

"Perhaps. That is one option I am exploring. My sister … but, anyway." He adjusted his hat. "Take care, Tomas." He searched for the right words. "Take care what you think, and what you do."

"Yes."

For the first time since he was a boy, a firm resolve took hold in Tomas's heart. He would audition for the Berliner Philharmonic. Tomas held Herr Solberg's gaze in thanks. The tutor smiled fleetingly, then moved nervously out of the doorway and down the street.

That night, Tomas wrote to his father.

Memory

A layer of ice on a lake, deceptive simplicity. The surface is so glistening and smooth that you can simply skate over it and ignore—perhaps even forget—what lies underneath. Shafts of light in the dawn sky, slices of water as the waves harden and then dissipate ... As the surface is forced to part each time, I glimpse a truth that I know is there. I am guilty.

I can say again and again to myself, to the immigration officials, to my children—should I have any—that I did not know. We were told only what they intended us to hear; yes, I can say that too. When you breathe in lies every day of your life, you can lose your reference point and, like Pilate, ask: what is truth? Or perhaps, where is truth?

I felt truth in the music I played. Sometimes I witnessed the look in a man's eyes as he died, and I saw truth. That Polish winter was truth ... but the swastikas—like terrible spiders, they invaded every corner of my world.

Pilate could have searched, moved beyond his question. I hate to think that I, too, could have found an answer—but, what then? Driven to silence, even to madness? I am no hero, and my own cowardice would have devoured me. Maybe.

There are some things now, no matter how deeply I search for them, that I will never know.

25.

Spring, 1936

There was a ferocious banging at the door, and Tomas jumped up from his desk with a start. For one mad moment he thought the Gestapo were coming for him, and he didn't know what he had done. He had an urge to throw himself under the bed, but before he had a chance to do anything, Gustav fell into the room, an ecstatic grin spread across his face.

"You've made it! Look!" he cried, waving a piece of paper at Tomas and galloping around the cramped space. He tripped over a pile of books and dropped to the floor, narrowly missing the bed frame. He laughed and rubbed his elbow.

"What? Where?" Tomas helped his friend up, eyes wide. Then he gasped. "Not Berlin?"

"What did you think? I wouldn't throw myself around your room for any lesser reason!"

"Berlin?" Tomas asked again. Then, "But, you've opened my mail!"

"Berlin! Berlin! They want you in Berlin!" Gustav serenaded, jumping up and down and punching Tomas as if they were boys again. "Of course I opened your mail. I've been waiting for this!"

He handed over the letter, panting, and collapsed heavily onto Tomas's chair. "I need a beer after all that."

Dazed, Tomas skimmed the letter. It was true. But how could it be? He wasn't that good, surely.

Gustav interrupted his thoughts. "Your father will be thrilled! You were always better than me. I never minded giving it away." There was an awkward pause. "Does he … does he know?"

"Ah, sort of."

"Sort of?'" Gustav cocked his head. "Does he or not?"

"He knows I've auditioned."

Gustav yelped and sprang up. "I can't believe it! Hey, I'll tell him! He'll be so proud!"

Tomas wasn't quite so sure, as it would mean his father finally having to accept that his only son would never be a great businessman or lawyer. For a moment he envied Gustav's seemingly unquenchable optimism. Then grabbed his friend's shoulders. "The Berliner Philharmonic! I'm amazing, Gustav!" He stopped, and frowned. "That means I'll be leaving."

"Yes, of course, idiot."

"When?"

"Check the letter. As soon as you can, I'd imagine. You could leave now if you had the fare saved up, but you don't." Gustav winked at Tomas. "You're acting like you're going to miss me!"

"I won't. And I want to pass exams." *I owe that much to Father,* Tomas thought. "There's only one week to go until then. I don't have all that much to do."

"No, not really. Just learning the entire course," Gustav gibed.

"Very funny."

Tomas knew his friend was right. He hadn't concentrated on anything to do with his studies for weeks. The preparation, the audition, the waiting—it had all taken so much time.

He soon snapped into the present as the excitement of the adventure started to take hold. He knew now where his destiny lay, and a thrill passed through his whole body as he imagined stepping off the train in the city where music would become his life.

He folded the letter carefully before putting it in his front shirt pocket, "I'll be too busy to miss you much, but you'll have to come and visit. Exams will be over, and then you'll have vacation." He raised an eyebrow, as his tutor had done. "I'll be able to show you around."

Gustav opened the door, waiting for Tomas to follow. "Well, come on, then, Mister Big-City Musician," he ordered.

"I'll buy you a drink." He looked serious for a moment. "I hope things are different there. I mean, you know, I hope they let you stay."

"What on earth do you mean?"

Of course he knew—they had endured too much youth indoctrination not to be able to guess what might be required of them. Perhaps even one day soon they would be summoned to prepare to defend the Fatherland.

Gustav laughed suddenly, and threw Tomas's coat at his face. "Forget it! I don't know what I'm saying tonight. Everything will be fine. Let's go!"

Tomas chased him out the door, and the two of them strode exuberantly down the street.

26.

Spring, 1938

The work was excruciatingly difficult, yet never before had Tomas felt so completely satisfied. It seemed that his world and his heart had joined forces. The changes around him receded and dimmed, until he could hardly hear them anymore. He was only twenty-one, but believed now that he had found life, true and complete.

Somehow music had remained apart, even pure, amidst the terrible devastation of culture on which the new government regime had embarked. Tomas averted his eyes from the signs proclaiming *Juden unerwünscht*⁸ that now encrusted most shop windows like scabs. The café that had become his second home had a sign so small that it was almost unreadable anyway.

His work had become his life. He rehearsed, practiced, performed, woke himself up over coffee in Rosa's Café—ate there many nights as well, as the food was cheap and the proprietor was generous.

Nearly two years had passed, and only the month before had he managed to finally return to Zweibach, where the joy of a recital had eclipsed any remaining resistance from his father regarding his son's choice of career.

"As long as my son swears no oaths to that imbecile, how can I complain?" he had said good-naturedly one night.

Gustav had been called up. Tomas had so far managed to avoid the military. He had been sent his letter once, but it had been quickly and expertly handled by someone who arranged such things for the orchestra. He had even, thankfully, been spared the obligatory Reich Labor Service. Tomas had asked no questions, just practiced more diligently than before.

"There will be no war. Hitler will be out by Christmas," assured his father as they sat by the fire, their cellos resting elegantly like reclining Romans. Tomas hoped he was right, although he

8   Jews unwelcome

had doubts. Unlike his father, he had heard Hitler speak, and he shuddered at the memory of the frenetic screaming.

"But the Rhineland, and now Austria," his father continued. "Nobody has fought back, and Europe is at peace."

"For now."

"Well, now is all we can be sure of."

Tomas fell silent and stared at the flames.

"What did Gustav say in his letter?" asked his mother, looking up from her knitting.

Tomas could remember every word from the recent correspondence from his friend.

"He says everyone cheered them. I think," he added with a grin, "that he took it all a bit too personally. I hope his helmet still fits him."

He didn't mention the other part of the letter, the part that worried him most.

March 1938

Tomas, you wouldn't believe the feeling here. There is a sense of pride in what we're doing. We're training, we're marching for Germany, for what we can be as a nation. I suppose everyone's got their own idea of what that is, but you and I know what it means, for us. We've always agreed on that. So far we haven't had to do any shooting. Well, only in training, but that's obviously not the same thing.

It's amazing! We've simply arrived, it seems, and everyone has made us feel so welcome. Of course there are some of the soldiers who have been making life difficult for the Jews here, but you can stay out of all that if you decide to. Anyway, there is a lot to be said for joining us. We're here for all of you, and there are definite advantages to being in uniform!

Well, until we meet, which may not be for a long while, even Christmas—my two years will be up then, and I'll take it from there.

Your friend,
Gustav

Tomas had always supposed his friend was immune from the propaganda; then again, he remembered the parade he and Gustav witnessed so many years ago in Leipzig—the power of the pounding feet, the vehement sense of purpose. Had Gustav, despite his angry dismissal of the march, also felt its fascination and power? Well, at least he would be out of it all by Christmas, and maybe gain a new perspective.

Warmed by the fire, Tomas and his parents laughed together at the idea of Gustav swaggering about Vienna and—according to his father, who had fought in the Great War—pretending at being a soldier. As he watched the flames, Tomas hoped that Gustav would be strong enough to not let himself be changed.

27.

Summer, 1939

Tomas stood with the rest of the orchestra to face the enraptured audience. He held his cello in one hand, while the other loosened a collar damp with sweat. Immense Nazi banners draped from the balconies and above the stage; they billowed from the applause that rose in waves across the auditorium. To Tomas they looked like gigantic, undulating spiders.

Although the performance was finished, music continued to course through him like the blood in his veins. Tomas packed up his instrument, heaved the leather strap over his shoulder, and joined the elated musicians leaving through the stage door.

To his surprise, he was recognized outside with a shout and grabbed in an enthusiastic bear hug. The force made him gasp. It was Gustav!

Tomas broke into a grin; any lingering dark feeling was immediately banished. "What took you so long to see us perform? Come with me. Now!"

Gustav, laughing, found himself being pulled along the street with a crowd of musicians dressed in black, clasping cases of various sizes.

"The night has only begun!" Tomas crowed, as they all squeezed into the narrow hallway of his apartment building, and climbed a dingy staircase.

Once inside Tomas's living room, wine appeared from nowhere, and the instruments were set free from their cases with the seamlessness of a dream. Somehow there was room for everybody to sit and play, and the banging on the walls and ceiling by irritated neighbors was drowned out in a continuum of glorious music.

Gustav leaned against a wall and drank. He sat at the foot of a swaying violinist and was caught up in notes that soared, keened, and painted the air with a sad and joyous euphony.

The long hours dissolved the stringed voices of Telemann, Vivaldi and Bach, with their rich, aromatic sounds.

Eventually, however, even the most energetic performer began to wilt, and the last strains of the improvised symphony faded. In ones and twos the musicians departed, clapping each other on the back and disappearing into the streets, as if their day were night, and night their high noon.

Finally only Tomas and Gustav remained.

Tomas yawned. "So, how does it feel to be free?"

Gustav started. "Free?"

"Too much music has made you deaf?"

"Not enough. There was not enough music."

"Well said, my friend, and if we hadn't been up all night, and if all the wine had not been drunk, I would propose a toast to that."

They both sat folded into their armchairs, watching the morning light seep through the windows. Tomas's eyes prickled, and he heaved himself off his seat and disappeared into the kitchen. There was a clattering, a faucet turned on and off, and Gustav could hear his friend grunt. Then the smell of coffee percolating on the stove wound its way around the door and into the main room. Gustav grinned.

"Is there food to go with that?"

"Hah! I'm a musician, not a hotelier!"

"Bring out what you've got!"

Gustav heard drawers opening. Soon Tomas arrived with the coffee and handed a cracked, steaming mug to his friend.

"Where's the breakfast?"

"We can go out for that. My café. Until then there is some bread on the counter. Get it yourself, I'm not bringing everything in." He scowled as Gustav kicked him in the leg before ambling into the kitchen.

"By the way, I'll answer your question another time, if I may," Gustav added on his way out of the room.

They stepped into the café, and the bell tinkled. A woman stood behind the bar with her hair in a lopsided hairnet, and a look of professional disinterest on her face. Tomas waved, and she glanced at him in semi-polite acknowledgment. He led the way to a table by the window.

"She seems hard, but she's kind. I get my food cheap because I'm a musician. Businessmen"—he nodded casually in the direction of a group of men in suits—"have to pay more."

The woman arrived with coffee and hot bread rolls, a mound of butter, and some slices of cheese.

"Thank you, Rosa," said Tomas, and Gustav nodded obligingly.

"Doesn't your friend here talk?" she quipped. Gustav spluttered indignantly, but she moved away before he could reply.

Tomas felt confident—this was his world. They fell upon the food. It was fresh, and they were ravenous. They finished the plate. Rosa deposited more on their table, and that too was devoured.

"Now, to your question," began Gustav, slurping gracelessly at his coffee. He was stalling for time—he had no idea what to say. Where could he possibly begin? How could he make Tomas see into what had become his world?

"There is a lot of waiting, preparing," he continued. "But I have seen some action … and I'm going to stay with it," he finished quickly.

"Was Austria action?" asked Tomas, surprised.

"You got my letters?"

"Yes, but … "

Gustav leaned forward, excited. "I cannot describe to you the feeling of being there—the cheering, the victory.

Tomas, people *want* this. And to think we can be part of it!"

"Part of what?"

"Part of restoring to us what is rightfully ours. Being strong again."

Tomas stared out the window at commuters passing. A silence fell between them like snow.

"I cannot imagine it," he said softly, almost to himself.

Gustav too stared out the window for a few moments, then looked back at Tomas.

"You may have to," he replied. "You can't hide forever."

Tomas swung his head around. "Is that what you think I am doing? Hiding?"

"What do you call it then?"

"Art. Sublime, simple, and truly important." He couldn't meet his friend's gaze for long, and took a gulp of his coffee.

There was another silence, this time broken by Gustav with his customary grin. "I've brought you something from Vienna. I won't see you for a while because I'm being sent East."

Tomas started. "What?"

Gustav dropped his voice. "Tomas, we must reclaim what belongs to us."

He fumbled in his pocket and brought out a compass, shiny and edged with brass. Tomas willingly accepted it into his hands.

"Gustav, this must have cost—"

"A small fortune? Of course! But … "

"What?"

Gustav shifted in his chair, then leaned forward again. "I want you to come. Why didn't you last time?"

Tomas shrugged. "There are ways. They like my work."

"There will be a next time. You have to come." He picked up his spoon, then dropped it on the table once more. "They'll make you, anyway."

"Perhaps."

"What's wrong?"

Tomas didn't know quite how to say what he was feeling. He held the compass in his hands and felt guilty. "I want no part in it," he admitted.

"Tomas, you *are* a part of it, and you know it."

The door tinkled again. Both of them remembered where they were, and glanced around cautiously. Tomas ordered two more coffees before Gustav continued, his voice lower.

"What was hanging from the upper balconies last night? Who was sitting in the most expensive box seats? To whom are you giving comfort?"

"Enough!" Tomas glared at his friend. "You don't know what you are saying. You have been away for so long."

"You don't want to hear the truth."

"You are the same," Tomas retorted.

There was a hard silence, a ceasefire. Tomas realized again how well they knew each other.

"Look here," Tomas lowered his voice still further and stirred his coffee, even though he had added no sugar or cream. "People have disappeared here, most of them Jewish. These are dangerous times, and I don't want to be part of an army that is defending this … this madness."

"Then you are a hypocrite," spat Gustav softly, "because you *are* defending it! Every note you play tells people there is nothing to worry about. With your music, they don't need to concern themselves with anything but feeling good. Can't you see that?"

"What I can see," muttered Tomas fiercely, "is that you have forgotten that you are the one who is shooting people. I am helping keep things humane."

"And I am defending us, Tomas." Gustav stole a quick look around at the other tables before he next spoke. "I am not fighting for Hitler."

Tomas stared at him, genuinely astonished. "How can you say that?"

"I am fighting for me. For us. There will be war, Tomas.

And if Germany loses this war, then we are all sunk. All of us. Perhaps it should never have come to this, but now that it has, we will have to fight. Defeat would mean the end of everything." He leaned even closer. "Hitler will die, things will change. But I want my Germany to remain."

Tomas just shook his head. "You keep fighting, then. I don't want such an adventure."

"That doesn't sound like you."

"What do you mean? I haven't changed. You have."

"Yes, I have. But I am living in reality. And you—"

"Yes, sheltered and safe," Tomas rejoined sarcastically. "Unlike you."

They were at a stalemate.

Gustav sighed and turned his cup with his hands. "You will join. You will have no choice."

"I am made for music, not guns."

"Sooner or later you will fight. I know you. You will want things to change."

Tomas said nothing but stared angrily out the window. They were both wrong, he knew it. They were deluding themselves. He rubbed the back of his neck. He suddenly felt exhausted.

"You're insulting me." He smiled ruefully. "But, I am glad you have come."

"Even though we're fighting," remarked Gustav.

"We have always fought."

"Yes, I suppose you are right."

But Tomas knew that they had never before fought like this.

From somewhere a clock chimed the hour, and Tomas checked his watch. "Rehearsal in two hours! I need sleep so I don't fall over my music stand and get slaughtered by Herr Konductor. He does not take kindly to his musicians going unconscious." He smiled, but tensely. "How much longer are you in Berlin?"

"You really didn't get my letter. Another three days."

"Where are you staying?"

"A boarding house I know. It is a good place for me. I can come and go as I want, and the meals are cheap." He chuckled. "Bad, but cheap!"

"Well, there is always my apartment."

"Thank you."

"I'm serious. Whenever you need it."

"Thanks again."

They stood up to leave, and Gustav waved Tomas's money away with an impatient hand. "It's on the Wehrmacht!" He winked. "And listen—when you do join, join me. It's not all terror and bullets."

Tomas shrugged and grinned, although half-heartedly. Their discussion had left him feeling even more tired than before. He needed to sleep.

"Meet me for supper tonight," Tomas told him as they parted ways a few minutes later. "Eleven, at my place. I mean to make the most of your visit here!"

Gustav shook his hand. "I enjoyed the music."

"Good. That is what I play for, that people will enjoy what we do."

They turned their separate directions, and disappeared down the busy Berlin streets.

Tomas wondered whether a new bridge was forming between them, or whether the one that had been there had just been torn down.

"But you must come!" I beg him urgently. "You who have fought with me, traveled with me!"

"I can't travel any more. I can't do anything."

He seems to lose height. His eyes slip from mine, while behind us the Wannsee laps demurely in the afternoon light. A boy rides past on a bicycle, and a pigeon churrs.

"You don't mean what you say!" I insist.

"How can I tell you that I do?" He is frustrated with me, banging one fist upon the other. "You do not understand!"

"You are afraid!" I know my voice is hitting him. But he is right. I do not understand. I do not even want to try to understand. All I feel is the drive to escape, and I have to treat anything in my path without mercy.

Now I am on my boat, and I feel this anger as I restlessly pace the deck, beating away memories that come again and again like cavalry charges. The only time this fury is stilled is when I am held by the flight of birds.

"You are also afraid, so you go."

We both realize the truth in what he has said. We stare at each other for a long time.

"Then we can escape together," I whisper.

"I don't want to go. This is my home."

He comes closer and puts his hand on my shoulder, as if that will help to transfer his feelings to me. "Tomas." He speaks levelly, almost firmly. "I have stayed alive because this soil, this land, this air still exists, and I can return to it. I am not about to leave it all now. This is what I have fought for. This is what you fought for, too."

"I did not want to fight at all."

"But now that you have, will you just leave?"

His eyes are on mine, in them. We will never be the same after today; we both know it.

"There is an adventure here, too," he continues. "We can rebuild, we can—"

"Don't say it."

"Say what?"

"I can never start again. Not here. I cannot."

Gustav knows it is no use trying to convince me, yet we continue to hold each other's stares.

"Then I must leave. And you must stay."

We stand at the edge of the lake, feeling the shadows shift and the wind pick up.

"And your cello? Will you take that?"

My fists clench. "I will not."

"But you say this now. What of later, when you have … healed?"

"Well, then, keep it here for me."

"What?"

He does not believe me.

"You must have it. Play it whenever you want, but … yes, do not give it away. Keep it safe, Gustav. I may need it again. Who knows?"

Gustav laughs. "I have forgotten how to play."

"You will remember."

"You think?"

"My father taught you!" I reply savagely. "How could you forget?"

"I'm sorry … of course."

"Then keep it here! Let it remind you that I may one day return, and be more at peace with the world than I am now."

Gustav stares down at his hands. "Then I will play, but not until then."

"As you wish. But will you … ?"

"Take care of it? Of course I will. You know you can trust me."

"Yes."

"Even though I am staying and you are leaving."

"You have something to plant here. I have nothing."

The sky is now a dull russet, like a dying rose. Evening has crept in, and we both shiver.

"And the concert?" he asks.

"Take the ticket."

"You might change your mind."

"No, I will not go."

"You keep it. It cost me enough! If I just knew you would hold onto it ... I thought it might help."

"Thank you, but no."

A few seconds later, however, I change my mind, although even now I am not sure why. Maybe it is sadness at what has passed between us.

"I will keep the ticket."

Gustav smiles. We shake hands. We both pull our coats more tightly around us and raise our collars against the cold air.

Perhaps we were never really one boy.

28.

Spring, 1942

It had rained overnight. The morning held no sun, only a pallid light that dulled the surfaces of buildings, lampposts and cobblestones. The street's personality was obscured in a damp haze; to Tomas, as he watched them from his chair by the café window, the *Strassenbahnen*[9] and early morning commuters appeared blurred.

Gustav's recent visit rankled, and Tomas remained haunted by the words they had cast at each other. Was he a hypocrite? Or was he, as he had believed, an artist doing everything possible to keep his world from disintegrating? Did he really believe that music could keep them from a war with Europe, or keep others from being imprisoned or deported? For a moment Frau Henkel's face misted the cold window-glass like a warm breath—opaque, and with a sadness that terrified him.

Inside the café, a waitress diligently tidied away the remains of the previous evening. As she tipped trays of crumpled cigarette butts into a metal bin, tiny puffs of ash escaped and then collapsed. To Tomas, it seemed he witnessed dying words, and that the waitress as she cleaned, efficiently dispensed with last night's encounters, memories and stains.

A tiny bell jangled above the café door, and a reed-like man the color of paper stepped inside. He was vaguely familiar, although Tomas struggled to remember how. The waitress glanced up for a moment, and Tomas noted that her face creased into fine folds, like the tablecloths heaped on the counter.

It was too cold for flowers. Two ladies clad in stylish wool coats sat poised by a far window, manicured fingers flipping pages of a fashion magazine; their gossip was reminiscent of bees in a summer garden, the sound of a foreign season.

---

9   Streetcars.

The paper-colored man glided over to a corner table and picked up a small, square menu. He gazed across it, his eyes barely moving. A cup and saucer clattered, then the waitress squeezed through the counter opening and clacked over to him in purposeful shoes, a brown teapot in her left hand. As she served him, the man spoke in a low voice. The waitress seemed absorbed, occasionally glancing around the café.

Tomas then saw her start and spill her pot of tea.

A few minutes passed. He observed over the top of his newspaper that the man reached into his pocket and found some coins. He lined them up on the table. From the look on the waitress's face, the coins might have been a miniature firing squad.

Tomas realized where he had seen this man before. Last winter, a composer whose name Tomas could no longer remember—a taciturn, brooding sort of man—had spent many evenings at the post-concert performances in Tomas's apartment. He knew the composer as one who spoke little, but whom the others revered—he had leaned almost surreptitiously against the door frame, as music was made around him.

One night the composer had left early, met at the door by the very gentleman who now sat chatting to the waitress with such studied casualness. Tomas had merely answered the door to him in the early hours, music and laughter blurring the memory. The composer had not appeared again.

From the dim corner of the café, the man's voice surfaced for a moment, like a whispering tide, long enough for a few words to make themselves heard.

"All I am saying is, consider carefully what you shall do. These are not idle rumors. And sooner or later, we must all stand before God."

Tomas was aware of a sudden arrest of breath and time: the gossiping women, the soft clink of metal spoons on saucers, even the diluted light seemed held.

Then the bell sounded again. A delivery man stood awkwardly on the threshold, his arms balancing two large crates. He coughed, and the waitress looked up. The heavy door thudded behind him, and the lull evaporated.

"I'll be there shortly," barked the waitress, and the ladies sipping their tea simpered, as the man passed by with an admiring ogle at their neatly coiffed hair. As that was precisely why they were sitting at the window, they then attacked their conversation with greater vigor.

The paper-colored man stood and brushed crumbs from his coat, leaving his drink unfinished. He paused for the waitress to step aside, and then he strolled out of the café, stopping briefly to doff his hat to the two women, who twittered happily behind their manicured hands.

He noticed Tomas and glanced politely at him, his eyes questioning. Tomas simply nodded briefly and watched the man disappear down the street, then quickly jumped up, left a handful of coins on the table, and followed him.

He found the man several blocks from the café, and caught up with him waiting to cross at a busy corner. Tomas coughed, but the man ignored him. He coughed again, and the man turned.

"The composer, where is he?" Tomas blurted out.

The man eyed him coolly. "I'm not sure I understand you, Sir. Good day."

He moved to cross the street, but Tomas now stood in his path. The man paused, then faced him.

"What is your business?"

"I'm a cellist with the Berliner Philharmonic."

The man nodded. "Oh, yes, I met you once, I think at your apartment."

"Yes, yes, that's right."

"I believe the man you are speaking of is seeking more permanent accommodation, but aren't so many these days? Rent is high."

"Yes, yes, I can barely afford it myself." Tomas found himself stammering. "However, if he was … stuck for a room, he could always sleep at my place until he found somewhere. I have a great many musical contacts who regularly visit."

"If I see him, I'll let him know. Now, if you'll excuse me."

This time, Tomas let him go.

⚡

At two in the morning, somebody pressed the doorbell. Tomas was sleeping, but lightly. He wondered if Gustav had his leave extended, and then felt a surge of annoyance that his sleep should have been so rudely interrupted; for once, he had been able to get to bed at a reasonable hour. The doorbell buzzed once more, and Tomas staggered out of bed and opened the catch.

"Yes?" he mumbled, only one eye open.

"Excuse me, but I need to come in."

Tomas didn't recognize the voice. "Who are you?" he retorted, apprehensive and more awake.

"An old friend. I have some music I have written for you."

Tomas suddenly remembered his conversation on the street corner a week earlier—was it only one week?—and he opened the door.

The composer stood in front of him, disheveled, his face thin and nervous. Tomas stared at him for a moment, while his stomach lurched in fear-induced nausea. He gestured for the composer to step inside, which he did promptly. Tomas shut the door and bolted it, his fingers clumsy and hot, his heart a drum.

"Coffee?" he offered inanely.

The man nodded, then sat—or rather collapsed—onto the sofa. Tomas stumbled into the kitchen to brew a drink for both of them.

"I only need to stay here for two or three days," the man called softly. His voice was tired. "Then I will be moving on—this time, hopefully, for good."

Tomas finished his task. He returned with two steaming cups. The man clasped his coffee gratefully, muttered a thank you, and raised his eyes briefly to his host. "You spoke to him?"

Just the smell of the coffee had been enough to jolt Tomas into alertness. He knew exactly to whom the composer referred, and nodded vigorously.

"Yes, yes. Of course."

"Good."

"What do you need?"

"Coffee is good, a necessity even!" He grinned wearily. "Even Reich coffee," he added. "Perhaps some bread … Please go to no trouble. I can sleep on the floor. I have my own blanket. I am not here long. Arrangements have already been made." He stopped himself from going further and sipped at his drink.

"I have spare blankets and a mattress," Tomas responded, leaning forward. "Please don't offend me by sleeping on the carpet." He thought for a moment. "Listen," he added, his voice anxious, "I will have people dropping in every so often, as usual, and some may recognize you. Who should I say you are?"

"An old friend. Passing through. A composer. But you know this already, I have been here before. I am familiar, and no one will be surprised."

There was an awkward silence before Tomas spoke, his voice tentative.

"Are you really a composer?"

"Of course."

"Then they don't like what you have written?"

The man weighed his thoughts. "Shall we say, they don't like *who* has written it. But one day, we shall see. They like my work in America." He fumbled in his pocket and offered what he had. "Not much, but hopefully it covers my bread."

Tomas hesitated before he allowed the coins to fall into his hand. He didn't know whether he should be feeling heroic, or fearful. He felt neither, just very tired. The silver rested on his palm. *Payment for a dubious act of bravery,* he thought numbly. And it was dubious. Tomas had the unsettling thought that perhaps what he really wanted was to prove himself to Gustav, show his friend that he was not a coward. *So really,* his conscience whispered, *this is not about saving others. This is about your pride.*

The composer drained his coffee. "We should sleep."

Tomas stood and closed his fingers. As his did so, the coins pressed into his skin, and accused him.

29.

The man stayed longer than three days. He was not only a composer, as it turned out, but a consummate violinist. This Tomas discovered in the course of their conversations over a glass or two of cheap wine after their evening meal, which was often around midnight, the time Tomas arrived home. The man had yearned for a chance to play again, and Tomas had managed to procure him an instrument—simply smiling mysteriously when asked how—on which the man quickly proved his prowess. He performed hushed, transcendent solos while Tomas camouflaged the sound with orchestral gramophone records.

Tomas had never played so much music. It filled his days and nights, so that he no longer had time to think. His argument with Gustav drifted further into the recesses of his memory.

As Tomas arrived one morning at the café, he noticed a thin man seated in the corner. His heart beat fast, but Tomas kept his eyes on where he was headed—to his favorite table by the window. Sunlight spilled onto his hands as he settled himself and opened his newspaper.

There was a hiss of steam, porcelain rattled, and then the waitress arrived, bearing a cup of coffee and a sweet biscuit. She placed them unceremoniously on the table in front of him. Tomas looked up quickly, bewildered at this sudden service.

"Don't you go getting any ideas about me, Mr. Musician," she muttered. "It's from him. And don't bother with any returns. He's just thanking you."

She returned behind her counter. The paper-colored man in the corner rose from his table, and departed. The bell jangled as the door closed. He did not once meet Tomas's eye.

Suddenly a fist thumped the window in front of him, and Tomas jumped, spilling his coffee. It was Gustav—when was it that Tomas had last seen him?

"Where have you been hiding?" Gustav admonished his friend, as he pulled up a chair and waved at the waitress for a coffee. Tomas ordered another for himself.

"Busy," Tomas murmured as he tore at a fresh roll. "And you? You didn't tell me you had so much leave time! I hadn't heard from you. I thought you had gone back!"

"The privilege of twenty-four days' leave—rare, but true."

"Where have you been, then?" Tomas demanded. "What have you been up to?"

"Busy."

"You? Busy? Here? Who do you know, apart from me?"

Gustav scowled. "I'm not a social outcast! I've got friends. And I am actually enjoying spending time by myself, too, just wandering."

"Things aren't all that safe here," Tomas retorted. "You need to be careful."

"You forget that my uniform keeps me safe."

"Of course. Your uniform."

There was a pause.

"Let's not argue again," Gustav insisted. "It is good to see you."

"You also."

"Although I must say, you look exhausted." He winked.

"Thank you. You look great, yourself." Tomas folded his newspaper. It was all lies, anyway—he didn't know why he bothered to buy it anymore.

"What have you been doing?" Gustav persisted, eating hungrily.

"Up late, up early, you know."

"You didn't look this tired last time."

"Well, maybe it hadn't all caught up with me."

"What?" Gustav glared at Tomas.

"What do you mean, 'what'?"

"You're hiding something."

"No, I'm not!"

"Are you still angry? I know last time we both said things—"

"That we meant. Let's face it."

"All right, so we meant them. Can't we move on?"

"That depends."

"On what?"

There was a longer silence this time, and Tomas shifted his weight uneasily in his chair. "On whether I tell you what has been happening."

"I know—music, parties, your crazy artist life."

"Things have changed."

"So, you have met a girl!" Gustav grinned broadly at him.

"No, it is not that."

"What, then?"

"A friend. Someone is staying with me at the moment. He is staying because he needs … protection." He stopped— was his face coloring? He suddenly felt that every eye in the café was on him.

Gustav leaned forward slightly, his face serious. He looked older, Tomas thought.

"What have you got yourself involved in, Tomas?"

"I don't really know. He needs somewhere, and he is with me. A wonderful violinist." He tried to speak casually. He realized that Gustav remained unimpressed.

"Don't you care what could happen to you?"

"Gustav, I thought that despite your uniform, you would understand!"

"What's there to understand? You're hiding some Jewish fugitive!"

"How do you know that?"

"Obvious, I would have thought."

It was bizarre, but it had not even crossed his mind. Was he that removed from what was happening around him?

"Either that or he's a Communist, or both. Tomas, you are risking your neck for a man you don't even really know."

"I know."

"No, you don't. I don't believe you've even thought this through at all. They could send you to a concentration camp for this. At the very least, interrogation or prison. They're brutal, Tomas. Believe me."

"I could pretend ignorance."

Gustav marveled at Tomas's naivety.

"Gustav, he really is a friend."

"Well, he is not a real friend to be putting you in so much danger. And you haven't ever mentioned him to me before. He can't be that good a friend."

"It is the least I can do."

"Since when did you start caring about what's going on?"

"You accused me of losing my sense of adventure!"

"You are crazy!"

"At least I am making a difference." It sounded clichéd, and he knew it. What on earth had he done?

"I cannot believe that this man has been staying with you, and nobody in your building has even noticed." Gustav took another bite of his roll, chewed, considered, then came to a decision. "Tomas, you have to tell him to go."

"I can't," he mumbled awkwardly.

"What do you mean, you can't?"

"I couldn't do it."

"Then I will."

"No!"

"His presence there will kill you."

"He'll leave when he can."

"And when is that?"

"It was supposed to be a week and a half ago."

"There." Gustav leaned back, definite, as if he had won his argument.

"What?"

"So he has lied to you already."

"Things are uncertain for him. He is waiting to hear from contacts in America."

"Hah! You have been taken in, and meanwhile you provide food, wine and a bed to a man who is making every day a danger to you, who brings you perhaps one moment closer to death."

"This isn't about me."

"Yes it is. You just said you are doing this to prove that you are not a coward."

"I didn't say that."

"You might as well have."

Anger rose up in Tomas, but fear rose with it. "Enough!" Tomas had so wanted the next time they met to be like it used to be, and yet they seemed to be more separate than ever.

Gustav looked resigned. "We are fighting again."

"You believe it is wrong to save a man's life."

Gustav sighed. "You don't know how to protect him. You are, in fact, risking two lives. You have no idea what you are doing, and you have no contacts to help you out if you are in trouble. You are a fool, Tomas." He paused. "And I'm leaving."

He threw some money down on the table. "My leave ends the day after tomorrow. If you want to see me, you know where I am staying."

The café door clamped shut behind him.

Tomas left soon afterward, his heart a racing torrent inside his chest. For the first time, he felt real terror. Again there was the question of what he had done and why. He suddenly believed it was the most childish, selfish action of his life. At what point had he failed to grow up? Gustav seemed so sure now of what was right, of what he wanted. Tomas, on the other hand, felt he had been cut adrift from whatever tenuous line had held him to a sense of security.

When Tomas arrived home, the flat was unoccupied, and tidy. He noticed that the mail had been left waiting for him on a small table near the door. There were two envelopes, both of them white, one with a handwritten address. He opened that one first. Enclosed was a single sheet of music, neatly folded. Tomas spread it out gently; he contemplated it. He then burnt both music and envelope in his kitchen sink, and rinsed away the pile of ash.

The second letter bore the Insignia of the Department of the Supreme Commander of the Wehrmacht, stamped in red across the top. Tomas could not pick it up, and left it sitting on the table. He reached instead for the compass he still had in his pocket, and knew, whether he opened that envelope tonight or in the morning, the orders contained within would not change. His time had finally come.

“The cycle of ice ages is the foundation.”

The man who loves birds stares into his fingers, deep in thought. “They recede, they advance … and the pattern of migration adjusts and adapts over many thousands of years. They are,” he adds, “in tune with the ages, whereas we consider only our own lifetimes. We are short-term thinkers, unfortunately.”

The hemisphere we have left behind seethes and cracks under such thinking. The man scratches at his beard, and shifts his weight. We are sitting once more on the thick coils of rope, watching the sea course by and letting ourselves be cradled by the rhythm of the swell.

“They molt before flight,” he continues, his eyes searching inwards—he is picking up one piece of knowledge at a time and fingering it like a treasure, savoring its rediscovery.

“They renew themselves, as it were, shed their old skins. What they need are strong feathers—feathers that are flexible enough to survive the varied and unpredictable elements. Their quality, you see, directly affects the way they fly. Healthy, resilient feathers will conserve energy and make for vastly more efficient flight.”

Thinking about the birds, I once again feel unprepared for my own migration. A seagull soars overhead, its call blunted by the wind. The man has forgotten me. My questions have pushed him into the museum of his memory, and he no longer needs my company.

“ … Although the young birds don’t need to do this at first, and they seem to know, without being taught, not only the way, but the return journey. There is always the return journey.”

There is another silence between us, a troubled one. Thoughts move in rapid and thick crosscurrents.

The man glances up, squinting in the way that is his habit. He is restless. Another bird sweeps past, and he stiffens, relaxes, tenses again. He is lecturing, remembering, trying to remember.

"How do they know when?" I ask softly.

He answers my question, but I am now just another part of his own mind.

"Zeitgebers. Time, environment, conditions of the weather ... all meet, as it were, and their intersection causes restlessness in the birds. They know that the time has come and they must leave. Their bodies feel it. Even in enclosed spaces, they turn to face the way their free companions will be flying."

I cannot help but think of Gustav.

30.

Late Spring, 1942

Tomas sat as if strapped to a pole, unable to move for shock and disbelief. It could not, must not be true. The Assistant Director of the orchestra looked straight at Tomas, her eyes dark with concern and frustration. He stared at the letter that now lay on her desk. He had delivered it to her in person this morning, hopeful that perhaps he could still avoid the Draft.

"But, why not?" His voice sounded faraway. He knew it was no use, but he asked anyway.

"This time it has not been possible." She picked up a pencil and put it down again, then swiveled slightly on her chair so that she could see out the window. "You know we tried."

It was raining, and the glass rattled under the force of falling water. The ceiling began to leak in a corner of the room.

"But why this time? Why could it not be at least … postponed?"

"It was just not possible." She turned to face him again, her expression taut. "Please, I know this is difficult for you, it is difficult for us, too. Normally things can be arranged, but you must understand. This time there was nothing we could do. Since Russia … " She trailed off, but both of them knew of the desperate need for soldiers since the last terrible winter.

They both found themselves listening to the frantic pattering of rain; both shivered as a draft caught them from under the sill.

But he couldn't just leave, not with questions burning inside.

"And my position?" He heard his voice break, and felt annoyed at his lack of poise.

"That is not for me to say."

"Will I have to audition again … when I come back?"

She looked at him, and he clamped his teeth together to keep his fear under control. Once he had served his time, who knew how things might stand—would he even be allowed to leave the Army? He had never believed the war would be over in only a matter of months, regardless of the optimism of the press and the government. And what if he—but he refused to ponder the unthinkable.

"Depending on the time frame, then, I presume yes, although you know it is not for me to decide." She sighed, and absently shuffled some papers on her desk. "He is very happy with your work, you must believe that. He is as frustrated as you are that he cannot hold onto to each and every one, but we have to tread so carefully."

The sound of rain rushed in once more to fill the silence. Tomas sensed that the audience was over.

He left the room feeling numb. He had only a week left. That was not enough, or maybe just enough time to organize his things, tell his parents. He shuddered inwardly. He decided to simply arrive home without any forewarning. Perhaps then his father would not close the door in his face before they had time to talk.

The road returns again, and then once more, cloaked in dust and muffled with ambient light. A dull thudding punctuates the silence, like a heartbeat magnified a hundred times and broadcast around me.

I look down and see with surprise that my boots are the cause of this regular thudding—but not only my boots. I am with others, marching relentlessly, stupid from no sleep and foul coffee in our otherwise empty stomachs.

Can all this dust be from our feet? It settles on every part of me until I can finally breathe it in and no longer notice the rasping in my throat. And there is the road—the road that yawns ahead, sprinkled at its far end with trucks, their hefty wheels churning yet more dust into the horizon.

It is the dream. With the wailing of planes overhead, a village starts to burn, and night falls suddenly, tipping blackness over us like the contents of an upturned pot.

There is shouting, and I have straw and mud in my hair. There is blood. There is an explosion. There is silence. There is the boat.

I am on a boat.

I am on a boat. It is night.

There is no dust.

The thudding is merely my heart, and the relentless dance of water.

The door banged shut behind him, sealed by a cold wind that swore at his back. The fire ceased crackling, its flames stunted by the sudden change in temperature. His eyes felt taut, and Tomas was aware that one of his hands was clenched, the other trembling.

His mother sat calmly in her rocking chair, her fingers poised above the shirt she had been mending. Her hair was fringed with light from the lamp behind her. She was not looking at him, but he knew that she was deeply aware of his presence. Perhaps she was refusing to look at him. Her hands quivered—he could see their silhouette.

The silence was heavy and oppressive. They were both waiting for his father. They heard his tread, and the door opposite Tomas creaked, and then hung agape like an open mouth. It framed his father like a word almost spoken. Their eyes met. Tomas felt the stern gaze travel over his neatly part-ed hair, the thick, dark uniform, and then, with slow and ter-rible finality, the shining knee-high boots.

There was an awful quiet, as if Tomas had become an abyss that had opened in front of his parents. He tried to speak—he had prepared carefully for this moment—but the opportunity was never there.

The father turned from his son, and the door creaked again, and closed. Inside himself, Tomas wept. His mother's cheeks shone with tears—they seemed to be the only things in the room that moved.

The fire spat suddenly, and the clock chimed, biting into the silence. Tomas wanted so very much to kiss his moth-er and tell her that he loved her, but he did not move, and neither did she. Was it a hundred days that he stood there like that, suspended in his grief?

"I will write," he said simply, and—like his father—he left the room.

He did write. He sat on the wall beneath his bedroom window, where Gustav had met him all those years ago, and under the moon he scratched out his thoughts on the back of a concert program that for some reason he had in the top of his bag. He wrote what he had not been able to explain: that he had no choice, that arrangements had fallen through, that he was threatened and was afraid, so deeply afraid. It was of this last aspect that he was so ashamed—he who had built his childhood on dreams of flight, could not think of one single way that he could escape this. It berated him, rebuked him, this past self.

It seemed to Tomas that he did not breathe as he wrote, and when he had finished and folded his letter, he placed it under his parents' front door, before turning back toward the station.

He had not gone far when he heard his mother's voice call out to him.

"You must stay here—where will you sleep?"

He faced her. She held the paper in her hand.

"Please give it to him."

"I couldn't help it this time … " He broke off, feeling wretched. "Believe me, if there was any way … "

"I know."

"But he doesn't!"

"Not yet. Please, he has feared this moment, and now it is come."

"But he thinks I am a traitor."

Am I? he wondered.

His mother moved toward him, her voice low and determined. "He loves you."

Tomas kicked his bag. "Would you give him the letter?" he repeated, not looking at her.

"Yes, of course, but where will you stay?"

"There is one more train tonight. I have a few days left in Berlin before I have to go."

"Please ..." She reached him and clasped his head to her breast as if he were once more a young boy.

His mother wanted to tell him to eat properly, to wear warm socks and stay out of trouble. She wanted to tell him not to die, but all she could do was cry soundlessly and clutch at him.

All that time, although Tomas did not see, his father was watching from his darkened shop window and crying, too.

Part Six: Menuet 2

31.

Autumn, 1943

Tomas wandered into the café as part of a bored and rest-less walk around the city of Berlin. The past few days had been his hardest; it did not feel like his city anymore.

"Excuse me? Waiter?"

The tapering, black and white figure slipped past the table and swiveled neatly on the spot. He quickly noticed Tomas's uniform, and nodded his head with respect—per-haps apprehension. Tomas felt his skin grate every time he received a look like this: a searching, anxious dart of eyes, or—what was worse—wide-eyed infatuation. This latter response particularly unnerved him; with each admiring glance, ghosts of the composer's silver coins pressed his hand and spoke their judgment.

Tomas realized his fist was clenched, so he relaxed his fingers. The thought of continuing his aimless meanders through the city exhausted him, and Tomas decided that he wanted a drink more than he was bothered with this man's attitude to his uniform. He indicated his need with a few curt words.

"As you wish, Sir."

Was it Tomas's imagination, or did the man click his heels before leaving? Suddenly the tray balanced next to the waiter's head became a strange metallic salute.

Tomas watched the waiter disappear to fetch his order. He absently watched people come and go through the swing-ing wooden door, while the fingers on his left hand rapped arpeggios on the tabletop.

Two army officers strode in. They glanced at Tomas, but he was not of their rank, and they looked away. Their neat figures crossed to a table at the other side of the café. They drank one cup of coffee each, talked for about ten minutes with very serious expressions, then departed.

A group of relentlessly cheerful businessmen claimed a table near Tomas. He could hear their self-congratulatory talk from where he sat. Oh, yes, Hitler's regime had thus far been extremely good for business. They had been able to make desired, necessary changes. Their polished faces reminded Tomas of well-preserved antique tables; all the pockmarks lacquered over with aftershave and success.

So that's who I am defending.

Frau Henkel's face appeared again in his mind, her shawl drawn about her shoulders.

He stood quickly, abandoned his order, and left. The bell tinkled above his head as the doors swung him onto the pavement. Frau Henkel's gaze pursued him down the street, a siren only he could hear.

The week after we were captured, and then rescued, I write a letter home.

Dear Mother. Dear Father.

I do not know how to begin. Perhaps with the way all myths begin, with *once upon a time*? So, I speak it first to myself before I write, whispering it to the tree I am propped against ...

Once upon a time, there was a brave warrior. He was powerful and strong, and when he raised his gun to his shoulder, the enemy trembled in fear and cowered in their trenches, their dens, their bunkers. On parade days his body sounded like it was covered with bells, from the medals that bellowed and swayed from his broad chest. It was a proud mother whose child was scooped to his shoulder, a proud father whose boy received a manly pat as the soldier strode by. Once upon a time.

I begin again, this time placing my pen to the paper.

Dear Mother. Dear Father,
We find ourselves once again with our own, after a brief time of imprisonment by a random enemy unit. Have no fear, they treated us well. They were scared. Our army is stronger than theirs, and they knew their hour of defeat was near. They fed us, and gave us hay for a bed.

It was our first meal in three days.

At first I did not know if they would shoot us.

No. I thought they would shoot us. They made us turn around, so that our backs faced the dark mouths of their rifles, and I—

I hummed Bach.

But they will worry if I tell them that.

Dear Mother. Dear Father.
I am alive.

32.

Early Summer, 1944

Gustav and Tomas stepped off the Berlin train onto the grimy, bustling platform. It was late afternoon, and commuters in fitted coats and gloves hurried about them, while pigeons hustled at their feet. Tomas felt invisible, or worse, that perhaps he had dissolved.

Many months had passed since he had been able to return to Germany. He could not visit Zweibach, could not even envision himself standing at the front door of his home. Tomas shuddered; he would never forget that night. Again, he promised himself that he would write another letter to his parents. He swore he would forget the terrible silence of his father's back.

It was good to have Gustav with him. This was not the first time they had been home on leave, but this transition from battleground to civil life immobilized him, every time. Here there was no longer gunfire, but shoe-heels tapping on pavement. Dust clouds from marching boots turned to train smoke, men in uniformed suits were now armed with briefcases. Standing on the platform, Tomas was an immigrant from another world, bereft, possessing not even the language to explain what he had seen in his old country.

At the front he and Gustav each wore a self-forged, inner helmet; it blunted the fear, kept them moving, surviving. As much as they counted the days and hungered for time away from the horrors of the front, once Tomas debarked in Berlin, his inner helmet evaporated. Again he saw soldiers clutch limbs no longer there; felt the sudden scarlet spray from a grenade; witnessed faces stripped of youth in less seconds than it took to light a cigarette. His mind became a helpless axis; on this axis the terrifying scenes revolved, like spokes on a malevolent wheel. It seemed worse, not better, every time they returned.

Gustav and Tomas glanced at each other, then swung their kit bags over their shoulders. Together they jostled their way to the station exit. Despite the feelings clouding them both, Gustav nudged Tomas and mustered a small smile. "Where to?"

Tomas shrugged under the weight of his bag. "Auntie Lonna's."

Gustav nodded, and together they headed off in the direction of the boarding house.

Tante Lonna was not her real name, although she quickly became substitute mother, aunt, and sister to all the weary soldiers that lodged with her when they had nowhere else to go. She never remembered their names, but that didn't seem to matter—she loved every tired young man that came through the door, even if she ended up calling all of them by the latest name she had remembered. When Gustav and Tomas arrived, she had just seen the film *Romance in a Minor Key* with Ferdinand Marian, so her boarding house was full of "darling Ferdinands" of all shapes and sizes. The young men let her kiss them at the door like long-lost sons, and then they wrote down their real names in a large, brown book at the front desk.

Tante Lonna's hair was tucked neatly into a bun, her makeup well-intentioned but skewed. Her lipstick was always smudged, and one eye seemed to be bigger than the other, although that was largely the fault of the asymmetrical lighting over her bathroom mirror. She smelled comfortingly of cheap perfume, lavishly applied. Unsophisticated generosity flowed from her as she served burnt-but-sizeable meals, and played loud, out-of-date records on the little gramophone in the lounge. Her hugs made every soldier feel he were sitting by a fire with a big bowl of soup in front of him, and the promise of never being forced to move.

Rumors trickled around Tante Lonna—her husband had been an army commander in the Great War and never returned; her own sons had been murdered in the tumultuous years following the Armistice—but these whisperings merely increased the gratitude the men felt toward her, and their belief that perhaps she understood some of their pain.

As Gustav and Tomas signed in at the front desk, Tante Lonna readjusted her glasses and repositioned the long strings of beads that had fallen over one shoulder. She blew a kiss at their backs, as Gustav and Tomas mounted the tiny, winding staircase to the left of the front desk. They clambered upward, finally reaching number 19. The room contained two sagging beds only an arm-span apart, and a pinched window between them. There was not even enough space for a dresser, but a row of hooks on the door sufficed. They never had much gear with them anyway.

Down the hall a few steps was a leaking, lopsided bathroom with a cracked basin, a narrow bath, and a slice of mirror wide enough to see most of one's face while shaving. One of the delights of this place, however, was the towels. Tante Lonna had made them herself. They were large and soft, and each soldier who stayed here seemed to be given one in a different color from everyone else's. The towels, the hugs, and the breakfasts were extravagant, even if the paint was peeling and the heating only sometimes worked.

Tomas peered out the casement, but could not see much with the darkening sky, and blackout curtains already drawn on all the windows. He and Gustav could smell charred soup, and this made them feel hungry. They deposited their gear and trudged downstairs again, joining a growing line of men anxious for food. The lodgers sat around a long wooden table, hardly talking, while Tante Lonna dished out deep bowls of soup. It was hot, and traveled happily down to their stomachs, helped along by thick slices of dark bread without butter.

There was no beer—one of Tante Lonna's rules, that nobody dared break, was that there was to be no alcohol on the premises.

"You are all dear boys and unhappy enough without drowning yourselves in that poison," she would lament, her brown eyes drooping melodramatically, and a heavy sigh emanating from her mouth.

The boys obeyed her while in the house, although they often returned late at night, singing and shouting too loudly. This was why she was forced to board them in such a forgotten part of the city, she would explain over breakfast, shaking her head at them in a scolding manner that none of them took seriously. But they never drank inside, or even out on the corner. They loved her too much for that.

Dinner ended spasmodically, with various boarders abruptly pushing chairs back, and departing for the evening. Tante Lonna never asked them where they went; she only hoped they kept away from "troublemakers" and arrived home before the sun rose too high. Gustav and Tomas were two of the last to leave the table. Tante Lonna gave them each a firm pat on the head and collected their bowls.

"You two boys take care of each other," she ordered and waltzed off, whistling, to the kitchen. They grinned wearily at each other and stood up, completing the evening exodus of tired soldiers.

Gustav and Tomas let the front door slam behind them, and strode down the dark street. A car screeched in the distance, and searchlight beams sliced the sky above their heads. They headed in a northerly direction, where a string of bars spewed light onto the pavement. A cacophony of music and chatter flowed into the cool night—a twisting, swerving symphony in which women's laughter formed a tuneless melody over the low hum of male voices. Glasses clinked, doors opened and closed, and—if you shut your eyes—you could imagine the war had never even begun.

They chose the last bar on the street, although this one seemed nearly devoid of revelry. The lighting was dim, the barman looked depressed, and a stooped piano player tinkered with the keys in a dispirited, chaotic fashion that suited their mood. They ordered two beers, and grabbed a table where they could nurse their drinks in peace. A few more stragglers came in, purchased drinks, and sat at the round, shaky tables. It was still early, and people were just beginning to emerge from restaurants and cinemas to while away a few more hours. Tomas and Gustav ordered something heavier, something to make their throats wince.

More people entered. On the empty stage to the left of the piano, a woman appeared, her dress sparkling and her face tinged blue under the sickly spotlight. Gustav and Tomas ordered another drink and watched as she lifted the microphone to her lips. The sound was perfect for the night and the time, and as she finished the first tune, everyone nodded and offered sparse claps of appreciation. The chanteuse, with eyes half closed, began to sing a sad, slow ballad about leaves turning to brown and the decay of love.

Tomas gulped down a piece of ice. The woman's voice scratched at him. Two more songs in the same vein, and the sound lay heavy on the room like a fog. He shifted his weight on the stool, and suddenly craved sunlight. To his relief, the next song was slightly more upbeat, and the woman even opened her eyes for at least one line and smiled jauntily at the hunched figure at the piano. His tinkering sped up, and so did the frequency of conversations around the bar. From that point, the evening livened up. The woman's dress glittered more brightly, the crowd filled out, and the piano player straightened his back and produced solos that swung out and over the room.

Someone pushed the tables back, and they watched as figures filled the impromptu dance floor. The singer leaned further into the microphone. Couples swayed and shifted, mouths open in smiles and shouted conversations. Tomas felt lonelier than ever.

Gustav shot him a grin, and then launched himself off his stool to wander over to a woman sitting at a nearby table.

She was with a female companion, and Tomas watched his friend talking and gesturing to where he sat against the window, clutching his now-empty glass. Gustav waved his arm at his friend. Tomas shook his head—dancing seemed impossible tonight. He felt fused to his chair.

Gustav was insistent, however, and Tomas found that he had to maneuver himself off his seat in order to escape. Before he quite realized what was happening, he was working his way through the sea of dancers in front of the stage. He could barely see their faces in the dim light. He had intended to cross to the other side of the room, to put a good distance between himself and his friend's strong will, but unfortunately he was unable to cut a path through the swaying, congested crowd.

Tomas felt absurd without a partner, but all he had wanted was to be able to watch and think, alone. He tried to push past a dancing couple, but then the gap closed, and he was trapped again, aware of the critical, uncaring stares of those pressing around him. He tried once more to break through the human maze, and strangely, as he did so, in his mind he found himself writing to his parents.

Dear Mother. Dear Father.
Today my left hand fingered Telemann on the barrel of my gun.
Today we rested.

It was an unusual thing to do at a time like this, perhaps, but it helped him feel less self-conscious. At one moment Tomas even forgot where he was, and didn't at first realize that he had finally managed to break through the crowd and arrive at the bar. A row of stacked glasses confronted him, and only then did he register where he stood, but also how physically exhausted he actually was. *Perhaps I should have stayed at the boarding house and slept,* he thought.

He stepped backwards and knocked a man standing with a full glass, who promptly spilled it all over his jacket and the dress of a woman cleaved to his arm. Tomas did not apologize, but tried to move away—he did not feel like speaking while he was in the midst of composing a letter. The man harrumphed and yelled at Tomas, who placidly ignored him.

The next thing Tomas knew was that a burly man in a soaked dinner suit had whirled him around and was about to punch him in the face. Tomas's mind was fixed on his letter, and it took him several moments to re-enter his immediate world. He dodged in time, however, and the man's fist missed by a few inches.

Tomas was suddenly angry—so what if this man had damp clothing? Tomas had seen death and dismemberment continuously for many months, and what was a wet suit coat compared to that? He flung his own fist at the man, grazing him on the cheek and sending him flailing backwards onto the floor. There were a few gasps, and the dancers cleared the floor while the singer protectively grabbed her microphone. The piano player darted a quick look over one shoulder and sped up his playing until a frantic soundtrack underscored the fighting.

And fighting it was. Tomas found himself lunging at this enemy, whose face now contained all his own sorrows and guilt. Two others joined the man in the dinner suit. Tomas was dimly aware of Gustav jumping in beside him, but it was so dark, and the experience so nightmarish, that he wasn't sure what was actually happening.

Then something clicked inside him, and he dropped his arms to his side. His own guilt rose up before him—the men he had killed, the grief he had inflicted, the uniform he wore—and he just stopped fighting. He moaned out loud and sank to the floor while his surroundings spun and buzzed about his head.

Tomas let the man—the men, whose faces he could not even see—punch and kick him, while he covered his face with his hands, and silently finished his letter.

*D*ear Mother and Father,
    Yesterday we were surrounded, and now I am fighting once more for the Fatherland.

See how in one sentence I have distilled the hours. I am lying in mud, and the stars mock me with their whiteness. The winds shiver over us, tonight we are no more than mounds of grass. Tomorrow we will move on the village. We will take it, we have been assured. The Polish soldiers are said to be hiding in the forest, so we will send in men to flush them out, and deal with them.

Yesterday I read a paper published for the soldiers, but that is all I have heard from home. Rumors, whisperings, speculation are our diet of information. But perhaps it is for the best. We move when the order bids us move, and we stop when we are told to stop. We shoot, we joke afterwards, we keep marching, and sometimes we bury the dead.

I know it must be autumn because there are no birds, only dying leaves.

I am writing another letter to my father, wearing my cut-off gloves. My fingernails are filthy, my hands shake as I write. My rifle vibrates violently as I shoot, and now my hands have been imprinted with the trembling movement of the metal. I wonder if this is a common occurrence among soldiers, at least here where the fighting is intense. We are winning, though; we are always winning.

I wake. It is night, and I am lying on my bunk aboard our boat. My cheeks feel wet. In my dream state I think I may have fallen asleep with the pen lying still on my face, and that the ink has dripped through it. I touch my skin, and my hand looks black when I hold it up. Then the shadows pass, and I see my palm, white and scarred, defying my imagination. Maybe my cheeks are not wet after all.

I turn and face the room, then turn again onto my back. My coat slides off, and I pull it back over my neck and chin. I think of the man who loves birds. In my mind's eye I watch him slapping his arms against his sides, and I wonder if he desires wings.

33.

Spring, 1945

The war itself was now mortally bleeding; each soldier knew it. Tomas both feared and hoped desperately for its end, so he could finally make his way back to Zweibach. Each day, each night, he fingered the stone in his pocket and longed for home.

His chance came one chilly night, amidst the confusion and clamor of rumor, gunfire, and sweep after sweep of planes that shattered the night air with their ferocious scattering of bombs.

We're surrounded, we're defeated ... we've surrendered. The voices, calls and whispers of bewildered men swooped through the night air like hunted birds. Their uniforms were as worn through as their minds, their nerves jittered, and above all they were tired—in a deep, desolate way that sleep alone could not alleviate.

One by one, or sometimes in pairs, they began to run. Villagers awoke to find clothing stolen, larders broken into, and sobbing men confessing in a driving fear. Everywhere in the night bonfires raged, and white cloth spluttered from trees, from gateposts, from any church spires that remained.

Tomas fled, too. His regiment had long since fragmented, and he was alone with only a few Reichsmark, his rifle, and his boots in good enough condition to still march. He traveled west.

The next few days he would not remember well. Somehow he was on a train, somehow eating bread from the hand of a fearful peasant. Then finally he was stepping onto the deserted platform of Zweibach station.

The old guard was conspicuously absent, and the gate swung eerily, as if humanity had been ousted and the buildings themselves had taken control. Tomas had no ticket, and there was nobody to show one to if he had, so he walked through the gate, and soon found himself standing in the town square, gaping at the destruction around him. The tavern was there, but so much else was not. A dreadful stillness had settled on the once-bustling village center. There were, reassuringly, a few people around. Here and there a woman ducked into a shop; a man in a faded cap trotted past, pushing a wheelbarrow of wood. Tomas turned down a lane and walked carefully toward home. He strode faster. He began to feel an excitement as if he were about to fly, and started to run.

Then the road ended, and he stood at what should have been a familiar place.

I was born in a small village. I knew so well its streets and lanes, its river, and the places where the trees were permitted to grow unhindered. I knew where to stand in order to see the sky in all its vast expanse. I could watch as the clouds came to pour dreams upon us. I contemplated the space from where, years later, the bombs carved desperate paths toward us. From this place, I saw many thousands of birds leave and return.

I was born in a small village where the church bells chimed out the hours, the sun and moon marked the days, and the years went by unnoticed.

34.

Where the shop-front should have been was now a wooden frame, risen amongst rubble, behind which a workbench sat empty and neglected. There was no glass, but the space where the windows had been was loosely barricaded with barbed wire. A heavy wooden plank bolted across the front door barred Tomas from entering.

He knew there could be nobody inside, but in spite of himself he knocked, then knocked again. Then he was banging his fists, slamming his arms against the wood. He threw his weight on the door, crushing his hands against it until the fingers were grazed and bleeding. The doorstep seemed to grasp him there, clamping his feet to its worn stones.

May God watch over your family.

Tomas felt he was melting as he sank to his knees—his emotions were lava that coursed out through his skin, welding together all his hopes, memories and fears.

A hand touched his shoulder, and he cried out. Dazed, he turned his head and recognized the intruder, even in the midst of his turmoil. It was Gustav's mother. Her face was ashen, her eyes shadowed with grief and concern.

"Tomas?" she murmured.

"Where are they?"

She shook her head, and knelt down beside him. "We wrote to you, several times."

He shook his head. "When?"

"Two months ago. Oh, my dear Tomas … "

She enfolded him then, as his own mother would have done, and he sobbed in her arms like a boy. His body shuddered. The same dreadful silence he had experienced in the square enveloped his shoulders like a shroud. He shook with sorrow, as if he too had been bombed, but he made no sound. A weary wind creaked the wood behind him, and paper caught in the wire flapped and sighed. No letter could have diminished this total onslaught of grief; it numbed him so that he could not even feel his own body.

🖎

It was not until much later that he finally ate some soup and bread, sitting at the kitchen table of Gustav's parents. He heard of the raids, the surprise, the bitter shock of that night two months ago. Gustav was alive, they assured him. He had been in Berlin; he had sent them word.

Tomas folded his hands, trying to hold together what was left of his world.

There was a lull in the conversation. He had to ask, but his voice sounded far away—as if another Tomas was speaking, a Tomas who was still alive.

"Is that the moon?"

It was an odd question, but as he asked it they all became aware of how late it was, that they had no lights on, and the blackout curtains were twisted tightly at the top of the windows. The moon's white disk had swung into their view like a faceless dial. It slid one bare, insipid arm through the glass, and across the table in front of them.

Tomas stood up. "I think I may go outside."

Gustav's parents stayed seated, and watched him leave.

Once the front door had clicked shut behind him, the night appeared much brighter than before. Tomas could see clearly where to walk, and he followed the street along the most familiar route of his life—from Gustav's house to his own. He had to go back once more, although he wasn't sure what it was he wanted to see—perhaps only that he had to stand there to say goodbye.

He arrived quickly. The stars shone like tiny frozen searchlights, and he wondered once more at the vastness of the space above him. Somehow that made it easier to stand here. He didn't want to get to the other side of the fencing; there was only this one room, then a crater beyond. Looters had long since visited the site, even with the barricades in place.

Tomas placed one hand on the wire. His boot kicked something loose from the dirt. He cast his eyes downward, then knelt abruptly. His hand quivered as he carefully picked up a twig of ebony, the size of a key. It was scratched and coated thickly with earth, but he knew what it was—a finely carved peg, fallen from the scroll of a handmade violin. Tomas cradled it in his hand before closing a tight fist. Then, his back to his childhood home, he traced the path to Gustav's house for the last time.

In the morning, he would leave for Berlin.

He has at once been apparition, teacher and friend. The man who loves birds. My one ship brother. The only one to whom I could relinquish, for a time, my silence. As we approach our final harbor, I scour the decks for him, pushing against a tide of flocking, exhausted travelers. I am in their way. I am shoved violently against the railing.

Finally, I have to resign myself to pressing with the others, straining with them, as if by our efforts we can move the ship faster to the end of our journey. I gaze with them as Melbourne's Station Pier extends its long, gray hand of ambiguous welcome. Like a vast colony of nesting birds, waiting friends and relatives jostle and cry by the water.

I never see him again. Perhaps, I wonder, he has never been.

Maybe he did, after all, grow wings. Perhaps my ship brother never stumbled with the rest of us down the gangplank. And perhaps, like the storm petrels he loved, he wandered across the waves and was lifted away, on his winds of chance. Perhaps.

35.

Over a breakfast of imitation coffee and hard bread, Gustav's mother handed Tomas a postcard. There was no ceremony. She did not meet his eyes.

"From your father. He never sent it. It was found—" Her voice fractured.

Tomas's fingertips gripped the gift, let it go, then frantically scooped it up and pressed it to his forehead. *He has sent me a postcard,* Tomas thought. *He wrote to me after all.*

Tomas placed the card like a butterfly on the table in front of him, frightened it would fly away.

I hope that you will soon be able to return to your position as cellist in the Berliner Philharmonic, his father had written.

I am very proud of my son, that you have worked hard and shown such talent. It grieves me that you have sworn an oath that I hoped with all my heart you would never have to swear. I only know that I cannot understand this new world, as I cannot understand what you have done. I had hoped that you might show more courage in the face of these "threats," as you call them, but then you perhaps have not learned that this may be possible. I only hope now that you return safely and can begin again, as we all will have to do.

You are still my son.

As he walked toward Zweibach station, the postcard lay close to Tomas in his clothes—where he could feel his father's words, even if he could not read them. As the train maneuvered its way north, the postcard swam in his head like a predator, gobbling up all other thoughts. He tried not to imagine the explosions, the bombs' carved path and his parents' blood mixed with fire and resin. Anguish surged, fell dormant, then erupted once more. He did not weep, only because it was no use.

With a sudden vehemence that frightened him, Tomas hated the Allies. For the entire war, he had wanted

Hitler's defeat, but now they were the enemy. He felt a tremendous urge to wreak revenge, to kill. Where to put the postcard—in his pocket, or the nearest gutter? Could he bear to hold it a moment longer? It burnt him, yet it seemed even more precious than before. He groaned aloud; the lady opposite him got up nervously, and left the compartment.

The train suddenly ground to a halt, and the lights went out. They were only minutes from the station, but he heard the sirens wail, and he could hear the thumping and panting as passengers burrowed down to wait out the raid. He felt confused and angry that the Allies would come back for more. Was Gustav in Berlin? They had arranged to meet at the boarding house again, if all went well. If it was even there. *If. If. Why should it go well?* he thought angrily.

The sirens whined, and everywhere people clamored for protection. They were not hit—the train rumbled and shook, but at some stage the vibrations passed, the lights went on, and it moved into the station. Crowds emerged from under the platforms, weary and dazed by what had now become such a horrifyingly normal part of their existence.

Tomas disembarked, moved along by the masses. He had to find somewhere to stay. As he wandered out of the station, he was incredulous at what he saw around him: the empty streets and the craters, the twisted trees, and rows of bombed houses like grieving, grotesque mouths.

Somehow he found his way to the address he was after, a friend who had managed to continue playing with the orchestra. Tomas had left him in charge of his instrument.

There was joy and fear as he first took his cello out of its case, the trembling that raced down through his arms and chest as he played in the dingy front room of his friend's flat, with its smell of old ersatz coffee grounds and cheap wine— and all he could think of was that this was to be the only homecoming he would know.

Tomas worked his bow gently, then violently, as his father had never played by the open fire, nor ever would play. He made music loud enough to drown out the sound of his mother singing in the kitchen, of the hammering and planing from the workshop, of a fire cracking with the suspended oils of the resin … but they were stronger than he. In a fury he pummeled the strings with his bow; but the sound was betraying him, it was not obliterating his childhood, but drawing him more deeply into its music. His mother's song magnified, his father performed *fortissimo*. Tomas was unable to continue.

His friend poked his head around from the kitchen, concerned and artfully casual.

"I've made us something to eat," he mumbled apologetically, and only then could Tomas bear to stop playing.

It was the last time, he knew. Unceremoniously he laid down his cello. His hands dull, he wrapped the neck in its sheet of silk, loosened the bow, and for the last time put the instrument away. Today, the case was a coffin, and the body he placed in it was his father's. It was his mother's. In some way, it was also his.

Tomas lowered the lid. Seamlessly the red velvet disappeared, bleeding rewound. One intake of breath. Latches clicked. It was finished.

I t is not a dream.

I am in a forest.

The thicket is tightly wadded with slender saplings, surging undergrowth, and a total absence of birdsong. I have been forced to come here. My boots suck me into the peat, and my straps and gear keep catching at branches, making my march a series of jolts and shocks. Ahead of me I finally see the tiny path I am following broaden, and there are others, blurred figures, silent. Perhaps, finally, it is my unit.

But, no—they stand at attention. Then I notice that their hands are behind their heads, as though they are resting.

But they are not resting.

"You there!"

A rough, unfamiliar voice summons me, and I step forward in automatic obedience, my rifle slung in ever-readiness, and my breathing harsh.

"At your position!"

My position? What is my position? This is not my unit. I am in the wrong place, and panic darts into my chest like a wolf and tears at my throat.

I call out my rank, my unit number, to the one who stands several feet away, ordering my steps like a miniature Führer. He ignores me.

"Orders! Position!"

I stare at the other soldiers who are dressed differently from me. How did I get here? These are SS uniforms. Surely they can see I should not be here.

The man's eyes and his gun fasten onto me, and years of unthinking obedience make me stand in position, my gun aimed—

—at the people with their arms held gently behind their heads.

One of them falls. He has fainted. It is an old man.

I panic. I cannot do this. They are peasants. The other soldiers scream at them, call them filthy names. The row of ragged people stands there, as if already dead.

Except one.

A woman. She turns and looks at me. Her gaze travels the terrible ground and brings me suddenly to a classroom far away, in a village that can no longer exist. She wears the dunce cap, and her fingernails are black …

"Two by two is four," we chant, while Frau Henkel conducts us with her long and frightening ruler.

"Three by three is six."

"No, Hanna!" says Frau Henkel in a voice somewhere between a sigh and a squeal. "That is three plus three. Three by three is nine. Think, Hanna!"

What is Hanna doing here? How did she come this far east? Then I remember—of course, she is Polish.

Does she recognize me?

I am cold and unable to move, yet something else drives my body, and I raise my gun. She looks at me. I cannot stand it. I cannot do anything. I cannot help her run. I cannot do a thing to alter what is about to happen.

But I can choose to miss my target.

The command is given. The bullets rack the air, tearing shreds through the sky and toppling the figures who stand so still.

Except the woman.

I have not shot her.

I wish that is how I could tell it.

"You—shoot!"

I realize I am now the fulcrum. I am in the schoolyard, with no Gustav at my back, no teacher to come roaring across the clearing.

Hanna looks at me. She will always look at me. My rifle cracks, her forehead bursts a rose.

She folds, and crumples. Hanna, wife of a Polish farmer, falls. All but her eyes—they terrify me still, and from now on I must look down at the earth, and forever see her blood mixing with the dust.

One of the Einsatzgruppen presses his own silver pin with its twin lightning bolts into my lapel, laughing. His eyes are holes. He tells me I am one of them. I am one of them.

... and two by two is four
and four by four is sixteen
and sixteen by sixteen is ...

Part Seven: Gigue

(n): A lively Baroque dance, often contrapuntal in texture, that usually appears at the end of a suite. Contrapuntist, or Counterpoint, involves the writing of different musical lines that sound harmonious when played together. A melodic fragment alone, makes a particular impression; but when heard simultaneously with other melodic ideas, or combined in unexpected ways with itself (as in a fugue), it reveals greater depths of affective meaning. Through this development of a musical idea, the fragments transform into something musically greater than the sum of the parts—something conceptually more profound than a single, pleasing melody.

36.

Berlin

Autumn, 1995

The poet's eyes were large and steady. She wore red, and one hand shook slightly as she gripped the edge of the lectern. To her left stood the Curator, with her thick-rimmed glasses, elfin hair, and Jill Sander coat. She had a tiny microphone pinned onto her lapel and seemed poised to speak, but people continued to enter the hall. The acoustics broadened the sounds of murmuring and rustling coats, until they sounded like a faraway river.

Anton shifted in his chair and observed the stage. It had been erected in the spacious foyer of the city's main art gallery, and on its far side autumn sunlight streamed through a sweep of windows. The walls were white, non-committal, barren. Anton had always felt chilled coming into the gallery, even in the middle of summer.

The poet turned her head toward the windows. The sun lit her face, softening its dramatic pallor. Anton thought how strange it was that poets always looked more like poets if they seemed sad. At least she was wearing red. He noticed that the Curator was now frowning.

Anton had missed acting class to hear this famed American writer recite excerpts from her latest work. His theatre professor had unofficially advised him to attend, believing it would benefit Anton's craft. He also sensed Anton would be personally interested. He was. His own grandfather's involvement in the Third Reich had bequeathed to Anton the haunting sense that maybe he too was implicated, in some distant way. The history of Anton's family, and his country, drove him to both obsession and repulsion. The few others he had confided in had nodded their heads sagely, and concurred with their eyes.

Anton looked at his watch. Good—they should start soon. He imagined the rest of his classmates, limbering up with morning yoga, and practicing vocal exercises in preparation for the day. Anton's muscles ached to stretch and move, too.

Eventually the crowd's drone and rumbling dimmed. He focused once more on the stage. After a brief introduction from the Curator, the poet smiled delicately, then began to read. Her voice was unexpected: strong, resonant, and warm. Anton listened with pleasure to the sound of it, and his English was strong enough not to need to Curator's translation.

He felt her words, caustic in their stark simplicity, flick at him like drops of boiling water. He listened as she calmly explained her connection with the material. Her own parents had survived Auschwitz—she enunciated the name with clinical precision, as if it were a medical term.

The poet continued to read. It was harrowing, as always, confronting the Holocaust, wrestling again his own demons of guilt. But there was something different about this work. As he listened to the poet, Anton realized—that although painful—these words were not simply another brutal re-telling, a past voice accusing him from a mass grave. This voice was different—it was from *now*, not then, attempting, just as he was, to make sense of something unimaginable.

The narrative wove on and he felt himself drawn to the warmth of the poet, the conviction in her words. Anton found he was able to experience his nation's past, for the first time, without drowning.

37.

The plane descended toward Berlin. Outside, the sky was the color of galvanized steel. As the wheels hit the runway with a lurching roar, Lara gripped the sides of her seat as her toes tensed inside her shoes.

Inside the terminal, she jostled her way to the luggage carousel—surprised that everyone seemed to be smoking as they waited with dour faces for their baggage. This detail alone made Lara feel foreign. She swallowed hard, as a panic that she had made the wrong decision rose and fell in tiny waves inside her.

※

When Lara had first announced her plans to visit Germany, college friends had been excited for her, if surprised that she was traveling alone. Her mother had been understanding, but apprehensive. Lara herself had been the most shocked by her decision. She remembered leaving the travel agent in a daze—it seemed too easy to book a trip so momentous.

But where was she really going? Lara felt fruitless and drifting, conscious of her twenties starting to roll forward without her. Maybe, she thought, this was grief. Whatever it was, Lara discovered it had many different textures. Some days it gave her the feeling of swimming endless laps through thick gray water, without ever finding a place to raise her head and breathe. At times it prickled like gully grass. Once it sang to her, and despite herself, she felt comforted.

Mostly Lara hated its dark pretense at friendship. Like a stray dog, it had a way of drawing alongside her, as if it cared—or even needed her. It then devastated her with a closeness that filled the room, so that sometimes she could not answer the phone, or even—on some mornings—open her eyes to begin the day.

It had begun as a way to anchor herself, fingering the objects. She had picked up first the ragged postcard and let the tears come afresh as she saw her beloved Opa rip up other postcards and grumble. She felt Oma's quietness near her as she held the lace and gazed out toward the hills. When Lara held the peg, in her mind she played her cello while Opa stood next to her, listening. Lara even dug out her book on birds and retraced the pages with her now grown fingers.

Where was she? Where was he? Had her grandparents taken something of her with them? Which part? In trams, walking along the street, drinking a solitary coffee in the music school café, she would berate herself for slipping down into numbness. And now they were selling the beloved house with the honeyed walls. Someone else would live there. They would subdivide the block, and Lara would never return.

She had wrapped and hidden the SS pin, separate from the other precious ornaments. From the moment Lara had touched the runes, it seemed that a fearful ghost mouthed words at her that she could not grasp. And that ghost was her grandfather. That ghost was also her love for him. Lara's roots grew from the stone house, and all it held. But now, a single, tarnished pin threatened her history—her childhood, her self, had been uprooted. Some days, Lara felt like a dry wreath, helpless before the wind.

It was easier to keep the pin where she could pretend to herself that she had never seen it, or touched it with her hands. Lara tried to forget it was there. Then steadily, the object had drifted over her life like a startling, delicate cobweb. Spider-like, it had bound her thoughts. She had to find a way, somehow, to untangle herself.

One afternoon, having cut class and stayed in her pajamas all day, she watched *The Sound of Music*. Perhaps this was foolish. But then, maybe Maria would look straight into Lara's dull heart, and wake up the child she had been. Perhaps she would find herself again.

The film's opening rolled into the mist and rocky back-stage of the Alps, with their chilling cliffs and veils of snow. Lara stroked the black mahogany peg. She heard the door shake as her flatmate arrived, with groceries and textbooks, to take over the apartment with her endless singing practice and overpowering scent of Ylang-Ylang essential oil. Lara paused the video, then stood to escape into the kitchen.

"You watching that again? You're so sweet!"

Her flatmate heaved the shopping onto the kitchen table. Lara prickled, but helped unpack dried lentils, flour and organic apples. She knew she was not sweet. She was sour, she was bitter, she was lost and she didn't know what steps to take to find her way.

Lara grabbed another organic apple, and noticed an especially dark bruise on its matte skin. In her peripheral vision, a frozen novice nun on the TV screen held her arms out, welcoming her to Austria. That was when Lara had the idea—the crazy idea of visiting Germany. Alone.

She left the groceries and disappeared to her room with the peg before her flatmate asked any questions. As she wrapped and returned the objects to her closet, she felt their presence under her fingers—they seemed to agree, to urge her onwards. Lara was frightened to fly somewhere on her own, but it was as if they compelled her to arrange the journey: the compass, the postcard, the feather. And the SS lapel pin. Especially the pin. Why was it in Opa's things? Its presence threatened them both. She needed to find out. She needed to find him. Just once more.

Lara had to wait for more than an hour until her pack rolled like a sedated animal onto the pleated conveyor. She was offered no help as she struggled to heave it onto the floor, and then onto her back—which ached from having slept on the plane.

Eventually Lara managed to move cautiously through Customs, and parked herself on a high stool in an airport bistro. She ordered an over-priced coffee, but didn't care—she needed to get her bearings and just sit for a moment before entering the world that was pressing its face to the glass doors. Lara couldn't quite believe she was here.

Her coffee arrived, and she again opened the envelope addressed in her mother's careful handwriting, re-read the card and examined the ticket for the Mediterranean cruise. This added gift had been a surprise that she had been instructed not to unveil until the plane had taken off.

Lara had first read the card as the hostess was maneuvering down the aisle with a trembling cart of drinks, and she had been both shocked and excited by her mother's generosity. As she had explained in the card, Mum wanted her to end her explorations in a way that she would always remember. Lara had experienced a moment of stung pride—saving up for the trip by herself had been a high priority—but she also knew that this would be a way to see a part of Europe that she hadn't even considered visiting on her tight student's budget.

Lara slid the card back into the flat canvas wallet strung around her neck, and tucked it under her shirt. Even if she had to rough it for the next few months, she would have a piece of relative luxury waiting for her at the end of it all. She drained the last of her airport coffee, and consulted her guidebook.

A couple of hours later, Lara found herself booking a room through the tourist desk at Zoo Station. She felt so new and awkward, so annoyed at how long it took to create German sentences, even simple ones that could convey her urgent need for a place to stay.

Her pack seemed to have fallen asleep on her shoulders and doubled in weight. By the time Lara clumped up the stairs to the tiny room in a Charlottenburg pension, she was wondering whether she had overestimated her stamina and capacity for adventure.

She spent most of her first day in Berlin sprawled on a creaking bed, her guidebook next to her shoes, and the sullen lump of a pack only partly open. Lara tried to catch up on sleep and will herself to be excited that she had actually arrived in Germany.

38.

Sleep made an enormous difference. Lara felt braver, if only because her vision was no longer blurry, and her German sentences were becoming increasingly coherent. She had arrived without much of an itinerary in mind. She wanted to wander Berlin, visit galleries, and improve her German. And somehow, find out something about her Opa.

The journey evolved during the first two weeks. Lara did simple things: caught public transport and watched people, stared at the river Spree, and bought a couple of pieces of eccentric clothing at one of the curious little shops near where she was staying. She traveled locally. She wrote postcards, read books, and learned German vocabulary at night. She kept a diary.

On the single wooden shelf in her room, Lara lined her objects, so they could catch the dreary November light. As she drifted off to sleep, and lay half-awake in the morning, she meditated on where they might have come from, and what they might mean. Could they point her in any sort of path, to find out something? Lara ached for Opa to take her hand and show her where to go—she needed to find some place where she could see a hand-print on the wall, and match her own skin to the painted stone.

Three weeks after her plane had landed in Europe, she began to feel lonely. It was a cold, overcast afternoon. As everything was always in motion in Berlin, it felt odd to be standing in her pension room looking out the window at the street, or lying on her bed thinking; Lara wanted to be moving, too. She decided to set off in the direction of the Cecilianhof Palace, and wondered how far she could get without catching the tram, or the light fading. She grabbed her coat and her diary, and walked out the door.

People moved purposefully past her—or maybe it was just that they walked fast, and this made them appear to have somewhere important to go. As she wandered, Lara sensed the movement of old buildings dying and being torn down. She heard and felt the rumble of earthmovers, of cars and vans, of trains. Sometimes it seemed that the sounds emanated from the very core of the earth and that all this activity was just reverberations, echoes of a deeper churning.

There was something profound about Berlin; everything seemed symbolic of a greater human story. It seemed to Lara that all the history she had studied had gone to her head, and taken over her imagination. She felt in the midst of a film, timeframes and images dissolving over each other. That man walking ahead of her transformed into a soldier, because in another time, a soldier passed that way. Bullet holes punctuated the walls, as if they had only just been fired, and warriors momentarily hidden themselves. And everywhere, her Opa walked before her, but Lara always arrived too late to find him.

It started to get dark. The sky began folding in on itself—there was no announcement, no big, gilded blast of color as the sun left, but immediately the gray hardened, and muffled the edges of things.

I had better head back.

She glanced at her map and realized that the path to her simple lodgings, although straightforward, was long. She began walking, and after twenty minutes or so she saw a bright sign indicating a bar. As she drew closer, she could see the warm, red glow inside and decided that the decor looked respectable. Suddenly she was aware of her legs aching. A beer would be good just now, just here.

Lara turned into the doorway, then stepped up off the street, and into a carpeted hallway. The interior of the bar looked like someone's living room. It was cozy and brightly lit by a huge glass chandelier—fake crystal, she presumed—that hung from the center of the ceiling. There were a few polished black tables, and plenty of high stools clustered near the counters and at the windows. Several people turned to look at her, but with no more than a cursory glance; there were no lewd once-overs, just the registering of a new arrival. She felt reassured. Yes, she would buy a drink.

The glasses were tall and thin, sparkling with golden fluid. Gripping hers, Lara perched at one of the windows. She heard voices nearby. They were young, laughing voices, mostly female. She half-turned her head and saw a group of young Germans watching her, smiling.

Great, she thought to herself, *I'm that easily identifiable as a tourist.* She stared out the window, although there was nothing to see now except a blur of misty headlights gliding down the road outside.

"Entschuldigung?"[10]

Lara's shoulder twitched with surprise, and she turned toward the voice—a woman her age, she guessed, with short blonde hair and a deep red scarf wound around her slim neck. She was tall, casually dressed in jeans and a wool sweater. Lara smiled politely, then in surprise as the woman spoke to her in English.

"You are American?"

Lara grimaced. "No, definitely not. And I'm not British either."

"Then Irish?"

"No, try again."

"Your accent is strange."

So's yours, Lara thought ungraciously. All she wanted was to enjoy her beer on her own, and then get something to eat. Then sleep. It had been an active day. The young woman, however, continued to stand next to her, smiling encouragingly.

"Ich komme aus Australien,"[11] said Lara finally, with a tired smile.

---

10   Excuse me.
11   I come from Australia.

The woman grinned, *"Du sprichst gut Deutsch. Komm, setz dich neben uns hin!"*[12]

She motioned to where the rest of the group sat sprawled in a relaxed way on the other side of the room.

Lara gave in to the friendly voice, and the promise of company. She walked over to the table, shyly keeping herself tucked behind the young woman, whose name turned out to be Annika. After she had introduced herself, and offered Lara the only empty chair at the table, Annika then found herself another one from across the room. This was kind, Lara thought. The others were also smiling.

Opposite her sat another young woman, her red hair short and perky. She was dressed in a cropped leather jacket. The young woman leaned forward, extending her arm carefully so as not to spill her glass of beer. She held out her hand to shake Lara's.

"Jacquie," she offered.

"Lara."

Jacquie winked at her. "We were trying to work out who you were. You came in with such a frown on your face that we became instantly curious."

Lara felt herself coloring. "I didn't think I was frowning," she murmured lamely. She could feel her mental gears clicking sluggishly into German, and she hoped that she would not make too great a fool of herself.

"You must have been thinking hard about something, right?" The voice came from another direction. Lara noticed that there were two men with them, sitting on Jacquie's left. They were dressed like students—old coats, faded jeans, scruffy hair. They grinned and also shook hands with her.

"I'm Zak, by the way, and you don't have to tell us what you were thinking! Not straight away, anyhow."

His free and easy manner made her feel comfortable, and she smiled.

---

12   You speak good German. Come sit with us!

"I *was* thinking, actually. I was thinking that I really, really wanted a beer."

They all burst out laughing at that, and the other young man hopped up and glanced around at everyone before introducing himself. His eyes held hers for a moment, and she was surprised by how green they were.

"I'm Anton. And I'm about to buy us all another round, so I'll see you anon!" He ran one hand through his hair, and left for the bar.

Lara settled into her chair and was very glad that she had been thirsty. These were nice people.

Three beers later, and they were really nice people. The two men were students. Zak was studying medicine, and Anton was at drama college. Jacquie worked for a magazine, and Annika was studying law part-time, and spending the rest of her time going out with Zak. Lara found with relief that her German was doing alright, and the few mistakes she made were amusing, and added to the fun of the evening.

"Why have you come here? Are you studying in Berlin?" asked Zak, reaching over to grab Annika's hand.

"Sort of." She paused, not quite sure how to express her reasons for being here—she wasn't even sure herself. She noticed Anton watching her. "I'm here for a vacation, really. Next semester doesn't start for me until March."

How could she even begin to explain? *I have brought a mahogany peg, a broken compass and a feather with me. And a Nazi lapel pin. I have lined them up on a shelf in Charlottenberg and am wanting to know what to do next. And have you seen my grandfather?*

"Fantastic! So, how long are you in Europe?"

"I'm only really spending time in Germany. I'm probably not going to see much of anything else."

She didn't want to tell them about the Mediterranean cruise that hung like a promise at the end of her trip; the extravagance of it suddenly embarrassed her.

"Pity. Paris is incredible. So is Prague."

"And Berlin? What do you think of our city?" asked Annika blithely, taking a gulp of her drink.

Lara thought for a moment before answering. How could she put into words—let alone German words—the tumult it had somehow produced inside her in such a short time?

"Pretty amazing so far," she replied finally, feeling awkward at her insipid response. "A lot of building going on. People look a bit depressed."

The others all looked at each other and broke into laughter. Lara joined in, since her statement suddenly seemed so ludicrous.

"Have you ever been to Australia?" she asked.

"No, but I really want to go. All that sun and the outback!" Jacquie grinned. "Camel rides! That's what I'd love to do … and surf!"

Lara raised her chin slightly. "There's much more to Australia than that."

"And much more to Berlin," added Anton.

Lara found herself feeling embarrassed. "Those were only my first impressions. I've only been here three weeks."

Anton smiled at her.

Jacquie leaned forward and touched Lara's arm. "Where are you staying?"

"In a pension."

Then something happened. The cog that shifts everything.

"You can come and stay at my place, if you like. My flat-mate has just gone on holiday and won't be back for weeks—months even—if she gets her way! South America or something exotic like that. There's a bed for you and everything." She looked at Lara eagerly.

Lara's eyes met Jacquie's, and the young woman laughed.

Do you work for a magazine? Can you do research? Could you help me begin?

So she said yes. She was dazed. It felt like booking the ticket. And yet Lara found herself somehow buying the next round of drinks in celebration. The trip to Berlin, the trip into herself, had finally begun.

39.

"What do you mean, you've missed the boat?"

Lara rested her chin on her hands, deeply interested. The glasses around her were filled to varying levels with glowing red wine, looking like hearts on tiny stilts, beating and thrumming with the flow of their talk.

The first course had by now been well and truly eaten. The plates had been cleared, and the chairs pushed back. In the middle of the table, a glass jar nearly burst with orange tulips. It seemed that the colder the weather became, the more colorful were the flowers Jacquie and Lara found to brighten up the room.

They were talking about Germany—again. They often discussed Germany. Maybe it was the questions Lara asked them sometimes, as they met together. Or perhaps it was that the Second World War seemed to be a history that refused to leave the present alone.

"It is not my history," snapped Annika firmly. "They were not decisions I made. Or my family. It is not my fault. I refuse to think about it as my fault."

"Is fault an issue?" asked Lara tentatively.

"Who said it was an issue?" Annika retorted. "I just said it wasn't my fault."

"We've been to Dachau," said Zak. Next to him Annika pulled a petal from part of the bouquet that had begun to wilt as they had sat there.

Lara wondered whether she shouldn't have spoken, and all the time she felt Anton watching her. Was he cataloging her responses? She tried to listen more carefully to what Zak was saying.

"We had to. Every German student has to come face to face with what happened."

Jacquie fiddled with her fork. "We are forced. Of course we feel bad about it."

"I don't," Annika interrupted, but Jacquie ignored her.

"We all feel desperately that it should never have happened. But what can we do now?"

"It's too much learning," responded Zak. "At some point it must stop, and we must begin to look forward."

"Like the rest of Europe," Jacquie added.

Lara noticed that Anton hadn't spoken. He seemed to carry himself as if in his heart he lived somewhere very far away, that he was constantly just visiting them. It made Lara wonder sometimes whether he didn't approve of her. She suddenly realized she had tuned out, and quickly focused again, in case a response was demanded of her.

"We can never be like the rest of Europe," muttered Annika darkly. "Europe will never let us be like the rest of Europe."

"When we travel, we say we are Berliners, not Germans."

"Yeah, that's right. Berliners," Jacquie nodded in agreement at Zak. "It's crazy, but you are given such a hard time, you know?"

Zak gave a sardonic half-smile. "People think at the back of every German is a Nazi, just waiting for the moment to come out and shoot them."

"It sucks," Annika added, twisting the stem of her wineglass. "You are not allowed to be proud of being German."

"No," Jacquie agreed. "That is dangerous. Patriotism is dangerous."

"Germany is a thing of the past," Zak said sagely. "We can never lose the Holocaust. It will always be here. We are always being reminded."

"Even though it is not our fault."

"It is not our fault."

This thing again, fault, wondered Lara, and caught Anton's eye. To her surprise he didn't look away. She turned her gaze back toward the others.

"Germany has forever missed its chance of being a part of Europe. We have missed the boat. We will never be forgiven." Zak continued, his fingertips cosseting the petals nearest to him.

Lara began to wish that she had never broached the subject.

"By others, perhaps. But by God—"

"Right, Anton. Whatever."

They were always like this toward him, Lara noticed—friendly, dismissive. They found it difficult, she thought, to relax and accept his convictions. Then again, so did she. And yet he intrigued her. Zak opened another bottle of Italian wine, and she watched her glass turn red.

Jacquie laughed suddenly.

"We are so intense … all of us!" She looked pointedly at Lara. "You, too, you Australian!"

She jumped up and pressed a button on the stereo, and jazz music soon wilted the fear and anger as the heat had done to the flowers. The night changed gear and, as often happened after such discussions, the conversation became frenetically light, the laughter bold and defiant.

Lara knew that things would continue well without her, and she slipped out onto the tiny balcony. Above the glow of the city, the stars were so faded that she could barely see them. She heard the glass door open behind her. She knew it was Anton, even before he spoke.

"Don't mind Annika. Her grandfather was very involved as a Nazi official, he was high up."

Lara kept trying to find the stars. "Was he punished?" She spoke hesitantly, trying not to sound as curious as she felt.

Anton shook his head. "No. Like so many others, there was not enough hard evidence to convict him. He was a … a … paper monster."

In spite of the seriousness of their conversation, Lara laughed and turned to face him. Behind them the room glowed with chattering faces.

"A what?" She wondered whether her German was as funny as his English.

Anton joined her at the railing. "He signed papers. A desk job. But he was just as guilty."

They both turned to face the street.

"I think I find that sort of thing harder to understand," she said after a while, wondering what it would be like to be Annika.

"What do you mean?"

"Well," she began, then wasn't sure how to continue. She suddenly realized that she was talking about real people—relatives, loved ones, of those she had become so close to in such a short time.

"People like that, you feel somehow that they must be the weakest of them all ... " She trailed off, trying to find the right words. "I mean—even though I find it hard not to hate those who actually committed atrocities—they did believe in what they were doing; I suppose at least they were being true to what they thought, even though it was so horrible. But ... but the ones who kidded themselves that they were not involved, because they wanted to keep their heads down, I think they are the ones I despise the most."

"I know," Anton replied.

The two of them stood there for a while, looking out into the night. Anton finally spoke.

"My grandfather was one of those," he admitted.

"Sorry," said Lara, feeling her face going as red as the wine. She was glad it was dark. "Trust me to put my foot in it. I really am sorry."

"Sorry that he was a Nazi, or that you may have offended me?"

"Both."

"Believe me, Lara, I wish so much sometimes that I could go back in time and convince him not to do what he did, but I've given up hitting myself over the head for something that I have no control over."

She wondered whether his decision to let it go had something to do with what he had said at the table, but she didn't want to ask.

"I found out as much as I could about him," he continued. He cocked his head, and smiled wryly in the darkness.

"German record keeping," he added. "Brilliant."

"You mean?"

"He left a diary, a day-by-day account. It disgusted me, the way he could comment on everything happening around him, and at the same time believe he was distant from it all. Even afterwards he would say all the same old things … you know, that he never knew, he wasn't responsible, that he had to do it, otherwise his family would have suffered. But really he was a coward. And guilty."

"Perhaps he was afraid?"

"No doubt."

"I wonder, though, whether I would have felt like that."

"Probably. I think everyone was afraid at some time or another. But that's the point."

"What do you mean?"

"The point is that it is not just being afraid of something, but what you decide to do about it."

"Oh."

He laughed gently. "Have I said something wrong? You've gone all quiet."

She noticed he had moved closer to her, close enough that she could feel the weight of his arm against her shoulder.

"Oh, no," she muttered hurriedly, "It's just, well … " There was no way she was going to tell him what she had been thinking. "I just hope I wouldn't have been like that. I like to think I would have done something."

"It is easy for us to say that. We were not there. Lara, we have no conception of what it would have been like to have been in such … bondage. That's what it was. Bondage. Slavery to a regime of terror. We have no idea how we would have reacted to that." He ran his hand through his hair, a habitual gesture, as if trying to knead his thoughts through his fingers.

"We can still say they were wrong, though. Annika's grandfather and … "

"And mine."

"Yes," she murmured. *And mine?*

"Of course. We must, or else we are not human. But you can't afford to think too much along the lines of what you would have done."

"Why not?"

"You go crazy after a while. That's what started to happen to me. You start believing you were actually there, and that somehow this is your fault too."

"Everyone keeps using that word."

He paused before he next spoke, feeling around for the right words. "You don't understand, Lara, what it is to be German."

She went cold. She so wanted to understand, to fit in with them.

"My grandfather was German," she said hopefully, then felt embarrassed when he laughed. But he was not mocking her.

"Really?" he asked.

It was strange to talk about Opa with someone else. She already recognized the choking feeling in her chest, when something brushed too close to her sorrow, and threatened to wake it. Lara felt that grief formed a secret core inside her, and now it so often seemed that she witnessed life around her through a thick glass barrier, while others were out there experiencing it. Suddenly she yearned to be in the sunlight too, to feel normal again.

"He came out to Australia in the late 40's. He was a soldier, I think, but he never talked about anything from his time before emigrating."

"His secret life, huh?"

She cringed at his words.

"Mum told me he wasn't a war criminal or anything like that."

There was an uncomfortable pause.

"I am sure he was a good man."

"He was."

They stood awkwardly, and Lara wished she hadn't been so defensive.

She recalled her objects, wrapped carefully in a special place in Jacquie's spare room. And especially the one that she would never show anybody. Lara sensed the cogs shifting again, and found herself holding the railing tightly.

"I just wish I knew more," she said softly.

Anton turned to her, and she was surprised again by how clear and steady his eyes were as they searched her face.

"Is that why you have come to Germany?"

"Oh I don't know. I just needed to travel ... "

"But you said you only have come to Germany."

There was the cruise, but for some reason that felt like a secret.

"I've always fancied myself as a bit of a gypsy, but maybe roots are important after all. I keep getting curious about my ancestors." Her words sounded so flimsy, thrown out like paper. She wished she could say what she meant.

"Is he still alive?" Anton asked gently.

"Oh, no. He died, a year ago."

"Were you close to him?"

"Yes." Lara's voice wobbled. "Were you to yours?"

"No. Well, maybe. I felt strangely connected to him, but I didn't love him. I don't think I could, after what I found out."

"Well, I—loved mine. I just want to know that he ... didn't do anything I wouldn't have done."

"Yes."

They were quiet again, thinking. Behind the glass wall, the others laughed and carried on, creating a blur of happy noise and color. Outside, Anton and Lara stood like trees, gently moved by the night wind. A car passed below them, and from somewhere a train whistled.

"Do you know where he lived?" Anton asked, his voice quiet, focused.

"No. I only have the most bizarre assortment of things that he left me. None of them make any sense."

She was amazed that she had so casually told him about the secret collection that lay hidden in her room.

A voice hallooed them from inside. "Hey, you two! What's going on out there?"

Lara blushed. Anton just winked at her, and then pulled a face at Annika through the window.

"We're talking World War Two," he called back.

"Again?" She groaned. "Do you have to be so serious?"

"Do they have to be so intrusive?" muttered Lara. Anton turned to her and touched her arm. Her stomach churned, and she wondered if he could tell.

"Lara, I will help you find your grandfather."

"Really? How on earth?"

"I want to help you try. You have come all this way."

"But I didn't come here for that."

"Maybe you didn't, or maybe you did. Your deepest motivation … ," he intoned mysteriously.

"Drama school," she teased, and he assumed a melodramatic pose. He opened his mouth.

"No! Don't start!" She giggled, as lines of Goethe began to pour forth with exaggerated eloquence. "Get me out of here!" she squealed and ducked inside. "Help! He's starting to act!" she cried as she threw herself between Jacquie and Annika.

Their response was simple, and the same as it always was. Ten cushions battered the young man as he came back into the room, and yet another bottle of wine appeared.

40.

The next morning, the phone rang. It was Anton.

"Hi. Let's get started."

"What?" She was barely awake, and her voice sounded foggy.

"Your grandfather. Let's find him."

"But I've just woken up!"

"Yes," he laughed, "I can hear that."

"But it's Saturday!"

"I'll be there in half an hour."

He hung up, still laughing, and Lara made a face. She swung her feet over the bed, and as her eye caught the thin wedge of sunlight on the edge of the blind, she felt excitement waken and roll around inside her, until she too was laughing. Anton was coming to get her, and they would explore together, and maybe they would find out something. She had no idea where to start, but his energy made her feel that they would do it.

Then she heard the whisper of the pin again. The haunted part of her, she knew, did not want to succeed. She was not sure she could not bear the discovery that Opa had been another man. Like her father.

Jacquie was still fast asleep when Anton arrived, but Lara was gulping down dark bread and cheese, waiting anxiously for the coffee to finish percolating on the stove.

"Enough for me, too?" he asked hopefully as she answered the door, and she nodded, her mouth full.

The two of them sat in the cramped kitchen, holding hot mugs and watching the slender park next door embrace the day. An old man meandered along with a tiny dachshund, and two children in red coats dashed across the grass to the only swing. Lara watched them fight, and then a woman in blue swept one small figure into her arms, while the other one clambered onto the swing seat and started slicing rhythmically back and forth through the cold morning air. She loved Saturdays—especially this Saturday.

She smiled at him. "So, where do we start?"

He looked out the window thoughtfully, and then his eyes brightened. *Like agate,* Lara decided.

"The objects!" Anton thumped the table.

"But they are so unhelpful, Anton. Really, they are not documents or anything—although there is a concert ticket."

"That's something! Where is it?"

Lara got to her feet and disappeared for a moment into her room. When she emerged he was pouring more coffee. She sat down, pulling a fresh cup toward her.

They were silent as Lara cautiously opened the bag. The plastic crackled, as the objects she had pondered so many times slipped into her hand—except the pin.

She laid out the items carefully on the table. Anton looked at the compass, but kept his hands around his coffee.

"These are amazing. Is that a compass?"

"It's broken."

"It is such a metaphor."

Lara didn't reply, but sat watching him turning it over with his eyes. She realized he was waiting for permission.

"You can pick it up."

He did, and examined it closely. Then he glanced up at her. "The feather?"

"Sure. Help yourself."

One by one he touched each item. "They are elements," he murmured, "elements in a design. This is wonderful!"

She watched him with a mixture of awe and amusement—and gratitude. He understood.

"We sometimes have a class, you know," he continued, with quiet enthusiasm, "where we take objects like these—I say 'like,' but they are ordinary, nothing like yours—and we then design a performance from them. They are catalysts, maps even, of character and action."

"Sounds like fun."

"Yes." Then he looked at her seriously. "But work, too. It is not easy."

"Okay. Please, I didn't mean—"

He laughed uncertainly then, and put down the ticket he had been holding. "Yes." He ran his hand through his hair while Lara's eyes followed the gesture. "All the jokes are getting to me, no?"

Lara wasn't sure what to say—they did tease him a lot, she had to admit, but they always insisted that they did it to help him keep his feet on the ground.

"But don't you mind always having to play other people?"

"It is a game. I play at being other people, I don't believe in becoming them. Oh Lara, the *ideas* we discover are so worthwhile." He was animated now, his eyes bright. "You get to explore the ideas physically, as it were, rather than just talking about them. But,"—he added lightly—"it is not what makes my life."

"Yes, I know," said Lara hurriedly. She did not want him to get started talking about his beliefs. For some reason it troubled her, and even more so because she did not understand why. She wanted to change the topic, and fortunately he did it for her.

"There is a history museum here—no," he corrected himself, "a library. Enormous. We can go there. You said he was a soldier?"

"That's what I think."

"Well, he will be listed there if he was one, and we can find out."

Lara shuddered. She thought again, that perhaps she didn't want to find out anything. What if she found out something she could never un-know?

"Don't be scared," he said softly. He stood up. "Let's go."

They left the apartment, and made their way to the library. It was a huge, intimidating building that seemed armed—appropriate for a military museum, Lara thought as they stepped through the doors.

After so many years of wondering and searching in her mind, it felt surreal to be standing at the microfiche reader, seeing her Opa's name and details staring at her in luminescent white. It had been so quick, after Anton had questioned the librarian and slotted the dark square under the screen. Lara had nervously steered the handle, and for the first few moments had been disoriented as names swirled in front of her, before finding her bearings and gradually settling the dates.

"I can't believe it!" she kept repeating. Something in her felt it should not have been this simple. But then, according to these records, Tomas Müller had not been anything other than an ordinary soldier. She looked again, closely. There was definitely no mention of any SS involvement. Confusion muddied the euphoria of relief. Where had Opa got the lapel pin, and—perhaps more importantly—why had he held onto it all those years? Even here, in front of the very information she had been seeking, Lara still had no answer to her questions. She could not help speculating whether the records had been tampered with, the truth conveniently imagined away. After all, she had been tempted. Could she visit his town, and find someone there who might know the real story? Again Lara was seized with both fear, and the compulsion to know.

"Zweibach. Never heard of it," muttered Anton, scribbling the word down with a pencil. "We can look at a map, that's easy. Taking time off college to go there, not so easy."

"I'll go. You don't have to come."

"Yes I do."

"No you don't."

"Yes I do."

"No you ... What's happening here?" She laughed.

"I'm on the case, Lara. I want you to go home satisfied."

Does he actually want me to go home? Lara wondered,

feeling suddenly lonely. If he felt like that, there was no way she wanted to invest any more time with him on this. She bristled—he seemed to think her Opa was a case, a file to be read and analyzed, unsavory conclusions drawn.

This was her journey, she decided there and then, not Anton's.

"Please don't come," she said abruptly, gathering up her coat and gloves.

"Why not?" He looked surprised.

"I don't know. You shouldn't miss classes, and I want to go during the week, when things are normal, and I can see what it was—is—like."

"Lara, I'm coming!" he insisted. "I want to find out now. You've got me feeling like a detective!"

"This isn't a movie, it's me!" she snapped, and he looked startled. "It's my past, my history, and I just want to see this by myself." Her lip trembled, as did her voice. "And my Opa is not a character in one of your plays."

Several others raised their heads from their books, and she lowered her voice.

"Sorry, but can you just understand? Please?"

Lara realized that Anton had hurt her, and that she felt angry, and that he had absolutely no idea. He put his hand on her arm.

"What have I done?" he asked, concerned.

She was annoyed because she couldn't tell him. She couldn't admit that she wanted him to keep her here, that she had nothing to go back to, and no idea where her life was headed. It was all right for him, she reasoned enviously—he had a direction, a purpose. He believed that his life had meaning, but Lara knew that hers was just drifting.

How she wanted him to know what it was like to have someone put his hand on yours, and help you see inside a cave, someone to hold you under the moon, when you had been forgotten. She needed Anton to know that a person who does those things cannot be so loving, and so terrible—someone like that can't have driven others into a great pit.

And how could she say all this? He had just made it clear to her what he felt, or at least she thought so.

"Thanks," she replied coolly, "but I'm going to go now, if that's okay."

She moved quickly out of the catalogue room and was soon out on the street. She wandered in the direction of the train station. She would book a ticket and just go—even go today, if it wasn't too far.

41.

It was a longer distance than she had thought, Lara discovered, as she checked at the information counter. But it was still early enough in the day. Lara paid her money and went to wait on the station platform. She sat down on a bench where she could watch people. She scuffed at a cigarette butt that lay next to her shoe. A piece of gravel skidded away from her, and a sparrow darted to the ground nearby. It cocked its head questioningly at her, and she was reminded immediately of Anton.

Had she been unfair? In the hard light of the station, the glamour of her exit from the library receded, and Lara felt a bit stupid. She knew she had been melodramatic—although, she mused, he should be used to that. Suddenly she wished she were back there. She had been so quick to judge his opinion of her grandfather, and maybe he was genuinely interested. And perhaps, she thought cautiously, he did like her after all.

She checked her watch—another fifteen minutes. Great. She was freezing already, and she was about to spend a day on her own, when she had been so excited about being with Anton.

Forget it, she berated herself. *Just go on your day trip and see what you can find out. Be realistic. He's being sensible—you're just here for a vacation, so why would he even waste his time.*

Brakes screeched, and dirt flew into her face as the train pulled in. Lara embarked and chose a seat near the window where she could watch the countryside emerge.

A fat woman in Bavarian dress squeezed in next to her, followed by a thin man, whom she assumed was the woman's husband. They were both panting. The woman muttered something in a dialect Lara didn't understand, and then pulled a bottle of lurid purple liquid from under her coat. It was as if Lara were not actually there. The woman produced two shot glasses from her handbag, and the couple began to drink. A pungent odor permeated the compartment, and Lara tried not to dry retch. Instead, she gave herself up to staring out the window.

The landscape began as flat, even dull. It was early December, and still too warm for snow, but the color had already seeped out of the trees and sky. The world seemed to be falling asleep—except for the cold wind that rubbed its hands with delight as it enjoyed its seasonal paths through the bare trees.

As they pulled out of the station, she noticed huge freighter containers resting at the sidings. All she could think of were cattle trucks jammed with human cargo, heading east. Those twin lightning bolts—she could not escape them. Lara felt she understood what it must be like for the others to live here with so many reminders, in spite of all the new buildings and landmarks.

The woman next to her belched. Lara stared more intensely at the land that now undulated with low hills outside her window. A thousand images marched across her mind in time with the rhythmic chortling of the train.

She thought first of Anton, then of her grandfather. She tried to picture her Opa in this landscape she was traversing. She pressed his gray figure into the backdrop of each town and village they passed. She wondered if he had even ridden the train as she did now, and then she tried to visualize him seated opposite her in the carriage, next to the thin, drunken man with his slurred dialect and puce-stained fingers. Had Opa ever been to Berlin? But of course he had—she remonstrated herself for forgetting—there was the concert ticket for the Berliner Philharmonic.

She combed through her memories of her grandfather for anything he may have said about where he came from, but all she could find today was an image of him carefully placing records of cello concertos on his gramophone, then sitting forward and gazing inward. He never leaned back and relaxed to listen to his music, and it was always impossible to interrupt him.

When she had given Opa a cassette of her own playing many years earlier, he had sat forward to listen to that, too, but she had felt embarrassed—his already obsolete tape player lifted and tightened the tone, so that it sounded like an old reed instead of her cello. Even so, he had listened closely, nodding his head to the pulse of the instrument. He had loved music, even though it always seemed to make him sad.

For the first time, the memory of Opa lacked a face. His hands were clear, wrinkled and strong, but his eyes, his smile, were the mist after a star dies. It had taken one year. In another year, what would have vanished? How long would his hands, his voice, survive in her mind?

The drunken couple pulled on their coats, and the woman held the bottle up to the light of the window, scrutinizing the thick fuchsia residue at its base. Then she popped it under her coat and wrapped the shot glasses expertly in a plastic bag. Lara realized they were nearing a station. As the sign swung into view, she read *Zweibach* and quickly flustered around for her own coat. She had not expected to have arrived so quickly. She could not even recall an inspector having checked the tickets, so absorbed had she been in her own thoughts.

Lara was forced to stand close behind the couple who had shared her journey as they pushed their way down the narrow corridor toward the door. She cringed at their odoriferous breath and noisy exit from the train. Lara then remembered her own exit from the library, and felt even more mortified. *Too late now,* she consoled herself, and tried to feel excited about where she had now arrived.

Lara crossed the platform and left the station, as her traveling companions inserted themselves into a taxi and were whisked away. She decided to buy a map, so she turned back to the station to find one, but it was Saturday, and the booth was barred with an iron grid.

Well, then, she thought, *I will just have to find the way myself*—although the way to exactly what, she did not know. With a sunken heart, she trudged toward what she presumed was the town center. Lara realized that she must be in the old part of Zweibach—the houses were propped up by huge dark beams. Dwellings crushed against each other, and cobbled lanes drove crevices between them. Empty window boxes hung from some of the windows, promising red geraniums in warmer weather.

Even under the drab sky, the place had a modest beauty, although the houses seemed resigned. They sagged under their eaves as if they knew they had been forgotten—or maybe it was just the winter light that made them seem so forlorn.

Where do I begin?

The uneven road bore her onto a bridge from where she could see a church spire, and the water rushing beneath her, foamy and determined. She could see the horizon, and another town strung upon its edge, with spires and buildings like so many fingers prodding at the clouds. Beyond Zweibach sat wooded hills interspersed with clumps of houses and brown fields, creased with old plow lines and bordered by shaggy stone walls and dilapidated fences.

From her vantage point Lara could view the main square. On the other side of it was the new town. Judging by the architecture, it had sprung up since the 1950s. She decided that it must have been bombed heavily during the war, which would account for the awkward juxtaposition of old and new.

Lara stood on the bridge until her hands began to ache, and her eyes watered from the cold wind. She realized that she had no idea where to go. *Maybe there's an information board by the station that I didn't see.* Because she didn't know what else to do, she meandered back in the direction of the station.

As she got close, she heard another train arrive and depart. Then she noticed a wooden shelter to the left of her eye line. It looked promising; its walls were papered with colored squares, and a large poster that could possibly be a map. She made her way toward it, and then paused. A young man in a dark coat was walking from the station toward the same booth—a man whose walk she knew.

He came up to her, looking slightly embarrassed, but he quickly regained his customary collected expression.

"What are you doing here?" she exclaimed, then quickly apologized for being rude.

"You apologize now, but that's nothing on before," he prompted her, and she blushed.

"Yes. I am sorry for that, too. I shouldn't have stormed out like that!" She looked over his shoulder at the darkening sky. "Just a bit melodramatic."

"Mm … "

They stood in front of a huge map with a fat red arrow indicating where they were.

"Look, Lara," Anton continued, "I respect what you said and everything, but I just didn't believe that you really didn't want me to come." He stopped and ruffled his hair, looking bemused. "So I came. I hope that's … okay."

Lara didn't reply but fiddled instead with the edge of her scarf.

"Oh stop being so difficult!" he exploded, exasperated.

She was so annoyed with herself that she felt like crying.

"You are feeling sorry for yourself," he declared, trying to meet her eyes.

"No, I'm not!" she retorted, but she knew he was right.

"Yes, you … hold on!" He shook himself. "Not this again!" He stepped closer to her. "Please, don't be like this."

Then he did something quite unexpected. He touched her face, ever so gently. She looked up in shock.

"Please," he said again.

She felt completely disarmed.

Then he leaned forward and kissed her quickly, quietly, and unselfishly. He stood back, then gave her a tentative smile.

Lara couldn't speak—all she could do was stand with her eyes wide open and with what she knew was a stunned look on her face. He lifted a strand of hair and moved it behind her ear, and she let him. She felt so overwhelmingly happy that she burst into tears. He gave her a hug.

She tilted her head to look at him, and he took her hand.

"May I take you out for a beer?"

"Hold on, I'll just check my schedule," she quipped and looked at her watch. "Oh, yes, that should be fine. As long I can make my train home."

"Of course."

Then she stopped herself. *Home.* Home would be too soon, and no matter how hard she tried just to be in this moment, her return to Australia haunted her. She wanted to tell Anton not to do this, that she would be gone, that she couldn't … but he looked at her again. Lara found herself slipping under his arm.

"Oh," she added lightly, determinedly quelling her own doubts, "and as long as you can work out where we are."

"That's easy!" He pointed at the fat red arrow on the map. "Look closely, Lara. We are *here.*"

"Hah!"

"Now let's just head … that way."

He steered her toward the lane she had followed earlier, and the two of them eventually stood side by side on the bridge, taking in the expanse of town, land, and sky, with the river heaving itself away from them.

Had her grandfather stood here, too? Had he explored the fields and forests she could see now, and had his hands rested on the stone wall that separated them from the water? If Anton had not been holding her, she felt sure that the force of her questions would have hurled her off the bridge and into the current swirling below.

The wind was forceful, so they turned from the bridge and made their way along what appeared to be a main road—albeit ancient and knobbled—that after a short walk delivered them to the fringes of the town square. The tavern seemed to be the only building in the center of the old town that did not wear scars from the war. Sadly the restoration of the houses and shops had not been sensitive—jarring colors and modern materials had turned them into a distortion, at best, and at worst, a mockery of what they once had been.

There were also a bakery, a stone fountain, and a kiosk in the deserted, windswept square. Racks of postcards teetered, bearing garish photos of the tavern in bright sunlight, with clusters of brightly attired humanity sporting dated clothing and huge sunglasses.

"An art-gallery day," Lara mused as she surveyed the low-hanging cloud, and the dimming light in the square.

Occasionally someone hurried past with shoulders rounded against the wind. From the kiosk a woman braved the chill to pull in the postcard racks, and from somewhere distant a bell chimed the hour. It was three o'clock.

They entered the tavern and found it nearly empty. A woman with a face as dull as the day outside was wiping the counter. They ordered, and then sat near the window with its thick, old-fashioned glass.

"It didn't cost much to eat here," Anton said as they devoured a bland, second-rate pizza. He wiped his hands on his jeans. "We could come back next week. We should look up some people, read a guidebook entry or something. This weather is shocking today for exploring on foot."

"Who could we look up? I assume people aren't listed by age in this country," she replied uncertainly, resting into his shoulder. There was silence as Anton thought, and Lara shut her eyes. She forced herself just to be there, in that moment.

"I know!" He sat up quickly, and Lara knocked her glass. "The cemetery." He sat back with a satisfied look, and then drained the rest of his beer.

The bells rang out again. It was four o'clock. Lara frowned at the table, thinking of the rows of graves. It felt too soon. She still could not help thinking of him as alive, just out of her reach.

"We should go if we're going to catch the train to Berlin and not have to camp at the station!"

Anton nodded, thoughtful. "We will come back here soon."

"You're right." Lara wound her scarf around her neck, getting ready to meet the cold. She needed to make herself strong, somehow.

He stroked her hair. "If you really want to come here during the week, let's come Tuesday. It's soon, but not so soon that we can't do some groundwork first."

"What about tomorrow?"

"No—it's Sunday ... "

"Oh, yes. Sorry."

She had forgotten for a moment what divided them.

"You could come with me to church," he suggested hopefully.

She smiled and shook her head.

"Not tomorrow. Maybe some other time."

"Okay." He shrugged, then winked at her. "You don't think it could be a cultural experience for you?"

"It would be the same as home, only I wouldn't understand as much."

"And you understood anyway, did you?"

She tensed. "No, probably not," she admitted.

He became still and stared at his fingers, before lifting his gaze once more. "I'm sorry. You don't have to come. Of course you don't. But if you are ever interested ... "

He seemed suddenly vulnerable, and she reached out for his hand.

"Take me there, then. But not tomorrow. Not when there's ... people around, if you know what I mean. But maybe sometime you could show me ... " She let the words trail off.

The waitress dropped a glass—it shattered, and they both jumped. They noticed the failing light outside, and without any more talk they burrowed into their coats, pushed open the old doors, and made for the station.

As they crossed the bridge, Lara told Anton of her traveling companions.

"You saw some real Germans, then?" he replied wryly, and she laughed.

"You tell me."

"All of us, Lara … " He paused dramatically. "We look normal, but we're all secretly wearing *Lederhosen*."

Lara giggled, but at the same time couldn't help hoping that there weren't any other, darker secrets waiting to throw her into some river to be hurtled away.

42.

Lara spent Monday leafing through her German guide-book, and trying to discover what she could about Zweibach. The entry wasn't very helpful. It confirmed what she had guessed about the damage from Allied bombing during the war, but apart from that there was nothing that distinguished Zweibach from any other small town—except that the book commented on the poor reconstruction of old buildings, and recommended somewhat sarcastically that visitors stay on the train.

She sighed, put down the book, and surveyed the objects that she had now laid out in an orderly line next to her bed. Lara picked up the postcard—the photograph was of the Zweibach town square. She recognized the tavern now, and the stone fountain. She turned the card over and fruitlessly examined the smudge where a message had once been written. It must have been important, she speculated, for Opa to have kept it. She traced a finger over the faded cloud of ink. She would never know. In frustration, she placed it back and wandered out to the kitchen.

Jacquie had left a note for her on the table, which Lara read as she made herself a coffee. Her flat-mate would not be home for tea, so Lara made plans as she heated milk in the small silver saucepan on the range. She would go to see the Reichstag. Strangely enough, she hadn't been there yet, although she had seen it from a distance in her other explorations of the city.

Lara caught the train to nearest station, and then set off on foot through the brisk air, her hands thrust deep in her pockets. She thought of Annika and Zak sitting in classes, of Jacquie absorbed in front of a computer screen, tweaking words and images that would appear glossy and polished in a few weeks' time. Then she thought of Anton, and imagined his arm around her.

She turned onto Unter den Linden and passed beneath the uneven skeletal canopy of branches. It was not long before she was facing the broad steps that swept upward toward the regal and intimidating doors of the Reichstag entry. Lara stood for a moment at the base of the stairs, her skin rippling with a sudden chill as she stared up at the eagles carved in stone. The enormous columns were thick and terrifying, dwarfing the humans flitting at their base. In her imagination she could hear crowds cheering, the bright, tinny melodies of a military band, and the rhythmic clip of marching feet … She shook herself, and proceeded briskly up the many steps.

Once she was inside, the thrumming of cars swirling around the base of the building outside receded, and even her thoughts seemed to echo in the empty space. From where she stood, Lara could see a café where only one party sat enjoying a late lunch—a group of elderly Germans, the men wearing tiny feathers in their hats.

She had planned to wander through the place, but now that she was there, the urge to inspect everything dissipated, and Lara stood aimlessly in the middle of the foyer, feeling vaguely like she shouldn't be there at all. She figured, however, that since she was actually standing inside the doors, she should at least walk around a bit.

It was unsettling to hear her own shoes click across the smooth tiles. Once more, another era slid up next to her, its citizens gazing with wonder at her ability to enter this forbidden place. It was, once again, surreal—another vibrant juxtaposition of time frames, which always came as a shock, even though it had become such a common experience of late.

Lara's exploration was abruptly curtailed. The remaking of the city appeared to be happening here too, and a barricade of gaudy tape prevented her seeing very much at all. Occasionally she could hear the sounds of machinery in the distance, but the industrial groans were muffled by thick stone walls, and the oppressive atmosphere. Lara found herself trying to breathe more deeply, and suddenly she longed to be back outside.

Her excursion had taken more time than she realized. As she neared the foyer again, Lara noticed that the sky had begun to darken, and her watch now read four o'clock. The group of elderly Germans remained in the café, boldly ignoring a waiter who had begun to stack chairs on the tables, surrounding the patrons with a black metal forest of upturned legs.

She could hear the men and women clearly—their tipsy voices tumbled and slithered across the marble. The figures gestured and threw back their heads like cartoon characters. To Lara, they looked like hulking, dribbling dogs. It was grotesque, and fantastic: here were Germans the same age her grandfather would have been, were he alive, lounging, drinking and indulging in the heart of what had once been a seat of power and terror. Lara felt as if she were being crushed. She made her escape, and with relief burst out into the open air above the main steps.

On her walk back through the linden trees, Lara wondered if she would gain anything from returning to Zweibach. What if, she thought anxiously, the only survivors were more of the kind she had just observed in the Reichstag? And December was already here—again, Lara experienced the breathless sensation that she was running out of time to experience Germany; perhaps her funds should be allocated to visit some other place. She remembered what the others had told her of Prague, and Paris, and wondered whether she should actually see more of Europe … or maybe, she thought as she trudged along, she was just scared—as frightened of not finding anything as she was of discovering some terrible truth, even though the official records had assured her otherwise.

She stopped and pushed a strand of hair out of her eyes. Perhaps, she told herself as decisively as she could, it was just that she had been in one place long enough for her old restlessness to re-emerge. Traveling seemed to hold her depression at bay, supplanting it with new sights, sounds and people. Maybe if she just did other things for a while, then she would be able to clear her head of questions. She could simply enjoy her trip, relax and forget about who her grandfather was—who she might be, for that matter. Yes, that was it. She should see some more art galleries, spend more money on concert tickets, hear the Berliner Philharmonic. Catch a train to France.

If only it were that easy.

Lara counted on her fingers the number of days she had left and felt her heart being squeezed. It was not very long. What had she been doing? Lots of long walks, lots of reading, a day trip to the Wannsee, visits to Munich, to Nuremburg. She had traced the map of her history classes, as much as her meager finances had allowed, even with the generous rental conditions that Jacquie had provided. In every place it was the same: her imagination feeding off ghosts.

She remembered the full moon that had risen above the old site of Nazi rallies in Nuremburg, the fortress of aged pine trees, and the cold air clamping everything fast, so that she was again in a frozen moment between times. Ghosts. Germany was filled with them, and their presence everywhere she went was beginning to make her feel she were being pressed underwater. At some point, Lara mused, she had to see this country for what it was today, now. But the wall had only come down in recent years; the place was still filled with such a turmoil of questions and hopes—the atmosphere sometimes encroached upon her very skin.

How surprised she had been to see a group of teenagers with green hair and worn clothing wandering happily past the old site of Checkpoint Charlie, as if soldiers had never stood there, as if the wall had been something from another lifetime. They looked so modern, so unencumbered by guilt

... what was it her friends kept calling it? *Fault.*

Maybe Anton was right about coming to an end of questions, but how had he made them go away?

Somehow she had ended up on the Kurfürstendamm, and it was now dark. Lara suddenly wondered whether she would be in Germany long enough to see snow. It was certainly starting to feel cold enough.

Her stomach rumbled, and she glimpsed a café through a veil of frantic pedestrians. Then Lara realized that from where she was standing she could also see the crater of an old church, crouched and hollow. She saw herself.

I don't want to live like that anymore.

She decided she would go once more to Zweibach. If Anton could skip classes, she would go with him tomorrow. She could even look in a phone book, see if any Müllers lived there. Lara owed it to herself to give things one more chance. She would not allow sorrow to turn her into a ruin.

43.

Where are you taking me?

She didn't say this out loud, but repeated the question in her mind, as she was pulled along by Anton's quick stride. He had arranged to pick her up at the flat and had even arrived early. He fidgeted while they had coffee, seeming eager to be on their way, so here they were, moving purposefully along the street.

"Do you have to walk so fast?"

"No," he replied, and slowed his steps. "It's just that I've been wanting to take you to this place for a long time."

"The station? Isn't that where we're going?"

He stopped suddenly and turned to face her. His eyes were tender and laughing at the same time. "You always want to know where you are going, don't you?"

"What do you mean?" *Was that a bad thing?* she wondered.

"You find it hard just to follow. You need to have looked at a map beforehand, or have someone talk you through."

"I don't get what you're saying. I don't always want to know, anyway. When I booked the flight to come here I didn't know why, did I?"

"But you were still the one who made the choice, Lara."

She loved the way he said her name—or, rather, she felt loved when he said her name. She dropped her eyes, and stared at their feet.

"Shall we keep going, then?" He took her gloved hand in his, and they set off once more, this time moving more easily beside each other. They walked in silence until they reached the square.

It was then that Lara saw it: the building towered majestically above them, its arches, curves and stones a triumphant cry to the heavens.

"You have no idea how hard it is to avoid school. They monitor you like it's a high-security prison sometimes.

We're going to make the most of today!" Anton grinned, and pulled Lara's hat down firmly over her eyes. "Come on. Trust me. I'll lead you." He laughed and held her arm as if she were blind, then pulled her forward. Her feet felt huge and awkward when she couldn't predict her steps, but today she didn't mind.

He led her up a broad flight of steps. She was aware of the chill of shadow falling around her. Anton lifted her hand, took off her glove and placed her fingers carefully on a cold stone carving. She pressed the pads of her fingers into the crevices and traced a smile and a small nose. It made her giggle.

"Can I see now?"

"All right, if you must!" He took her beanie off, messed her hair, and then replaced the hat, back to front.

"Wait!" She tried to wriggle her head away so that she could look at the stone face. It was a smiling biblical character, holding a staff and clasping a tiny animal in its arm.

"He's holding a dog!"

"I think," replied Anton with a hint of irony, "you'll find it's a lamb."

"Oh." Lara leaned forward to look. He was right. The tiny face with its frozen curls of wool gazed up at her with a serene expression. The stone man had a cheerful, beaming face.

"He doesn't look serious enough to be posted outside a church." Lara cocked her head quizzically at the carving. "He looks like he's up to something."

Anton patted the lamb on the head. "Who says he should look serious?" He paused, then added, "How could he when he's staring at you?"

Lara punched him playfully in the arm, then righted her beanie. "I'm getting cold! Give me my glove!"

He waved it, and it tangled in her hair.

"Please …! "

"Okay, okay."

He tried to put the glove on back to front, but she

wrestled his hand, and he finally gave up. He put his arm around her shoulders.

"Come on, it's freezing!"

He propelled her up the last great step that curved across the front of the church like an eyelid. It was worn in the middle; her feet dipped down as she entered. So many others had come here, she thought, so many thousands of footsteps—and the lamb had greeted them all from his master's embrace, with his welcoming eyes.

The huge cathedral opened its doors to them, and they stepped into the cool silence. She had been expecting the inside of the church to be dark, forbidding, but she found the opposite. The light from outside made the stained-glass windows burn with color. Someone was rehearsing a piece on the organ, and Bach's sublime triads and runs filled the reverential atmosphere with joy. Lara caught her breath. Something deep within her had stirred for a moment, lifted its head, opened one eye from sleep.

Then it was still, inside and out, because the organist had stopped playing. Anton squeezed her hand. "Come," he said simply, and led her over to a wall covered with faded frescoes.

Lara's first impression was that the wall was plastered with eyes, all vacuous and dreaming. Then she could make out the faint lines of faces, chins and threads of hair. As her vision adjusted to the light, she could then see their bodies—triangles of once-warm color, dried many times under a full sun. *An Australian sun,* she thought. Now she knew what they looked like—as if the faces had actually *lived,* not merely been preserved.

"They're beautiful," she murmured. "And warm, somehow."

Anton squeezed her hand again.

They didn't stay much longer, although Lara could have sat for the rest of the day in front of the frescoed wall, bathed in organ music, and the peace she felt there. But they had a train to catch, and some detective work to undertake.

They returned to the bright, harsh light of the outside world, and then they were striding toward the station. After they bought their tickets, they had to race onto the platform to board the train in time. They scrambled through the narrow door and nearly fell into the carriage. They were laughing as they located their seats, and a middle-aged businessman opposite them glared over the top of his briefcase, which lay rigid across his lap.

Gasping, Lara and Anton settled themselves while the traveler opened his case with two sharp clicks, and produced a newspaper. He raised it like a curtain across his face, and sat back in his seat. A photograph of a demonstration caught Lara's attention, and she leaned forward to try and read the caption. The man seemed aware of her, however, and rattled his paper threateningly, so that the words jiggled, and Lara lost her thread.

Anton waved his hand in front of her eyes, and she turned.

"Thank you for coming to church."

"Oh," she replied, surprised.

"You have now done your 'duty'." He smiled at her.

Lara said nothing. The truth was that she had forgotten about her promise.

As the train rumbled forwards, Anton slipped into his own thoughts, and absently took her hand. Lara leaned her head against him and gazed out the window. She watched the platform recede, the station buildings blur and dissolve as the train gathered speed.

In her mind, however, Lara did not move with the train, but stood motionless, her face to the frescoes, savoring their serenity and their gentle summer color.

44.

It was harder to locate the old cemetery than they had expected. Anton and Lara had purchased a map that led them through the modern landscape of the "new" Zweibach. The houses formed dreary avenues, punctuated with the occasional cluster of shops. Even the post boxes seemed to stand by the roadside as if wanting to hitch a ride to somewhere else.

They eventually turned onto a dead-end street, where the rows of blunt-faced houses suddenly stopped, and thin pines filled the spaces. The concrete under their feet was cracked, then chipped. Eventually they reached a point where the dirt road beneath had broken through, and had become pockmarked with ruts and muddy craters; it was clear that not many people passed this way.

The cemetery gates were fused open, bound by weeds. Beyond the entry lay a wooded park. The trees were mostly birches, gathered together in loose bunches, their frail branches trailing like string. The path between the headstones was difficult to see—hidden among dormant roses that tangled in mounds of rotting leaves. The place had been so neglected, that tiny birds remained poised and curious atop the graves as Anton and Lara passed. The place had the respectful silence of a library, only here the stories lay buried.

They moved carefully and thoroughly among the gravestones, reading the inscriptions in silence. Each epitaph seemed to breathe for the briefest of moments before sinking back into damp earth, as Anton and Lara passed on to the next. Becks, Schmidts, even a Goethe lay here, but there were no names that Lara could claim. The search continued, grave after grave. Dry leaves clutched at their feet, while fitful, tiny bells of birdsong accompanied them. It was not the brooding, fearsome place Lara had imagined; something in the atmosphere brought her peace.

Then she saw the name: *Müller.*

"Hey, Anton!" she whispered.

Together they bent towards the words engraved under the lichen.

In memory of Joachim and Charlotte Müller,
now in the hands of God,
February, 1945

That was it—no explanation, no mention of their age or loved ones. Was it the grave of her great-grandparents? Had her grandfather come to Australia as an orphan? Lara scanned her memory for anything he may have said about his parents, but she had never asked, and he had not offered any information. His life before Australia remained a vast, engulfing silence.

A surge of resentment coursed through her, but also—for the first time—the idea touched Lara's mind, that perhaps silence was Opa's right. Anger abruptly blocked the thought, as the pin's memory pricked her. No, the truth belonged to her. Excavation was a duty, or the ghosts would colonize her, forever.

"They shared a grave," Lara murmured. "They must have died together."

Both of them instinctively thought of the bombing raids, and Lara shuddered. She had read brutal accounts of Allied bomb attacks toward the end of the war. She hoped that her great-grandparents had not been burnt alive, but the headstone gave no clues.

"Müller is a common name." Anton straightened up and glanced around at the other headstones. "But not common here. These are the only two Müllers so far."

"There were none in the phone book," Lara added. "Let's finish here, though. Just in case."

Slowly they completed their circuit of the graves. There were two other Müller inscriptions, but the dates were in the very distant past.

"I'm sure he was an only child." Lara sank onto one of

the drier stones. Her back ached from all the bending. There seemed to be nothing else they could find.

Anton sat next to her and took her hand.

"Food, then?"

Lara found the energy to stand up. The headstones had closed ranks; she and Anton had discovered all they would ever know. They both felt it was time to leave.

The two of them made for the tavern in the old town. They had both seen enough of post-war architecture and wanted to pass the rest of their time here in the sunlit square, perhaps going for another walk around the old part of Zweibach. They came close to the square, but for some reason the road they were on veered sharply to the left, and they found themselves in another cobbled clearing between sagging houses. The sky was obscured by their teetering roofs, and an old water pump stood aloof nearby.

Anton and Lara looked at each other keenly, and Anton hurriedly produced the map.

"No—wait!" she interrupted, and he looked at where she pointed.

There stood a stone obelisk, bearing no statue, only dark, carved lettering. They rushed over to the war memorial—she quickly found *Tomas Müller*. Lara noticed little stars carved into the granite, alongside most of the other names listed. *So many young men never returned,* Lara thought sadly.

Aside from her grandfather's name, there were only five others that did not have stars. Anton grabbed his pencil and wrote them down. The tavern was forgotten, and they studied the map to see where they had got to; then they headed back to the information booth they had found in the center of town, in search of a phone book.

The rest of that afternoon was spent in fruitless phone calls. One old woman hung up before Anton could even finish a sentence. Lara sighed in frustration, then grabbed the phone from him.

"I'll try."

"You?"

"Yes. My accent and my gender should help."

She felt slightly annoyed that Anton didn't contradict her about the accent, but she let it go. He grinned, though, and leaned forward.

"You're waiting for something?"

She scowled. "No."

He laughed. "You are so serious!" he teased. "All right! Your accent won't give you away!"

"Do I have an accent?"

"Just a bit."

"Really? Everybody tells me how good my German is."

He looked pointedly at her until she had to start laughing too.

"Don't be so obsessed with perfection. I like your accent, and your German is good. Now, dial!"

She smiled back at him and dialed the last number on the list. She asked for Herr Ecker.

To their shock, he answered and then agreed to see them.

Lara put down the phone in disbelief. She stared blankly at Anton. "It worked!"

He laughed and spun her around. "Thanks to your idiosyncratic German!"

She shrugged him off happily, and then they turned their attention once more to studying the map.

❧

The house where they arrived twenty or so minutes later was a divided prefabricated arrangement, its stucco exterior painted the palest arctic blue. To the side of the little gate—which did not squeak as they opened it—a prim letterbox stood guard, the street number neatly engraved on its polished surface. A concrete path led to the front door. It was lined with geraniums crouched in black pots. Lara looked around her; it was a bland, well-organized garden.

They knocked on the door, then had to knock again, and wait a few more minutes before somebody answered. When the door finally opened, a strapping elderly man with a cane greeted them with a cool smile and a nod of the head.

"Come in, please."

He led them down a dark passageway. Lara couldn't help noticing the smell—mildew and cooked cabbage, musty and unpleasant. She wrinkled her nose, and behind her Anton coughed.

Herr Ecker limped in a stately fashion through an open door, and they found themselves entering a dim, but well-kept parlor. To the left of a glowing gas heater, a fat sofa sat puffed and ready for them.

The man motioned for them to be seated, and they sat. He offered them tea, and they accepted. While he disappeared for a moment to put on the kettle, they surveyed the small room. The mantelpiece above the gas heater was strung with photos in polished frames. There was not a speck of dust anywhere, Lara noticed.

They said nothing to each other.

"He was your grandfather," muttered Anton finally, and Lara knew it was fitting that she opened the conversation.

The man returned. He passed them their tea, and placed a jug of milk and a little bowl of sugar on the table, before reclining opposite them in a worn but well-cared-for armchair. The man rested his cane, and picked up his cup of tea. An upright lamp lit the top of his face, and a marmalade cat curled, well-behaved, at his feet.

"And what is it that I can do for you?" he asked politely. The question was aimed at Lara. He seemed to ignore Anton.

"I'm after anything I can find out about my grandfather. I think it was his parents'—my great-grandparents'—grave we found earlier today in the old cemetery."

"Ah, you have been there? Once a beautiful place, but now sadly neglected."

"Yes."

It was still beautiful, Lara decided. She remembered the stiff geraniums lining the path outside his house, and was not surprised that Herr Ecker did not appreciate the cemetery's wild and wooded setting.

"They take so little care of it, as you must have seen," he continued sadly, shaking his head. "It was a regal place once, but now their attention is turned only to the new one on the other side of town. I find it frustrating … the lack of order, the chaos of that cemetery. But then, I knew many of those buried there."

"Did you know my grandfather, Tomas Müller?"

The man focused his eyes at the glass behind them, and then smiled faintly. Lara decided that it was not a benign smile.

"Yes, I did … only slightly," he replied. "He was a year below me in school."

Lara sat up, her heart beating. She felt she had become a moon in the gravitational pull of an enormous planet. Anton tensed beside her.

"What do you remember about him?"

"He left to study somewhere else for entry to the University. I didn't see him after that. He was a quiet boy, not given to being very sociable, but he worked hard, I seem to recall, as did his friend."

"His friend?"

"Ah, yes, that is someone who knew him a lot better than I. You see, I did not have much to do with him. He was in a younger year-level, and he joined the army much later than I did. Did your grandfather ever mention the name of Gustav Klaubert?"

"No," she admitted awkwardly, shaking her head. There was so much about Opa that she had never known.

Anton cut in. "I noticed there was a name like that on the memorial, but he had a star next to his name, and we thought ... " He paused respectfully, not sure how to finish his sentence.

Herr Ecker, however, seemed not at all affected.

"No. Gustav survived. I don't know why that star has been left there. I heard from someone a long time ago that he moved to Berlin after the war. He certainly was not here when I returned home. But perhaps it was only a rumor."

He stopped talking and shifted his cane to the other side of the chair. The wood landed on the head of the cat, who jumped, then resettled itself once more at its owner's feet.

"This town was a happy place," the elderly man began again. He patted his cat, who began to purr. "But many couldn't resettle here. It was heavily bombed, and there was not much left of the place where we had grown up. Your great-grandfather, he ran a music shop—mended cellos, violins, that sort of thing. I sometimes walked past it."

"Did you ever go inside?"

He paused. "No."

"What were they like?"

He sipped at his tea. "They kept to themselves. Kept odd company sometimes. Had a Jew living with them at one stage, I remember, but I'm not sure what happened to him. No, I didn't really know them. But this other man, if you can find him, he should be able to tell you what you need to know. They were—inseparable."

The man yawned, and they knew the audience was over. They stood as the old man clambered to his feet, and reached for his cane.

The three of them retraced their steps down the hall.

As they arrived at the door, Anton and Lara turned once more to face their host.

"Thank you, Herr Ecker," they said in unison, and then the three of them laughed in a weak, embarrassed way.

"Please," he replied, with the same cool politeness that made them feel obliged rather than grateful. "Please," he repeated, "call me Hans."

45

"Well, did you ask him? Was it Gustav Klaubert?" Lara demanded when Anton returned to the borrowed car.

There was ice on the road. The sky was frosted and deep gold, as the sun shifted above the buildings behind them.

Several weeks had passed since the visit to Herr Ecker, and they had finally been able to trace her grandfather's friend. The search had become, for both of them, an engine that drove them forward. It had begun with Lara's journey, but now it was as if in this final interview, the ghosts that crowded both of them might finally be put to rest.

"Yes, it was him. I'm sure of it. Lara, I'm glad I went in, instead of you. It doesn't feel very safe here."

They both sized up the apartment building. It was in the former East Berlin, part of a decrepit area that looked as if the Wall had never come down. A group of bitter young men lounged against a wall further down the street, hurling drunken insults at the winter wind. Newspapers tumbled in drifts, and loose wires drooped from power lines. Not far away, a contained square of park played host to pigeon sentries, and a woman in a dark coat pushed a stroller. A slide hung down in a sad curve, like a discarded slice of melon.

Lara felt exhausted, with everything. She longed for somewhere to simply *be*, where there were no ghosts, no tiny lapel pin to mock every memory of her Opa, no armies of anger and sorrow to fight over the possession of her heart. She felt in her coat pocket. Today, she had chosen to bring two of the objects with her, not sure if they were talismans, or keys.

"It did not go as we hoped," he admitted. "I did not have even one chance to mention your grandfather."

"But you were in there for over half an hour."

"Please, it is not my fault—I don't think you could have done any better. I think," he paused, reaching for her gloved hand as, in spite of herself, Lara began to cry, "that's just how it has to be for now."

Anton stared out through the windshield. "Do you know, the moment I mentioned that I knew Herr Ecker, he just closed down—he told me there was nothing to say, about Zweibach, or anything else. In fact, the only thing he did was give me a message, for both of us." With his free hand he played with the lock on the door. It cracked the air as it clicked up, then down. He locked them in again. "I don't think it worked, trying to make him like us."

"What was the message?"

Anton shifted uncomfortably in his seat, and pursed his lips together. He touched Lara's arm, and when he spoke, he sounded sad.

"It was: Please go home."

Lara gripped the steering wheel and pummeled the sides of it with her gloves. She was breathing out steam because the air was cold, and she was angry. They had done so much searching, tracking, and now they had met with a fortress. Somewhere up in that gray apartment block was an old man who was gripping his silence as if he could find his salvation in it.

Perhaps she shouldn't be surprised. Herr Klaubert had seemed a taciturn, difficult man, from the first telephone call.

"I'm sorry, but I do not talk to Australians," he had responded, his voice hard and graveled.

Lara had only just introduced herself, thinking that the distance she had traveled would convince him to see her. She had not even mentioned her Opa, and how could she now?

She had pulled back from the phone in shock, terrified of losing the chance to know anything of Opa's past. Why did he hate her country, what had made him so angry? Lara had to get the interview with him. Maybe, she thought, Anton might succeed, where she had failed. He, after all, was German.

So it was that Lara found herself telling Herr Klaubert confidently that she and Anton were doctoral students, undertaking research on Zweibach before the war. Instantly his tone changed—he clearly respected the University. Herr Klaubert had remained guarded, but to Lara's enormous relief, he did not hang up.

Her face was hot with guilt as she ended the call, but she had secured the interview.

"You have to make him like us," she had begged Anton, as she was trying to explain her ruse. "If he likes us, then maybe he will talk, maybe you can ask him about my grandfather."

But Herr Klaubert had not liked Anton. He had discovered nothing, and they had been told to go home.

Lara thought she might explode.

Anton put his hands under his arms, to warm them.

"We ate cake, though... He believed me about the PhD research. He tried to put on a good impression, until I put my foot in my mouth."

She guessed Anton had sat there bewildered by the way hospitality and rejection could meet him in one person, in one moment.

"How were you to know," she muttered. "He shouldn't blame you for something you had no control over."

"Let's get breakfast," Anton suggested.

They found a café, and managed to park the car nearby. They sat at a table next to the window, shoulders hunched in disappointment. Lara absently traced a finger across the opaque glass and drew a circle, then two eyes and, with a glance at Anton, a sad curve for a mouth.

The coffee arrived, and the waitress smiled at the artwork before moving on to another table. Together Anton and Lara pondered the latest roadblock.

"It is his right not to talk," began Anton, then instantly regretted his opening as Lara's gray eyes flashed at him.

"It is our right to demand that he talk!" she snapped back, and viciously turned her cup around in its saucer. Coffee splattered onto the table.

"He owes it to us—not just you and me, but to all of us—you and all of your friends who have missed the boat." Her voice hardened with the force of angry tears behind it. "I can't just give up now and let him win. You don't understand, it's like our pasts and futures are teetering here, like two people walking across a ravine with their fingertips touching, about to be blown apart or flung together."

"You are getting poetical again."

"Poetic."

"Sorry."

"Don't be." Lara pressed her fingernails into the paper napkin. She looked up suddenly, her eyes darting across his face. "Yes, be sorry! Be sorry for your whole nation and every old man who's holed up in a concrete prison and won't talk!"

She stirred her coffee while Anton stared at her hand. She moved the froth around on the surface and focused intently on making the swirls move faster and faster.

"What are you doing?" he asked her gently.

"Making a whirlpool ... big enough to suck us all in."

She got up suddenly, and raced out through the door. The icy air hit her face and put a clear glass wall between her and the sound of Anton calling her name.

Her feet pounded the sidewalk. She was counting the cracks as she ran: *1, 2, 3, 4, 5.* Then she was moving too fast to count. She tore down the street, then stopped short at the curb, just in time for a cyclist to skim past. The shock of the near collision made her body sway and her heart stop for a second, but then she glanced both ways and ran across the road.

She slipped under the rail outlining the park, and then paused for breath. She knew she had run too far for Anton to follow her. She also knew how to get to Alexanderplatz from here. There was the wooden slatted tower, and the orange slide. She could see a small green figure moving down it like a pea.

Lara filled her lungs and stretched before taking off again across the slippery ground. Snow was spread intermittently; the sun was starting to melt it, and the brown slush tried to grab the soles of her shoes and throw her toward the earth. Several times Lara slithered and fell, but she got up and kept moving. Her cheeks burned and her fingers felt numb—her gloves were back at the café, next to her abandoned coffee.

Finally Lara recognized Gustav Klaubert's apartment block in the distance—a communist castle, its sides uneven with cracked rendering, its windows rows of crushed squares. It sat a block or so behind what had been the old Teachers' Building, once. Before the Wall had come down, the disseminators of knowledge had been grouped there, and perhaps together they had tried to forget that they were hollow men.

One side of the Teachers' Building was painted an immense mural: a hand reaching upward, fist clenched. Lara hated that fist with every muscle. She strained toward it, longing for a crane with a huge iron ball to smash and crack the image, until it fell.

Must everything on this side of Berlin look like the end of the world is only ten minutes away?

Strange men in leather jackets and cropped mustaches paced the streets here, men from whom Lara did not want attention. She slowed herself to a deliberate hike, trying to read the numbers on the buildings as she passed, but many of them had fallen off or been stolen.

We parked the car over there, she thought.

Lara finally stopped at a metal door with bolts across its edges. She recognized the entrance. To her relief, the young men no longer idled on the street corner. Old newspapers, however, still trembled in the gutter, amongst wet cigarette butts. The park was deserted.

She noticed a line of buttons on the wall, with empty slots beside them—spaces where there should have been names. Clearly, one just had to know who lived where, and in her flustered state, she could not recall the number of Herr Klaubert's flat.

In desperation, Lara pushed one of the buttons. She heard a metallic click, then a husky voice.

"*Ja.*" It was more a grunt than a word.

"I must get into the building. I am looking for a Herr Klaubert."

There was a long pause.

"*Sind Sie allein?*"[13]

Lara wasn't sure how to reply. She took a deep breath and lied. Again. There was a brief pause before the male voice crackled back at her.

"*Schade,*"[14] grunted the male voice, "Too bad. You sound cute."

The metallic click repeated and was followed by the silence of the street. She was starting to feel very cold.

"*Sie sind doch nicht allein.*"[15]

She flicked around. A man watched her from a ground-floor window, his head near the intercom.

"You see, I can see you, and this means you are not alone. I could let you in the building."

Her heart started to thump very fast. Was this the man who had spoken through the first intercom? She pulled herself up to her full height and answered bravely. "My boyfriend is in the car around the corner. He is waiting for me. I need to speak with a Herr Klaubert."

The man was smoking. He dragged on his cigarette and blew to his right. The smoke disappeared into the building. "You speak good German."

---

13   Are you alone?
14   Too bad!
15   You are certainly not alone.

"Ich bin Deutscher."[16]

"I hardly think so."

She turned to leave. She felt scared, foolish, and flat. It had been a stupid impulse to come here, and even more stupid to engage in that conversation.

She took five methodical steps, paused, then took five more. Her breathing was quick and light with fear. Was the man still watching from the ground floor window? She didn't dare look around, but kept up a studied, casual pace until she had crossed the street and covered enough distance so that she could no longer see the apartments. Then she turned around.

A bedraggled cat slunk across the bitumen, and she heard someone slam a car door. Adrenalin had made her hot, and she concentrated on forcing herself to breathe more evenly: counting and breathing in for three seconds, out for three. It didn't really help—it just made her dizzy.

It was ludicrous, just standing here. She knew she had to find Gustav Klaubert, and make him talk. She had so little time left in this country, and who knew when she would ever return? It had to be now.

A calm rose within her and settled her heartbeat. She made her decision. The number she had needed several minutes ago now appeared in her mind, as if it too knew it was time.

Slowly, Lara walked back in the direction of the building. She recited under her breath the number they had so painstakingly discovered, that had slipped her memory and now returned: number 217.

She would buzz number 217. She would just press the button, and see what happened.

---

16   I am German.

46

Lara approached the entrance cautiously, as if she were hunted. She scanned the windows—to her relief there seemed to be no shadowy figure watching for her approach. She poked her finger at the button.

"*Ja?*"

"Herr Klaubert?"

"Who is this?"

She was about to be polite, but then realized that around here that could be a dangerously foreign attitude.

"I represent the Berlin Tenants' Union." She tried to sound clipped and official. "We are currently doing a survey regarding the effectiveness of the heating system in this building, so would you mind if I asked you a few questions? It should only take about ten minutes of your time."

Lara held her breath, and waited. She tried not to look at the ground floor window.

The door buzzed. The sound startled her, and Lara dashed through, anxious that it would lock again before she was inside.

The foyer was dark, and for a moment she stood and blinked, waiting for her pupils to dilate. After a few moments, she could see there was an elevator nearby, but she heard the rattling of a lock behind her, and without another thought she bolted up the stairs. Thankfully she heard no footsteps apart from her own. The lift creaked as it opened, but Lara ignored it, and kept moving.

The corridor stank of mold and urine, and she covered her face with her sleeve. *How could anyone live here?*

Above her, lines of battered florescent lights flickered and hummed. Graffiti littered the paintwork, so that in the dismal light the wall was a bizarre map that led her eventually to number 217.

The door handle was shiny, the paint clean. Lara knocked.

There was the muffled clatter of a safety chain, and a slash of light appeared at the edge of the door.

"*Ja?*"

"Thank you for your time," Lara lied again. "The survey has only a few questions. Can I come in?"

The latch clicked.

"Are you from the government?"

"Representing the Berlin Tenants' Union. We have had complaints about the buildings and need to take official statements."

The door opened fully, and she saw a thin, streaked face.

"Where is your notepad? Your pencil? Your identification?"

She felt like a cop on TV. She pushed past him and whirled around.

"Herr Klaubert. You gave my friend cake today."

It sounded so lame, and she felt ridiculous. To make things worse, he smiled at her—albeit a tight, hard smile that could have been just a preliminary to his reply.

"And you want what?" he asked in an unfriendly voice.

She didn't know what to say now, how to begin.

Somewhere a clock ticked; it squeezed out the seconds, drop by drop. Each tick was a tiny release of hatred into the air—a betrayal, followed by the next one, and the next. She thought of the fist on the Teachers' Building.

"You have no right to come here," he continued.

"You have no right to lie." Lara couldn't quite believe her own rudeness.

He laughed—a hoarse, brittle sound.

"Please, sit down," he said smoothly, politely, and motioned toward a brown vinyl armchair. "*Kaffee?*"

His gentlemanly manner caught Lara off guard, and the tirade that had been about to emerge, stuck in her mouth.

"*Ja, bitte.*"[17]

"Please, sit down," he repeated, "I will not be a moment."

---

17   Yes, thank you.

The bent form shuffled out to the kitchen alcove.

She could occasionally see part of his dark blue shirt shift into her line of vision. He was very old, and he snorted and rustled like a tired horse. Lara could smell the bitter reek of twice-brewed coffee, and heard the clumsy sound of metal hitting metal as he dropped a saucepan.

"*Milch? Zucker?*"

"*Milch.*"

She couldn't bring herself to say *please*.

Herr Klaubert returned with two mugs and handed one to her. Her fingers were frigid from the outside air, and they stung madly as she clasped the hot china.

They sat in silence for a full two minutes.

"My right to lie," he explained in a listless voice, "was awarded to me a long time ago. A lifetime ago. You cannot strip me of this right."

"Anton asked you questions. You told us you would answer them. You promised. How could you lie?"

He looked at her with a mixture of pity and surprise.

"How could I lie," he repeated, and Lara colored at the sarcasm in his voice. When had she become such a moral crusader? She had lied to set up Anton's interview, and then lied her way into the building, and now into this man's home.

Herr Klaubert shook his head, and tried to speak calmly. "Anton—is that his name? Anton? And yours?"

She stared at her coffee. "Lara Davies."

He sat back in his chair. "That is not a very German name." He darted a look at her through eyes enveloped in creased white skin. His eyebrows hung like jagged balustrades across his face.

"You speak good German, Fräulein Davies."

This was how every conversation had begun since she stepped off the plane those many weeks ago.

"I am of German descent."

"Really?" He raised one furry brow.

"My grandparents ... you—"

"I, Fräulein Davies, am none of your business."

She spilled her coffee. "How can you say that? You knew my grandfather—Tomas Müller!"

She had blurted it out, all her self-control gone. She felt like a blundering child.

He stared at her for a long time. "Is that why you have come?"

She nodded.

He was silent again for a moment. "Your friend said the research was important, but I did not realize ... So. It is a personal matter. You are not from the University."

He paused and considered his hands, before he raised his head and glared at her. "Or the Berlin Tenants' Union."

Lara waited nervously, watching the old man's face as a thousand clouds passed across it. Herr Klaubert tensed his eyes, until they were only slits. All the time, the clock attacked the air with its tiny gunshots, and all the time, Lara angrily willed the old man to speak.

"He is dead?"

"Yes."

Another few minutes passed. The old man breathed, the sound like paper tearing. Lara was reminded of ice floes, of canyons of frozen water plummeting into the sea.

"So, then. He is not coming back," Herr Klaubert murmured. He opened his eyes, and held her with a long, dark look.

"Your grandfather." He said the words slowly, with precision, as if repeating something he had learned in another language. His gaze focused backwards, deep into his head, then turned outward again, but not to Lara.

"Your grandfather," he said again, shifting his stare to a ring on Lara's finger. She knew, however, he was seeing her Opa's face. There was a pause.

"He hated Hitler."

"Did he tell you that?"

"He didn't need to. We all did. We were … what can I say? An unusual regiment. But we loved Germany."

"Did you shoot people?" she breathed.

"Of course, little girl. We were soldiers. But shooting people in the head or the arm or the gut doesn't mean you admire the man making you do it."

"How could you," she stammered.

"What else could we do? It was shoot, or be shot for subversion."

Lara, distraught, half-rose from her chair. The old man plunged one fist into the other. His eyes blazed.

"Yes, we shot peasants. Yes, we shot soldiers. Yes, we shot Jews. Does that answer your question?"

Lara no longer knew what the question was.

Herr Klaubert stood now in front of her, a smoldering volcano.

Lara stiffened. His "little girl" had lit something inside her. She groped in her pocket, and for the first time, the SS badge pricked her skin. Deep. She stifled a cry as blood ran down her finger. Biting her lip against the sting, Lara placed the lapel pin on the palm of her outstretched hand.

With this tarnished black disc, she accused him.

"Where did he get this?" she whispered, hurt and hate clouding her voice.

She watched his face narrow and fade.

"Where did you … "

"It was in his things. Hidden. Nobody ever saw it."

Gustav was shaking, then his breath rushed out of him. "He was never with them. I do not know where he could have got this."

"It makes him guilty!"

Lara could no longer contain her anguish.

Gustav stood abruptly. He threw his heavy coffee cup onto the floor so that droplets flew into Lara's face and legs, and again he crushed his fists together. Lara withdrew her hand.

"Little girl," he trembled. Lara winced.

"You know nothing of war. You know nothing of hate. You know nothing."

He paused briefly, trying to collect himself.

Lara recoiled into the chair. She stuffed the pin back into her pocket.

"Tomas and I, we knew how to fire a gun, and keep our mouths shut." Here his voice dropped. "We heard what happened when you said "no" to them. We knew they interned people ..."

Lara had nothing to say. Her Opa kept holding her and letting go, his face distorting.

"We have seen the footage on the television," the old man continued, "We are doomed by our age as murderers, aligned with those who planned everything. But—" He turned his eyes to her, almost pleading. "We were soldiers out on the front. It was *different* for us. We were expanding Germany. We were fighting for a new world order!"

Herr Klaubert threw his hands to his head and shut his eyes, furrowing his brow. "We were," he added quietly, "obeying orders."

Lara tore methodically at the hair that had fallen around her face. A hand from long ago would have tucked those strands behind her ear. The one that had held the pin. What vile orders had that hand once obeyed?

Lara held her fingers in front of her face—edged in white, they were hand-prints. She wanted, right now, to push through the wall that separated her from her Opa. A wall made of human sheaves.

"Fräulein Davies," Gustav whispered, "your grandfather was a man who followed orders, but I can swear to you on his memory that he was never with the SS."

He wiped his eyes. Lara continued to stare at her hands.

"But was he guilty? Yes. We are all guilty. You are a slave of what you obey, Fräulein Davies."

He looked up at her, and this time she held his gaze. The violence had gone, the volcano now a coil of smoke. The hand-prints folded, and came to rest on her lap. The wall, Lara knew, would never come down.

He leaned forward. "He told me he would throw everything into the sea on the way to Australia, but, Lara—"

When he spoke her name, she started. The word jarred before it reached her; in his voice, she thought she heard the man he had once been.

"Guilt does not drown."

Opa.

Lara bent her head, and sobbed fiercely into her arm. The spiders had always been there—watching, waiting. Now, they had won.

Gustav Klaubert could say what he wanted, but the pin had drawn blood. Nothing—not a single question, not a peg, a postcard, nor even a feather—would ever bring Opa back, or change what she now knew. The Opa Lara loved was dead: his voice urging her to listen to the birds, his arms, strong to swing her, protective, to hold her against loss—they had gone.

Herr Klaubert, she knew, would never unwrap the lies from around the secrets they hid and protected. To do so would destroy her grandfather's ... life work.

Lara had once wondered whether to keep those you loved whole, was more important, more precious even, than truth. She had been wrong, or maybe deceived. Herr Klaubert was right. Guilt would always return, caught forever in a spiraling tide. Opa had protected them from what they could not bear, for a time. But it hadn't worked. Lara had splintered into shards, the moment she held the pin.

Gustav absently kicked his coffee cup, then walked to the window and stood completely still, staring out at the gray sky.

"I hate Berlin in the winter. Your grandfather wrote to me once. He said the sun shone much in your country.

Your grandfather married. I could not. I worked in the same factory for forty years. I live in this one room. I cannot answer your questions."

He paused. "Please—destroy that pin."

Lara's heart turned, and her hand involuntarily moved to her pocket. She felt the lighting bolts under her fingertips, and surveyed Herr Klaubert's silhouette against the window. He seemed smaller, almost no longer there.

Lara absently pulled out the ticket to the Berlin Philharmonic Orchestra.

"And this?" She barely raised her voice, but he heard and moved to her chair. He trembled slightly, like a cold breeze, as he took the scrap of paper.

"Tomas—your grandfather—could not go again to hear music after the war. A great sadness, he was a brilliant cellist. He performed so many times with the Berliner Philharmonic."

Her love of music, then, had come from Opa. This unexpected knowledge caused Lara a new, deep pain.

It was then that she noticed a dark shape in the corner that looked like a person, or the shadow of one. It was a closed, upright cello hard case. It looked exactly like her own—Lara's heart jolted, and with it, she felt a violent urge to open the latches. It was all she could do to stay seated, her arms still.

"I bought him tickets, hoping he would change his mind." Herr Klaubert looked away. "I wonder why he kept this one ... He must have sailed with it in his pocket."

"Do you think he would have played the cello again, if he had not left Germany?" Lara whispered.

"No."

"Why?" She paused, and then asked in a low voice, "Is that your cello, or his?"

"Drink your coffee and go, Fräulein Davies," Gustav replied sharply. "Go home."

Lara didn't ask for the ticket. She looked one long,

last time at the cello in the corner. She wiped her face with her sleeve, and replaced the cup on the table. Then she stood up quietly.

Herr Klaubert had walked over to the window once more, and seemed no longer aware of her presence.

"*Auf Wiedersehen.*"

He did not hear her. Lara turned her back, and left him.

47.

The door roared shut, but it was nothing compared to the tumult inside her. Fragments of the afternoon, with its fervid storms, buffeted her thoughts, so that her shaking hands could barely manage the buttons on her coat. Lara didn't know whether she wanted to scream, run, or throw herself against Herr Klaubert's door until he let her back in—he had told her so little.

Had that been Opa's cello?

Lara clenched her hands; if it were, then surely it should belong to her, by right? If only she could take the instrument with her, give it breath again, honor the one legacy of her grandfather's she was prepared to own.

The jaundiced bulbs above her wavered and hissed, and she noticed once again the acrid smell. It was unbearable, and she covered her face with her hand. The whole place, the whole situation, now revolted her. The cello was locked inside Herr Klaubert's flat, and no matter how hard she willed it, she was powerless to set it free. Lara knew Gustav Klaubert would not open his door to her again; nor, she realized now, would she ever try to make him.

It was finished.

As Lara turned to face the corridor, she remembered another object in her pocket—one she knew now she could not bring back to Australia. It had led her to a story as reticent and sorrowful as the empty church on the Kurfürstendamm, and failed her.

Slowly Lara took the broken compass, and laid it on the floor, just outside Herr Klaubert's apartment. She knocked once, fixed that glistening handle in her memory, then turned and walked away.

The walk became a jog, then she began to run down the stairs. She kept stumbling; the walls were a dirty gray, and barely any light from outside penetrated the tiny glass slits at each stairwell. She needed to get home.

But where was that? Her bed at Jacquie's? Lara's personal photos were stuck to the wall, her clothes strewn on the floor—surely a sign. But it was not "home."

Australia? Lara felt a sharp yearning for vast skies, for white light, vivid enough to reveal the veins of trees and dismantle shadows on the streets. She wanted to smell crushed eucalyptus leaves after rain, and hear magpies sing. But all this didn't make her country "home."

Lara arrived at the last step. She worked frantically at the huge door, heaved it open, and nearly fell out onto the street. She stood on the curb, dazed, unsure of where to go next. She finally decided to head towards Alexanderplatz.

Once there, Lara kept walking, until she came to the enormous boulevard that rolled out through the Brandenburg Gate. On the large concrete spaces around the monument, street vendors with restless eyes sold remnants of East German army uniforms, and pieces of rock from the Berlin Wall—*Yes, really,* they assured buyers, as they traded the souvenirs for cash.

Lara watched as too many people, cameras strung around their necks and grotesque moneybags at their hips, bought the lies. The fake relics, she supposed, were props in their own personal drama of being here in Berlin, a city that had seen so much lying.

Lara recalled how she had burst into Herr Klaubert's apartment—indeed, the way she had demanded an inventory of her grandfather's past, as if she had the right to break his silence ... and she felt ashamed. Lara was no longer sure she even had a right to the cello. Anton had said, the first night they talked together, that Lara had no idea what it was to be German. He was right, she thought. She wasn't German. She was just another tourist, demanding pieces of someone else's history to carry home.

Under the linden trees, Lara felt closer to peace, but only slightly. She wanted to throw her arms around one of their worn, noble trunks and hold it until her muscles gave way. She longed to place her ears to its skin and hear the sap coursing between branches and roots, but anguish and the biting cold kept her moving.

Lara found a phone booth. She had one coin, and on impulse decided to ring Anton.

The phone's blurred, inhuman bleat pulsed rhythmically for too long. He was not home. She didn't even know what she would say, if he answered. Lara placed the receiver back in its cradle, and leaned against the smudged glass.

In the distance she could see the Reichstag, its sombre gold, red, and black flag shuddering in the winter wind. The traffic rumbled around its base like a sluggish river. The branches of the linden trees formed a thick, spiked layer across the distance, so that she almost didn't see the church steeple. She knew she needed to go somewhere where nobody knew her, where she could cry without anyone interfering. She set off wearily toward the spire.

The portal of the cathedral was enormous, like a pair of giant closed eyelids. Lara had to push her whole body against the doors to shift them enough to enter. Once they fell shut behind her, she could no longer hear the clamor of the street.

The stone interior was cold, and the air fragrant with incense. Rows of candles burned at the far end, and they reassured her that something was glowing, alive. Lara sat down on one of the long wooden pews. Like a basket, her lap caught the light streaming through a huge stained-glass window above her. The melting, vibrant reds, purples, and blues fell across her skin, and released her tears. With her face lifted to the colored glass, something cracked inside. Lara's breath escaped clumsily, along with her tears. She found herself kneeling on a cushioned footrest. For the first time, Lara prayed to a God she wasn't even sure was there.

A man in a white collar moved past her pew, and stopped.

"Can I be of assistance?"

Lara stood quickly, confused at his offer. She felt calmer, so his words struck her as strange.

"I'm fine, really. Thank you." She mustered a smile, and sat back down on the pew. So he would go away, she grabbed a Bible from a slot in front of her, and fell to reading intensively. At least, she hoped that was the impression she gave. The man moved on down the nave.

Lara was exhausted, and wanted something to eat. She tried to wipe her face inconspicuously, before replacing the Bible. She navigated her way through the pews, trying to reach the aisle furthest from the clergyman. Her progress, however, was annoyingly slow—the corners of her coat kept catching, so eventually she had to encounter the same man at the church doors.

He nodded his head at her, then unloaded a collection of red hymn books onto a carved table. He found a small square of white paper with a picture of the church on the front of it. He held it out.

"In case you wish to visit us again," he murmured casually, then held the door open for her. "We are open for Vespers nightly at six pm."

Bewildered, Lara said nothing as she wandered out onto the street, and found an underground train that could take her back to Jacquie's flat.

48.

Lara had not seen Anton since leaving the café yesterday morning. Today she had spent the afternoon wandering Berlin, sitting on the Reichstag steps and marveling at the flag, the voracious, swirling traffic, and the bare trees. She had read, and reread the inscription above the building, with its chilling irony: *To the German People*. Again, ghosts. She had returned to Jacquie's for dinner, but was too restless to spend the evening at home; it seemed a North wind was blowing her out to the streets.

Now it was nine pm, and Lara was back on Alexanderplatz. It was the closest landmark she could remember—she had irritated the taxi driver enough, with her jumbled instructions on the way here. He had veered left, then right, performing geographically the internal leaps and starts of her memory. The decision to be dropped here had been a relief for both of them.

The pavement stared up at her like a lonely face. The air was frozen and silent—nobody else was around. Lara was caught again in the *what if game*. What if she had been in Opa's world? Could she have prevented him from joining the Wehrmacht? She hated to think that perhaps, like him, she would have donned a uniform instead of standing alongside those who spoke out, and were—how had Herr Klaubert put it—*interned*. Interned, as if they were sick. What a terrible, unimaginable paradox.

Lara plunged her hands further into the pockets of her coat, and set off toward Herr Klaubert's apartment block. She should be scared of being here, at this time of night, she thought. Instead, she simply felt responsible: for Opa, for those he had hurt ... for that abhorrent disc pinned to his chest. It felt like her fault. That word again: *fault*. It sickened her.

Lara arrived outside the building, and quickly moved to the opposite side of the street, where she could watch the apartment from a distance. She pulled her scarf closer around her neck. All along the pavement, saplings stood taut in rusted cages. She wondered why she had not noticed them before. Lara looked up at the second floor. Somewhere in there was an old man enslaved by his past; trapped, like one of these trees. Her heart hurt.

And then, she heard it.

From very high up, a tremulous sound crept cautiously, but beautifully over a windowsill. It floated down like the first delicate and reassuring snow of winter, settling on the stunted saplings in their rusted pens.

The street held its breath. It was a painful sound, an animal voice, that was from no animal.

It was wood singing, infused with life from a master's hand. Gustav Klaubert was playing the cello.

⸎

"I thought you would be here."

Lara started, prepared to run. But it was Anton who stood in the darkness. He took her hand, and together they listened to the melody that poured over their skin.

They were still for a long time—until the music shivered and paused, then finished ... one last tender, aching note. The night air remained full, and Anton moved closer to her. Lara's throat tightened. She remembered the melting of color from the stained glass.

"Where did you go?" he asked softly.

Lara's sudden sobs raked the air, and caused her whole body to shake. Anton simply held her. She didn't know where to begin, what to say, or how to speak.

"Lara," Anton said in a firm voice. It was a statement. It meant *We need to do something, move forwards.*

"Lara, we need to talk about this, but not here. It is too cold." He glanced up once more at Herr Klaubert's window, and then continued, "Zak is at Annika's place. We can go to my flat to talk, and then I will take you home. Okay?"

Lara nodded, subdued, and let his arm guide her down the street, into a taxi, and then out again, and up the many stairs into his flat. Anton switched on a light.

"Sit," he ordered kindly.

As she placed herself in a worn armchair, Anton boiled water, and warmed some milk in the kitchen. The heaters clicked and creaked; it was a comforting sound, and Lara gradually stopped shaking.

Anton switched off the kitchen light, and returned to the living room. He handed her a hot chocolate, and for the second time that day her fingers stung against a scalding cup. Lara took a sip. Her lips, then her throat and her insides, re-laxed—it was like sinking into a hot bath.

Anton pulled up the other chair, ragged and with one spring curling out from underneath.

Lara's eyes opened more widely, the cocoa had a tinge of fire.

Anton grinned at her. "Hot chocolate with something special added."

Lara smiled, and took another sip. "Medicinal purposes?"

"But, of course."

Lara glanced down at her hands, and in those few seconds the lightness between them disappeared. She lifted her gaze, and found Anton's eyes searching intently into her own.

"Please, talk to me. Tell me what happened. I was worried about you."

Lara looked at a black-and-white photo on the wall. A piano sat in a waterfall. Music was drowning, or was it an island?

"I was very angry," she began, so quietly that she wondered he could hear her. "He shouted at me. He told me

terrible things. He told me how they ... how they shot Jews."
The words had their own foul taste as she spoke them, but she
found she had to continue.

"Oh, Anton, it was unforgivable—but it was me, too. I
dragged it all from him. I pushed him. He was so injured. I
couldn't bear it as I left. I felt his hatred. And it was me who
caused it." She lowered her voice even further. "I didn't know
where to go. I tried to telephone you, but there was no answer. I even went to a church."

"Why did you go there?"

"I don't know. To be somewhere quiet. I thought—" and
here she broke down again, "—there might be more frescoes ... "

There was silence, then Anton leaned forward.

"Lara, can I tell you something? It is hard for me ... "

Lara suddenly felt very cold, even though her hands were
clasped around the hot mug. Today, she thought, everything
had plunged into a writhing ocean, and she was desperately
afraid she would drown in it all. And now here was Anton,
with his serious face and green eyes dark with feeling, about
to cut some sort of lifeline, she knew it. She jolted upright.

"You know I don't believe in God," she said, trying to
look somewhere other than his face. She felt angry again.

The fridge buzzed in the kitchen, and somewhere out
in the night a siren whined.

As Anton shifted in his chair, the springs squeaked, and
in spite of the situation he could not repress a small smile.

Lara felt embarrassed at her outburst. "Sorry ... tell me
whatever you want."

Anton took her hands, and she let him. He stared down
at the mug of hot chocolate near his foot, before raising his
eyes slowly to meet hers.

"Lara, I used to feel exactly the same." He spoke in a
soft and earnest voice. "Really. I was driven to find out about
it all ... but we are not to blame for what they did."

"What do you mean?" Lara looked up at him quickly.

Another silence fell, tempered by another siren, another electronic rasp from kitchen.

She took a sip of her hot chocolate, noticing that Anton's sat untouched at the side of his boot.

"You should have seen me two years ago, Lara," he continued. "Or maybe, you shouldn't have. You wonder why Annika put up with what I said that night you and I were out on the balcony ... you know, when we were talking about forgiveness. She wanted to hit me, I think. What stopped her was that I am in the same ... *was* in the same position. Oh, Lara, you have no idea what it is like to be taught again and again, the same terrible things that have happened in the lifetimes of people who are still here, and that someone you loved was responsible."

"No. I can't imagine it," she admitted.

"Some things, I have decided, are unimaginable," he said with sudden firmness, picking up his mug and turning it around, "and that is because they should be. No human mind should be able to imagine things like—"

He stopped, bit his lip. Lara discovered that she was clasping his hand. He drank some hot chocolate, then put the mug back down on the carpet.

"We had a workshop one day," he continued, "a class where we were experimenting with some Stanislavski theory."

"With what?"

"Emotional recall, going deep inside yourself to find real motivations and emotions, and then transferring those to the character you are working on. Well, it was a fairly intense session. I can't remember all of it, but we had the lights off, and lots of meditation time, and the teacher talked us through while we put ourselves back into different situations from our past. Anyway, after all that, we rehearsed a scene in a play we were doing—about Anne Frank, would you believe it?"

He shook his head, then continued. "I don't know why on earth they chose that for us. I had to be a Gestapo agent hammering on the door. The whole thing turned into a nightmare. The girl who was playing Anne went crazy. Literally, you know, she started to sob and scream, and was really frightened. It was scary that we could get so deeply into ourselves and the scene that we weren't really acting anymore."

He glanced up with a faint smile. "This was first year, what did I know? I was pretty shaken. And being a class of professionals-in-the-making, there was no debriefing or anything. The class ended, we went to get coffee, and some people talked. That was it."

"The girl—was she okay?"

"Eventually," he replied. "She wouldn't let me go near her for the rest of the day. It was horrible. I felt horrible. I like to think I didn't make a very convincing Gestapo agent," he added somewhat wryly, "but I suddenly realized how easy it could be to become someone I hated—and I started to ask a lot of questions. I couldn't escape my past now. It had come back with claws."

"So what happened?"

"I found this."

He got up and searched in the shelf for a book. She didn't know what to expect he might show her, but she was relieved when it wasn't the Bible. He sat down again, flipped through the pages, and then read a simple, terrifying poem.

Marilla[18]

When
Marilla
who'd
taught
you

patience
and
colors

---

18 "Marilla." In Brett, Lily. *The Auschwitz Poems.* Melbourne: Scribe, 1986.

at
kindergarten

threw
herself

against
the
electric
fence

it
gripped
her

and
left

little
shreds

of
flesh

fried
to
the
wire

she'd
thought

if
God
was
watching

she'd
join
Him

for
a
better
view.

Lara flinched. Anton closed the book and put it down next to his cup, allowing the poem to linger in the air before he spoke again.

"That started me." He paused, ran his hand through his hair. "I knew that somehow I had to see everything with this objectivity, with this realism. I had to know everything. So I found out as much as I could, but through poetry. I decided that was the only way I could do it, and not be completely overwhelmed." He raked his hair again.

"Even then, that was not enough. Then, in some war history section of a second-hand bookshop, I found this."

He leapt up and pried another book from the shelf. Translated, the title meant *The Hiding Place*.

"I read the title, and I thought, 'That's what I need, a place to get away from everything.' But this lady was a believer. In God. Not a fake one. This lady, I don't even know if she's alive now, she talked like she knew God. He was like her best friend. She hid Jews, lost her family, and nearly died in a concentration camp. She asked God to carry things for her because she couldn't deal with what was happening. She had to learn to forgive ... Oh, Lara, when I read this, something in me became so thirsty for peace."

Lara thought of the frescoes with their beautiful, faded eyes.

"I found a Bible," he continued. "I went home to my parents' house for a meal and discovered one—forgotten, dusty, all of that—I stole it, actually," he admitted. "I took it home, and it sat in my room for a week before I had the courage to open it."

Lara remembered her Oma singing to her, of fire shining on the decorated tendrils of wild cherry. She thought of her dream, of hiding in the cave and knowing there was no further place she could run to. Anton watched the memories flicker across her face.

"So, what happened?" Lara asked finally, tentatively.

"I talked to God," he said. "I looked up at the ceiling

of my room, and I asked that if He were real, he would take all this mess away from me. I didn't know anything, except that this lady had gone through the worst of that terrible war and had come out whole, and I … I wanted to know what she was talking about. It's so funny, once I started I just couldn't stop."

He touched her arm almost apologetically, "A bit like now."

In the dim light from the kitchen, all Lara could really see were Anton's eyes glistening like tiny streetlights in the darkness of the room. Time slowed—this one moment expanded to fill the entire space.

Her voice came from somewhere very far away, but perhaps it was instead traveling up from somewhere very deep inside her. "And then?" She wondered if perhaps she hadn't really spoken.

"It felt like … coming home."

There was a long silence. Anton's pulse played an uneasy rhythm in his wrist, and he felt it flickering up his arms and into his throat.

Lara let go of his hands, and stood up. She walked over to the window, and touched its surface. Inside, her whole life—memories, feelings, hurts, and yearnings—rushed, and fought and grasped at her.

When she spoke, her voice sounded cold and flat, like the glass in front of her fingers.

"Could you take me home, now, please?"

Lara watched in the reflection of the window as Anton pulled on his coat, and opened the door. He then moved quietly over to where she was standing and lightly, respectfully, placed his hand on her arm.

"I love you," he said simply.

Lara's heart jumped. The wild ocean inside her froze, and for a moment she felt like there was solid ground underneath her, not a cauldron of angry water.

She let him guide her out the door, and down the stairs.

That night, in her bed on the floor, Lara dreamed strange and chaotic nightmares. She was running down a corridor of eyes, the sun was shining, and as she ran, machine gun fire formed a spattering soundtrack. Herr Klaubert appeared from a doorway, wringing his hands, and then disappeared. She was seven years old, trying to climb an alp, and she kept falling over because she had no shoes. She asked a woman she met how she could get to the top, but the woman pointed to a sign that read "Zee," and then turned into a bird.

Lara was in the ocean, she was in the sky, she was in the Reichstag ... but throughout the whole dream, all she really wanted, was to be home.

Prelude

(Revisited)

The Gift of Water

I stand at the edge of a lonely breakwater that crouches stoically against the beating of the tide. My shoulders are rounded against the hard wind. I force my hat close over my ears. From a distance, I can hear the rumbling and moans of a tired city, as she stirs in her sleep. It is not yet dawn.

I pull out a parcel from under my coat, and my fingers fumble in the early morning chill. The gray water slaps the stone below, while the North Sea wind assaults me with the stench of rotting fish.

I hold the bundle awkwardly in my hands. I must drown it. Now, if possible—certainly before I leave.

In an instinctual movement, I touch in my pocket the papers that contain my new life.

Although I hunch my shoulders for warmth, it makes no difference; the wind breathes harshly at my back, as well as in my face.

It seems ridiculous, a waste of time, but I unmake my bundle, only to gather it once more. I fold each item—even straightening the edges, before laying one down flat upon the other. In this way I build a tier of the remaining parts of the uniform that was my skin—my hated skin—these terrible few years. Across them I place letters that I do not read, even for one last time. It is enough that they bear my name. They too must go.

And the most hated one of all.

I balance the metal in my fingers; I am instantly in pain. Yet I do not let go; I am frozen, captive, while memories tremble over me. They finally drain away like liquid, borne downward by gravity, and sink into the pile of fragments at my feet. I place the small steel pin across the top, hoping that its guilt will help it drown quickly.

Its guilt? I am mocked by the tarnished eye. My guilt.

I suddenly know, or perhaps the pin itself tells me, that one can drown evidence, but not guilt. And with what I have done, I do not deserve to walk free.

I do not know whether this makes me a worse or better man, but I pick up the metal pin. With this, I choose to be always reminded of the person I am now, and the musician I am no longer.

As I press the pin into my pocket, it pricks me, spindle-like. My finger bleeds into the lining of my coat.

We are blood brothers now. Perhaps we were already, from the moment I accepted my accursed bounty.

Low clouds spit on my wad of brown paper, scarring it and interfering with my hands. The day whitens, and I hear rough voices, and metal on wood. I pull a length of string from the pocket of my coat and clasp it in my teeth, as I remove my foot to fold the brown, now damp paper.

I blow on my hands to warm them, and as I do so, I hear the first fishing boats of the morning putter out of the harbor.

The bundle lies wrapped at my feet. Should I hurl it into the waves? I gaze at the tide swelling and rising toward the pier behind me, and imagine the parcel swaying with its current.

Suddenly I am sure that if I loosed it to the water, the hated sheaf would simply return to the beach, or the breakwater, and somebody would discover its contents.

No, there needs to be another way.

A seagull skims above me, and I watch the bird land sound-

lessly on a gray wooden pylon. I shift my eyes back to the burden; then I hastily bend, and pull it under my coat.

I know when my ship sails. I had hoped to leave this behind, but it will need to accompany me for some of the passage. When our boat is no more than a thread upon the surface of the sea, then I will choose a dark hour, and cast it over the side.

Yes, I will have to take a boat.

49.

It was morning. Lara turned over uncomfortably in bed, her legs sore from all the walking of the last two days. She kept wanting to weep, but couldn't remember why. Then last night roused itself in her mind.

She lay there, staring up at the little glow-in-the-dark stars that Jacquie's flat-mate had arranged before she left for South America. It was daylight now, so the tiny shapes that had sent Lara to sleep with an alluring glow these past weeks now seemed just what they were—grubby little bits of paper sprinkled across a cracked ceiling. As she realized this, one actually fell off and landed on her bed with a miniature hiss.

Lara burst into tears, and pressed her face into the pillow. She imagined, from the light slipping through the blinds, that Jacquie had already left for work, but then there was a tell-tale creak outside her door. Lara held her breath.

"Lara? Are you okay?" The voice traveled like a thread through the keyhole to touch her face.

She paused, sniffled. Her own voice scrunched like old paper. "Yes, thanks. Fine."

"You and Anton didn't have a fight, did you?"

"Why?"

"No reason."

Another pause, then Lara's voice became more definite. "We're fine."

"Just asking. I'm off now, but there's coffee for you out here. Oh, and I don't know what you two have planned, but just don't go out tonight, okay?" She laughed, and tapped conspiratorially on the door.

Lara sat up suddenly.

"It's my last day."

Somehow saying the words out loud made her wake-up fully.

Jacquie groaned, and banged the door with her boot. "I repeat my instructions. See you then."

She went off laughing, while Lara rubbed her eyes. Her own words rang in her head as she tugged at the blind. It was her last full day. Tonight was her last night. Tomorrow morning she would make a late run for some form of public transport, and a huge jet would gather her up, along with her baggage and memories, and take her back to Australia. *The cruise first,* she reminded herself. Suddenly she felt even more thankful for her mother's present—it put off going home.

Lara rocked back and forth in frustration, grabbing her head with her hands. What on earth had she done? Why had she come here, and what was she going home to? A wave of self-pity engulfed her, and she cried again, more freely now that she had heard the front door shut, and Jacquie's heels click down the stairs.

Finally she just lay there, breathing heavily, her nose running and her hair sodden.

Get it together! she admonished herself.

Lara swung herself determinedly out of bed, opened the window, and let the cold air shock her into facing her life. To Lara's surprise, it was a gloriously sunny day. Birdsong surged from somewhere to blend with the traffic and trains, and the sounds of building. *Always the sounds of building,* she thought. From down at street level, she heard someone laugh, a dog bark, and the singsong of children's voices as they traipsed to school.

Another day. Her last day. She swallowed hard. She couldn't leave Anton.

The front door buzzed. Lara hurriedly pulled some clothes over her pajamas, and blew her nose, as she moved as slowly as she could to the door. It would be him, she knew. Her heart was tripping away as if she were scared, and she felt foolish about it beating so fast.

"Lara! It's me! It's your last day! Open up!"

She wondered that he could sound so normal, so cheerful, after a night when she felt like a train had ripped through her.

She found herself opening the door, and even attempting a smile. She knew she looked like a mess. Anton took one look at her, and burst out laughing.

She blushed, and then grinned. "This is to help you not miss me," she replied, stepping backwards. Then suddenly she was in tears again.

Anton took her gently in his arms. "Hey, enough," he murmured, then kissed her. "I skipped classes especially to take you out today, so don't thank me like this!"

Somehow Lara couldn't stop, and she just sat down where she was, and cried as she had at six years old. Anton sat down next to her and simply waited, holding her hand. The sobs ran their course.

"About last night," she stammered.

"What about it?" he asked, his eyes steady.

"Um … "

"We don't have to talk about it."

"Do you still … ?"

How could she ask him? She needed to hear him say that he loved her—just one more time, before she left. She had to make sure, but she just couldn't force out her question.

Anton squeezed her hand. "I like writing letters," he said intently. "And when I get money," he held her eyes fast in his gaze, "I'll come there."

"Really?"

"Of course."

She etched every detail of this moment into her mind: the hard floorboards, the warmth of Anton's fingers, and the framing of his gentle, strong face against the white door. She started to choke up again.

"Enough!" he commanded. He stood up, and pulled her to her feet. "I'm going to have some coffee. I met Jacquie on the stairs, and she said there was some."

"But—"

"Yours can wait!" he laughed. He stared at her night-clothes and chuckled. "You've got other priorities right now!"

She blushed again. "Okay, okay," she muttered and quickly retreated to shower and dress herself.

When she finally emerged, she felt calmer. She grate-fully accepted the mug of fresh coffee that he held out to her. She was reminded again of the previous night by the heat on her fingertips.

"Will you really come?"

"I meant what I said to you." He paused. "Now don't … !" for her eyes had welled up again and he brushed the tears away with his sleeve.

"I'm just all weird today," she muttered in a useless at-tempt to explain.

"That's why we're going out. And anyway, I'd feel weird too if I was about to go on a cruise." He ruffled her damp hair.

"It wasn't my idea!"

"You are so easy to tease today! So then, I will need to be careful. Oh, Lara … " He hugged her to him. "Enjoy it! And remember what I said." He leaned forward and kissed her, and she knew, for some reason she couldn't quite understand, that he really did love her, and he would find a way to come to her.

She looked up at him. "It's like we're saying goodbye now."

"Yeah, well we're really going to do this with the others around."

He kissed her hand and put it in his pocket. "One last mad dash around our glorious city, avoiding anywhere I might be recognized. I am," he added with a frown, "severely ill today."

She smiled.

"Oh," he muttered as they put on their coats, "In case I don't get another chance before tomorrow morning."

He shyly fished a little package out of his pocket.

"For you." His fingers around Lara's tightened. "For some time. From me. You don't need to open it now."

For the second time that morning he pulled her to him. "About last night," his voice became a muffled whisper in her hair, "I didn't want to *change* you, or anything, Lara. I love you. I just needed you to know my story."

50.

It was a strange time, that last day, filled with half-hysterical laughter; the city blurred in Lara's memory with the tears that kept threatening to spill over into every situation, every time she saw something that had become familiar, every time she looked at Anton. They went to a café and an art gallery, and then spent the afternoon wandering around the Palace of Sans-Souci. The still winter sunlight coated the stone walls in soft gold, and the trees arched over the deserted gardens, monumental and serene.

This was a good place to be. Somehow the stately buildings steadied her; they had endured, their wrinkled rendering giving them wise, dignified faces. Fascism, Communism, so many other ravaging tides had washed across them, and yet here they were, peaceful and lasting. Perhaps, she hoped, she and Anton would be like this, too. She just wouldn't think about it all, yet.

The day faded, and her promise to Jacquie led them both homeward. Even so, they were late arriving. Lara wondered whether part of their afternoon had been a ruse planned on behalf of her friends.

When she entered the front door, Anton pushed her into a maze of excited whoops, tacky streamers, and confetti. She was handed a German flag on a kebab stick and a glass of Glühwein that nearly burnt her eyes with its fumes. Tears were forced into a tiny corner of her heart, and she found herself laughing, eating and even dancing, as her friends made her spend her last night whirling from embrace to buffet to balcony, from corny joke to raucous jazz music.

Midnight passed, and then came the presentation of a book of photos, notes she was not allowed to read until she was on the ship, and a beautiful, glossy history book of Berlin that would probably mean the end of any hand luggage. There was another toast, more hugs, some tears this time, and eventually all but Jacquie and Anton had left.

Annika's scarf hung like a tired banner around Lara's neck as she dropped, exhausted, onto the sofa.

"What time again are you leaving?" asked Jacquie, yawning, and casting a discouraged eye at the mounds of glasses, plates, and tattered streamers.

"I don't know," replied Lara sleepily. "In four hours I think."

"Oh." Jacquie rubbed her eyes, then plunked herself down next to her friend, her voice suddenly wobbly. "I want to come and visit."

"You can always stay with me. Always." Lara lay her head on Jacquie's shoulder. "Go to bed now," she said groggily. "You have to work tomorrow."

"Yeah." Jacquie laughed wryly. "Work. I don't know about that. I think I'll probably just prop up the coffee machine."

Anton stirred himself and came over to Lara. "I'm going now."

"Whoa, then!" Jacquie raised herself off the sofa and winked at them. "Enough. I'll have some of your coffee in four hours, Lara." She grinned and wandered out of the room.

Lara was too tired to think, even to feel. Anton pulled her to her feet and hugged her tightly.

"I won't be able to see you off," he murmured into her hair.

She just couldn't speak anymore.

He lifted her face and kissed her one last, long time.

"Oh, Lara," he said, with a slight choke in his voice, "who would have thought my winter would be like this one? And an Australian, of all people!"

She traced one finger over his face, drawing it for herself to remember.

"I don't know what else to say," he finished.

"I don't, either," she replied.

They looked at each other and laughed softly.

"We can't say goodbye."

"No."

"Then we won't," he said firmly.

"No."

They kept hold of each other's hands as he backed away from her.

"Don't see me out."

She stood as he had left her, listening for the click and rattle of the door, his last footfall on the concrete stairwell. She moved quickly into the kitchen to see if she could watch him pass under the streetlight. There he was—so tall, with his springing, energetic step, long, dark coat, and hand ruffling his hair before he turned the corner.

Then he was gone.

Suddenly she felt a bit sick, and turned for her room.

Although she was exhausted, Lara picked up the package and opened the wrapping.

It was an antique, nautical compass, rimmed with burnished brass. Underneath its glass face, the surface was laced with inked markings, like miniature bird prints. The compass was protected by a leather case that clicked shut with a tiny latch. The instrument felt heavy and smooth in her palm. Lara turned it over, and saw that the base had been engraved. She held it up to the light, and read the inscription:

To Lara, for the journey. Love, Anton.

The Gift of Dreams
Spring, 1947

I was born in a small village. I grew to know its streets and lanes, its river, its two streams, and the places where the trees were allowed to grow unhindered. I knew where to stand in order to see the sky. I could watch as the clouds came to pour their dreams upon us. I watched also the space from where the bombs would later carve desperate, murderous paths toward the trees, and I saw many thousands of birds leave and return. I have never ceased to wonder at that great depth of space, and the way it is the ocean, but not.

I am on a boat traveling over the sea. It is not the first time I have traveled over the sea on a ship. I traveled once to England, over the Channel. The vessel was sturdy and dark, creaking through the waves, and trailing a thick mass of white foam that quivered in the moonlight. I stood on the deck all night, marveling at the fragility of light and water.

I am not sure, anymore, of my name.

I am on a boat traversing the sea, a huge ship that engulfs the space around it, causing a wake that surges like a tide behind the stern. I am standing as far toward the sky as I can, yet still the deep thrumming of the ship, and the churning of the sea affect my gait, my stance, and my vision. If I look up—and I often do—I can see the privileged upper decks, and above them great dark funnels like the crest of a proud bird. Around me the earth is liquid, constantly shifting, so deep as to render me insignificant on its surface, like a finger held up against the moon.

Today I lean on the railing, staring until my eyes shimmer and dots ripple across their surface. I am searching for dolphins. I scan repeatedly the furrows of water, my neck tense because I keep thinking that I see a slip of gray—but then it turns to foam, and I am again disappointed. I have been here since dawn. I watched the horizon turn waxen, then alight as the sun tilted its face toward our part of the world. The clouds lifted from the sea, like birds leaving their nests for a day of fishing and flight.

There was a lady out walking here this morning in a thick coat, armed against the wind that seems to wake with the sun. We conversed briefly. She laid her gloved hand on the railing, shined the surface, and admitted she possessed a photograph of a ship's bow with dolphins bounding alongside it. She confessed she had always longed to see this sight for herself, which was why she had bought a ticket for this ocean liner. Then she became embarrassed, because we had spoken for longer than was necessary, and about things that were significant. She stiffened, bobbed her head at me, and walked on.

As she tells me of dolphins dancing alongside ships, I feel sad at the heaviness of this boat. But, then, everything these days seems to drive home the futility of metal, speed, and other human discoveries. Oh, yes, and war. But that is assumed.

Mostly I do not enjoy meeting people. Not at present, anyway. To meet people means I must talk, and to talk means to give away my accent, and to give that away means that people will ask questions, and then no longer wish to talk.

As yet I have not seen any dolphins, so I shift my gaze to admire the horizon, now frosted and the color of my eyes, traced across the edge of this world like a breath on a cold morning. The sky is frail blue and windswept, with horsetail clouds high above, strung like frozen scarves on the neck of the atmosphere. A flock of storm petrels passes overhead, on their way to a warmer place, as I am.

Then unexpectedly the birds decide as one to alight on the many gleaming surfaces of our enormous boat. They fold their wings, then stretch them again, all the time chatting and seemingly calling to each other, "What a marvelous opportunity, finding this ship! What a view from the railing!"

I nod in quiet agreement. Apart from seeing no dolphins, the view is overwhelming. So much water—but it is not the expanse, as much as the depth that fascinates me. Hundreds of miles reaching downward. I shiver as I realize it is all of my country tipped sideways—all those miles of darkness. At what point is there no more sun, where the fish flicker like ghosts, forgotten, in the closest thing to eternity that we have on the earth?

I threw my uniform into the sea. I threw away most of my papers. I am trying to throw my past into the ocean as well, but it floats too easily, and I am afraid some fisherman will hoist it up in his nets, and journalists from around the world will flock to see the amazing fish with its blood-red scales and mad eyes. Oh, yes, the past is a fish that will swim through the most treacherous waters to survive. Perhaps that is why I am now afraid to swim.

Suddenly there is a sound as if the sea is breathing out, as if everybody on the ship has sighed at exactly the same moment. The cloud of birds has swayed off the railings and toward space. They are drawn upward; they move so beautifully into their pattern of flight that every other movement is hushed: the boat, the sea, the wind. There are only the birds, a thousand leaves tossed skyward, flowing with the rivers of air.

Then they are gone, and the ship returns to its heavy breathing as it steams across the sea. The wind reminds us again that it is only very early Spring. In this hemisphere.

I take my fingers from the railing, clench them to release blood back into my hands, and turn from the view. Then begins my half-hourly promenade of the main deck. I am intrigued by the fact that the deck's surface is entirely wooden boards. I find all the lines fitting perfectly together very satisfying, like a completed jigsaw puzzle. Each board has been created, polished, tested, and placed; together they form an appealing physical texture. I enjoy the thick coils of rope and the lifeboats like babies strapped to the flanks of their mother. I always reassure myself by counting the lifeboats as I walk past them. I have chosen mine already, if the moment should come.

But I want to see Australia.

I have a new country to explore. I have a brochure in my pocket, and a map inside my shirt. There is a picture of a beach rimmed with trees. Underneath is the caption, *Untamed Coast*. There is a picture of a range of hills, termed "mountains," which I find amusing.

Then there is a picture of a very clean house with a picket fence. There are exactly two windows, and a door in the middle of them, like a doll's house. There are even little white curtains in the windows, if you look closely. It can be assumed that there is a small-but-productive vegetable patch around the back, adjacent to a small-but-functional outdoor entertaining area.

A young woman in an apron and manicured hair stands waving, as you wonder at her neat and perfect house. Beside her, with his suited arm around her waist, is a successful man. He wears a very clean shirt. He is smiling. His eyes say to you, "This is all mine ... it's all mine," but he says it so nicely that you want to move in next door, and have tea with him and his wife, perhaps even stand with them to wave next time the camera comes by.

The brochure is not a promise but a lure. Anyone who believes what he sees in brochures has not lived the past fifteen years. I knew somebody once who responded to the promise of golden beaches at an unnamed Eastern European seaside resort. When they arrived, the sand was merely concrete painted yellow. A true story. I conclude my opinion on brochures.

The picture I like best is the one I have drawn and colored in my own mind. It is of a big stone house surrounded with trees. Bread rises, and a woman sings. There is a large and over-productive vegetable plot behind the house, where peppers and artichokes grow (it is warm, and one is not forced to grow potatoes). Chickens murmur and scratch at the dirt, and give eggs all year round; because they are never afraid, the supply is plentiful. There is a field for sheep and two cows. In the garage next to the house there is a modern car, smooth and powerful, able to take me exploring wherever and whenever I want to go. This is my Australia.

Back in my cabin the other men, my fellow travelers, smoke and play cards, and tell jokes that I would not choose to retell. There is a forced laughter, a comradeship without substance—I know it will close like a door when we leave this liner.

I sleep in a tiny bunk that slams me up against the wall. My blanket stinks, and I am grateful for the coat I can drape over myself at night. There are other things I would love to share. If only I had a pen and paper. If only I could write to people who were no longer here. If only I could write to Gustav. I would tell him about the Spanish man with the balding head and one silver tooth who plans to open a restaurant and have seven children …

I try not to dream, but the last two nights the room has turned into a corridor, white and empty. Photographs line the walls, each a face from my past: Frau Henkel, Herr Solberg … Hans. I hear chamber music, but frustratingly harsh and fragmented, notes scattered like ticker-tape at a military parade.

I remember so many places at once, and am filled with a very sudden pain. The corridor narrows to a door. In my dream I pass through it, and enter an utterly empty space. The music becomes a relentless, distorted fugue.

I sit in a wooden chair. I am now the audience for my own dream, for my own life that I have just witnessed on the journey down the corridor. The concrete floor gapes holes, and large patches of damp. Bits of roofing dangle precariously.

A soldier enters calmly, followed by a woman with her face covered. They commence a tentative, elegant dance.

I feel the pain once more, and realize that in every age, in every time, a man dances with a woman. What a simple, beautiful ritual in which the two halves of the human race join together and move in graceful flight. It has the potential to be exhilarating, but to be so the dancers must forget about the steps and themselves, and simply lead, and be led.

The woman turns to me, but her eyes are dead. The floor opens, and a man dressed as a musician, with violin in hand, offers me a sheet of music and asks me to play—but how can I? I have no instrument. I am in an empty warehouse, and the music is water dripping, and the musician is a rat, and—

I am alone.

Tonight I will walk the deck, and watch for falling stars. I hate dreams.

But I do not walk on the deck. I lie here instead, curled uncomfortably on my cramped piece of the bunk. My knees press together, and I feel the bones in each one touch the other. They feel sharp, and I slip one hand between them for warmth, and cushioning.

Tonight I am counting the seconds between the snores of the man above me. I am counting the miles we move through in the darkness, counting the fingers on my hand, counting how many times I must clench my hands to warm them. I count the crash of waves. I count how many people I know who are left.

And I try to count to infinity.

The Gift

It is very early morning, and Lara stands on the deck of a large cruise ship, gazing out across the Mediterranean. A rough wind tousles her hair, and the clouds scud above her like migrating birds. Her face is a cold mask.

A fountain, seamless and silent, pushes up from deep within her. A clear, cold flow seeps through her skin and eyes, but strangely not her voice. She is muted. She is crying.

The objects rest in a bag at her feet. The mahogany peg. The smooth black stone. The postcard. The feather.

The pin.

"What was Opa like when he was young?"
"Where did he travel?"
"Where, exactly?"
"When?"
"Forgotten."
"Why?"
"Don't ask so many questions."

Don't ask so many questions. Don't ask so many questions.

But so many, many questions. Anton and his questions. God and His questions … an unceasing, eternal *Why? Why? Why?* His calls like the scream of an albatross, searing through hemispheres, following sailors until, crazed, they cry out, *A curse with wings pursues us!*

The why of the human sheaves, shoveled into the grasping, hollow earth. The why of a broken compass, so many broken compasses, crushed together in a ship bound for the Antipodes.

Still crying, Lara picks up the objects, those tiny burdens.

Dear Opa—

She holds them for a moment against the sky. She unlocks her fingers and lets the wind take the ornaments from the shadow box, spinning them through blue space.

The metal eye falls first. It blinks once, then is gone—the hated lapel pin vanishes beneath the swell, as if it has never been.

Dear Opa—

Lara buries her face in her hands. A seabird skims the air beside her, then glides away across the waves.

The cold wind blows a gull's soft plume into her hair. She untangles it, and laughs as the breeze fights her fingers.

The feather sighs into her palm—and she suddenly recognizes the beating of her heart.

Then quietly, with only the wind as witness, Lara drowns her grandfather.

There are some things, no matter how deeply I search for them, I will never know.

Lara turns her head once more toward the ocean—and she sees dolphins.

Xo

There are those whose stories are the heartbeat of this novel, who have left their hand-prints on its walls. Many of these lost their precious lives in war, which continues to be the scourge of our earth. To these ones, I keep this tiny flame burning for you.

May we never forget.

May war cease throughout the earth.

Acknowledgments

Art is borne from community, and I have many to thank.

The State Library of Victoria, Melbourne, Australia, provided resources, peace and the domed research space that inspires me even remembering it, and on the following pages I gratefully credit the texts there that informed my own.

My family and friends are my universe—convoluted, rambling, troubled, joyful, spreadeagled across the globe ... thank you for ensuring that I had a deep well of memories and shared histories to draw from, and for all the encouragement along the way.

I particularly honor my two sets of grandparents, particularly Lorna Burnard (nee Mengersen) to whom this book is dedicated.

I cannot thank my parents, Alexander and Rosemary Wearing, enough. For everything. They know.

B. & N. Burdack, for not only housing us in Berlin and driving us around in that old VW bug with jazz blaring, discovering illegal bars in the newly opened East Germany, but sharing their lives and incredible hearts with us over many years.

My Kickstarter community, friends met and unmet, ensured this novel was fledged. Their belief in this project has inspired many independent artists around the planet to trust the importance of their work, and I gratefully thank and celebrate each one of them. They have made this happen.

I humbly acknowledge my greatest human teachers: Richard Murphett, Simon Meighan, and Mr. Jimmy-Lee Moore.

I continued writing because of mentors, friends and teachers, who believed in me when I didn't: Amanda Johnson (Gustav to my Tomas), Tony Knight, Jo-Beth Allen, Joel Taxel, Melisa Cahnmann-Taylor, Cecil & Gretchen Bentley.

Sean Doyle, for being the most understanding agent ever, and a compassionate and skilled editor.

Stephen Knight, for your time, endorsement and mentoring.

Deanna Brady for your detailed and exacting editing in the initial stages of the "finished" manuscript.

I honor Arnold Zable, for your writing, heart and encouragement, and for reminding us in each of your books that stories are what keep us alive—thank you.

My sister in art and spirit, the brave and beautiful Janet Frame, a constant inspiration and whisper.

To my four precious children, Jade, Corrina, Molly and Ari, for giving me the best sort of manuscript deadlines as each one came into the world, sleeping generously during the day, and at night handing me enough waking hours that it also made sense to write while the moon watched me through the window.

My husband Mark, fellow artist and kindred spirit, whose music, humor and faith form my raft. This book belongs as much to you.

And finally, Johann Sebastian Bach, for prophesying, through music, all pain and its transcendence.

References

The following texts were invaluable in the researching and creating the stories and details in *Shadows and Wings,* and I wish to credit them accordingly:

Akbar, Saiyid Ali. *The German School System.* UK: Read Books, 2006.

Bidermann, G.H. *In Deadly Combat: A German soldier's memoir of the Eastern Front.* Lawrence: University Press of Kansas, 2001.

Bielenberg, Christabel. *The Past is Myself.* London: Chatto & Windus, 1968.

Brett, Lily. *The Auschwitz Poems.* Melbourne: Scribe, 1986.

Boyle, Kay. *The Smoking Mountain: Stories of Post War Germany.* New York: McGraw-Hill, 1951.

Craig, Gordon A. *The Germans.* USA: Plume, 1991.

Diehl, James M. *The thanks of the Fatherland: German veterans after the Second World War.* NC: University of North Carolina Press , 1993 .

Dawidowicz, Lucy S., *The War against the Jews 1933 - 45.* New York: Penguin, 1975.

Elphick, Jonathan (ed), *The Atlas of Bird Migration: Tracing the great journeys of the world's birds.* London: Harper Collins, 1995.

Engelmann, Bernt. *In Hitler's Germany.* London: Methuen, 1986.

Fletcher, A.W.. *Education in Germany.* Cambridge: W. Heffer, 1934.

Fritz, Stephen. *Frontsoldaten: The German Soldier in World War II.* Lexington, KY: University of Kentucky Press, 1995.

Harmstorf, Ian, and Peter Schwerdtfeger. (Eds). *The German Experience in Australia.* Adelaide: The Australian Association of von Humboldt Fellows, 1988.

Hedin, Sven Anders. *Sven Hedin's German diary, 1935-1942.* Dublin: Euphorion Books, 1951.

Hope, A.D., "Death of the Bird." In Colmer, John and Dorothy.,(Eds). *Mainly Modern.* Adelaide: Rigby, 1975.

Klemperer, Victor. Chalmers, M., (Ed.). *I WILL BEAR WITNESS: A Diary of the Nazi Years 1933-1941.* New York: Random House, 1999.

Klemperer, Victor. Chalmers, M., (Ed.). *I WILL BEAR WITNESS: A Diary of the Nazi Years 1942-1945.* New York: Random House, 2001.

Kursietis, Andris J. *The Wehrmacht at War 1939-45: The Units and Commanders of the German Ground Forces During World War II.* AD: Aspekt B V Uitgeverij , 1998.

Laffin, John. *Jackboot: The story of the German soldier.* UK: Sutton Publishing, 2004.

Panich, Catherine. *Sanctuary?: Remembering post-war immigration.* Sydney: Allen & Unwin, 1988.

Pruller, Wilhelm. *Diary of a German Soldier.* London: Faber, 1963.

Richardson, Horst Fuchs. (Compiled, edited and translated by). *Sieg Heil! War Letters of Tank Gunner Karl Fuchs, 1937-1941.* Hamden, CT, USA: Archon Books, 1987.

Sax, Benjamin, and Dieter Kuntz. *Inside Hitler's Germany: A Documentary History of Life in the Third Reich.* MA: D. C. Heath Publishing, 1991.

Spielvogel, Jackson J. *Hitler and Nazi Germany.* New Jersey: Prentice Hall College Div, 3 edition (September 27, 1995).

Stahlberg, Alexander. *Bounden Duty: The Memoirs of a German Officer, 1932-1945.* UK: Brassey's Ltd, 1990.

Thompson, Peter D. *Soldbuch : A guide to the German military identity book.* Annerley, Qld: P.D. Thompson, 1990.

Weidensaul, Scott. *Living on the Wind: Across the Hemisphere with Migratory Birds.* Portland, OR: North Point Press, 2000.

Zaslavsky , D. *The Face of Hitler's Army.* Soviet Union: Foreign Languages Publishing House, 1943.